BUS 64 ROMA

by
UMBERTO BARTOLOMEO

Bus 64 - Roma

By Umberto Bartolomeo

ISBN: 978-0-9907097-0-1 (paperback version)
ISBN: 978-0-9907-1-8 (Kindle version)

Umberto Bartolomeo is a pseudonym for an actual person described in the biographical information on the back cover.

Dedicated with Affection
to the
People and Spirit
of the
Eternal City
Past, Present and Future

Our Itinerary on this Bus Ride

Rome - Caput Mundi - MCMXCII (1994 AD)
July 19th, 10:12 A.M.

Welcome aboard this book about a bus, and some people and events that intersect its slow forward roll through this famed ancient *urbs*. Before we begin, though, may we suggest a cup of coffee?

After all, this is no snack-barred, dentist-chaired tourist bus we'll be taking. It's a public bus, frill-less and elemental - no refreshments once we've begun. And we do well to speak of coffee now lest we forget it later - a real oversight. For this lively bean's brew is one of our ride's guiding spirits.

Much can be said about coffee in this often oriental city. About the finicky multiplicities of its preparation. About the barman's robotics in his chromed Pavlovian kennel. About lazing guiltlessly in outdoor cafes, as workless days drift by. But this is no travel brochure, no slick in-flight magazine. It's a book about a bus that is soon to start rolling. We've no time for detours, however sweet. Let's turn then, to one cupful that's about to be drunk. The cup is not unique: just a thick-lipped bit of crockery with a chip nicked out of its handle.

Nor is the man who drinks from it. His name is Vinzo, and if he weren't our driver through these pages, you would not wish to meet him.

Rome has 893 churches - and 2,509 coffee bars. *Hisssss!* says the coffee machine, as its spout drips dark juices. "*Ecco, pronto!*" barks the barman, whacking the cup gracelessly on the counter.

Waiting for Our Driver

Vinzo, our driver, sat in the bar near the bus-stop. In the pudgy fingers of his meaty hand was the thimble-like cup of his fifth espresso of this no-longer-young morning. Though the cigarette smoke curling from his mouth was being drawn into his nose holes, little else about him might suggest he was alive. One might forgivably see in him just another sluggish, paunchy, mustachio'd, unshaven Roman, subsumed in his pleasures. But this was not so for Vinzo. Taking place inside him was quite real supplication - as fervent as had ever been felt by the priests standing near him, at the counter. Yes, his beckoning was quite real, though to what could hardly be called deity.

In five minutes Vinzo would be shutting himself in the driver's cubicle of Bus 64, which was standing outside in the *piazza*. And for two hours he would be without recourse, should his bowels choose to move for the first time in four days. Should his sphincter pinch in mid-journey he'd have no choice but to ignore it. And like yesterday, sit there helpless as it dove back into the Deep, lost again, like Ahab's whale. For two hours then, he'd be navigating Rome's torturous traffic, which was aggravating in the extreme to his torporous state.

Beneath its dark heavy lid, Vinzo's left eye stared sullenly at the clock behind the bar. His right eye strayed hopefully to the door marked WC. A third inner eye, meanwhile, gazed steadily bowelwards. Drawing smoke into his lungs, he saw crowds of bronchioli being lashed to a frenzy. Swallowing his coffee, he saw his blood being whipped into torrential currents. Surely his rectum should surrender now, what it was so spitefully hoarding. But time was running out, and the second hand ticked on...

The waiting bus was full, its 20 seats occupied, and 63 standees

filling the aisle. A sign near the exit said 85 standees was the capacity
- 22 more than were already crammed together. But we've no cause
for complaint. This is not, after all, Cairo. There'll be no youths sitting
on the roof, clinging to the sides, or riding the bumpers. No - many
more Romans than this, along with their guests, could share such a
cramped space as this one. And sustain their dignity and goodwill on
this tight stress-filled ride.

But… what feels amiss here? People don't seem too happy. All
stand silent and still, like dumb animals in their stocks. The forward
motion of the bus will lend this circumstance some meaning. But just
parked here, with its doors open, it's an anomaly, disquieting.

A dense fear pervades the air, such as one feels upon entering
a barn full of chained cows. The comparison is apt, for this bus is
odoriferous. A medley of smells swarms here, composed of disparate elements. There are commingling exhalations, from the mild
nuances of clean breath to the strong accents of halitosis. There are
breaths rife with garlic, onion and cheese, soured coffee, and tobacco. Blended with these are winds blown from the body's sundry
shores: decaying bacteria from dank to pungent, and the aromas of
arm-pits, from salty to toxic. There are fumes rising up from hard-
working urban feet. And fumes released furtively, inaudibly, but with
still fearsome impact.

This bouquet's not ambrosial but at least it is natural. Though one
needs a brave nose to confront it, these familiar smells are somehow
tolerable. True, a sewerish pyorrhea, or some excrescence in the draw-
ers of a pensioner can peeve one beyond measure. But *natural* foul
smells remain acceptable, and even strangely reassuring - like the whiff
of manure one receives like a caress as one drives past a farm.

What provokes us more are the smells of those products we have
sprayed, dabbed and doused ourselves with, to render ourselves pre-
sentable. An acrid hairspray can flare our nostrils and bite deep into
our sinuses. Brightly colored soaps and perfumes remind us that God
made the polecat. Even the deodorants that white-coated clinicians

say render us benign, wrinkle the nose more than the smells they expunge.

Now if bus-driving were sport, entertainment or politics... If there were glamour in being propelled through Rome's video-game streets while reacting like a robot, then our Vinzo would be famous. He would proudly mount the bus steps, take a smiling glance round the *piazza*, and flick his cigarette away with a flourish before taking the wheel. He's the captain, after all, of Rome's Bus 64, whose route starts at *Vaticano*, the fabled heart of Christendom, then crosses the legend-steeped Tiber before passing through famed centers of fashion and culture. And its final destination is *Stazione Termini*, portal to this city that lies at the crossroads of continents.

Some five hundred buses weave and crawl through Rome's labyrinth streets. Some pass ancient monuments, others historic churches, while others skirt the hem of still-surviving ancient walls. But no bus passes through quarters as celebrated as does Bus 64. Alas - if only our Vinzo felt the nobility and grandeur of his humble task.

But alas again - such was not his nature. And so, with the shuffle of the gallows-bound he left the bar, crossed the *piazza*, took a last drag on his cigarette, then climbed the stairs coughing to take his place at the wheel. He looked groggily at the meters and buttons on the console. On the dust-encrusted dashboard was a postcard someone had left there. It showed Mother Mary rolling her bulging, grief-shadowed eyeballs up to heaven. Beside her stood that frocked saint with the neat ring of hair round his otherwise bald head - the fellow who's always smiling, despite the hatchet sunk deep in his skull.

What, wondered Vinzo (as he had so often wondered before), was all the commotion about pictures and churches and pictures and churches? 'Beats me,' he concluded, as he pressed a green plastic button.

At once there was a brief high-pitched whine. The bus was convulsed as its engine turned over. In the space of but seconds it became

15

remarkably animate. Its motor rumbled, its windows rattled, and black smoke billowed out from its small toy-like chimney. At the press of another button, its three doorways slid shut with a loud pneumatic hiss.

And the bright orange bus lumbered slowly out of the *piazza*.

Maria Luigia's United Colors
of Benneton

As the engine roared to life, homemaker Maria Luigia hugged her pocketbook more tightly against her barrel chest, as if protecting a baby from danger. This was an uncomfortable way to stand, but surrounded by such people at such close quarters, what choice was there really? And who would do otherwise? Now if these people were all family - well - that would be another thing altogether. She had no problem with family, sitting four five and six on the couch, snacking, watching TV with the children crawling all over. That was just normal, after all, for family is family. In family you all look the same, you come from the same blood. But on a bus such as this one, in a city like this one...

Before her was one of those ads for those clothing stores for kids. Wherever you went these days, you seemed to see one. She never looked at them too closely, but since there wasn't much else to be doing now, she pushed her glasses up on her nose and focused in. Five pleasingly formed teens were leaning against each other in acrobatic postures, all smiles and easy intimacy. One was a negro and one was oriental. One was a redhead, probably Irish, and another a pale blonde from Scandinavia. The fifth teen was some muddy-colored breed; she couldn't guess from where... but then who could keep up with all those new sub-races, that seemed to pop up each week now?

As she studied this ad, something rose up inside her to reject it. 'Fantasy' was the word that came to mind, and a dismissive snort to go with it. Fantasy fantasy fantasy. Just a colorful juvenile dream. It was an okay dream for the youngsters, and for the businessmen who were cashing in, to be sure. But for a woman like herself, who had lived as long as she had lived, and seen as much as she had seen... well... there just comes a point when you're too old for Walt Disney.

The negro in the ad had an even-toothed smile and bright sparkling eyes. With his geometric haircut he seemed a cartoon figure come to life. What did *that* fellow have in common with the real negro right beside her, leaning against the pole in the stairwell, tuckered out already in mid-morning? He was no milk chocolate brown like the bright fellow in the ad. He was black. Black to the point of being purple. Like the skin of an eggplant. No sparkle was to be seen in *this* negro's rheumy eyes. They were yellowed like old ivory, and so sad you would think he'd been born sad. His hair too, was no showpiece — an uneven bush full of lint-balls. And what a terrible overbite he had, behind lips so enormous they seemed to take up his whole face.

The image came to mind of this negro sitting on the divan in her living room, surrounded by her family all eating, talking and laughing while he sat there so purple and shabby and unutterably sad. As her thoughts ran in this vein she became suddenly querulous. God is supposed to have created man, is he not? So why didn't He have the good sense to make us all look the same? And if just one family boarded Noah's ark, then why were we all so different, and so stupid, yes stupid, that we needed billboards and ads like this to remind us we were all brothers? In such a damnable confusion of creatures, who could be expected to feel brotherly? She clutched her handbag more tightly, and turned from the negro with tiny unseen steps

And all that was just on the outside. On the inside things were even worse. The fact is, she couldn't feel sure of anyone, not one, in this whole busload of people. She looked at the nun standing to her left. So okay, she was Christian. There was no doubt about *that*, with that dark habit and starched wimple she was wearing on this broiling hot day. And that wood cross on her chest with the little twisted figure, where other women just wore pretty decorations.

But how far did a wood cross go, and what did it mean actually? She may well be Christian, but she's got a ram's sullen eyes and a jaw that looks mean, verging on cruel. With that dusky red skin, who could guess *where* she came from, let alone her mother, or the mother before her? Maybe just one generation ago they went to witch doc-

18

tors, danced around fetish figures, sacrificed animals – or even worse! Who could say? We go running all over the planet baptizing primitives in droves. But you don't go from witch doctor to Christian from one day to the next. It takes years, maybe centuries for it to become part of your blood, of your soul.

Maria Luigia surveyed her fellow passengers. Here was a woman her own age whose cheap house-dress had sweat stains big as dinner plates round the armholes. Here was an aged man with a hump back and jet-black dyed hair. Beside him were two young blonde men with that cheap, coarse look of Poles. Why was it she imagined them in helmets and uniforms carrying rifles with bayonets? Gripping the rail nearby was a gaunt young man with an old man's skinny neck, and wide haunted eyes in raccoon-like dark sockets. He looked like those AIDS patients she saw in the magazines. Then it struck her: maybe he *had* AIDS. She looked at her own hand gripping the same rail, and vowed, with a chill, to wash up just as soon as she got home.

She looked now at Imogena, who stood beside her holding her shopping bags. Her very own Imogena, who had helped her each morning for five years now. But who was this *filippina* really, she now wondered, apprehensively. After those first several months she had stopped really seeing her. With her quiet timid ways and that ready simpy smile, Imogena had become a household fixture, like some polite useful pet. She'd come well recommended, she had a brother who lived in Rome also, and a tan little boyfriend who picked her up on his *motorino*. But apart from that, what did she know about her? In fact she knew nothing. Nothing about her life here, or what she felt, what she dreamed or what she thought. Looking at her impassive tan face and expressionless sloped eyes, it now struck Maria Luigia that her little Imogena, as well, was one of *them*: this menagerie of passengers who were dirty or ignorant, diseased or unemployed, strangers or foreigners, whom she wished to be away from and have nothing to do with.

It was not that she was hard-hearted. She was glad to help Imogena. And glad that the Church let this dusky nun nestle into it.

And she didn't mind, as did others, that her tax-money helped this poor negro. But as for this "family of man" propaganda, well – it was here that she drew the line

She looked back at the ad now.

Yes, a nice enough idea - a nice picture, nice theory. But she'd lived too long to be taken in by it. Thanks just the same, but my only family is my *own* family - flesh of my own flesh, and blood of my blood. It's not that she didn't wish everyone well. She really did, her thoughts argued. But that didn't mean the whole world had to be brought into her living room.

Maria Luigia's thoughts now turned plaintive, demanding, confused. Why couldn't she just go out and do a few simple errands without getting herself upset about the state of the whole world? It seemed you couldn't turn your head these days without some fresh problem staring you in the face. And if you shut yourself in, it found you just the same. It seeped through the floors and the walls; it came under and through doors. "I didn't make this world," she said defiantly, to Whoever Was in Charge and might possibly be listening. "I didn't make it, and I didn't choose it. So why then should I be the one who's supposed to fix it?"

Maria Luigia sighed heavily and felt suddenly weary. How she hated it when she felt this way - with everything so distressing. Distressing things outside and distressing thoughts inside - and no chance of escape till this bus brought her home. She glanced about for something to soothe or distract her. Her eyes settled on two priests sitting together down the aisle. Now these were *real* Christians, two *good* priests, both white and she'd also bet Italian. Seeing those black coats side by side with those white collars and white faces, she felt a touch better already.

The older priest looked good-natured but unwholesome, on the declining side of a middle age that little in him seemed inclined to resist. His hair and hands were unclean. He had a pot belly. His greasylensed glasses sat on a bulbous nose from whose nostrils sprouted black hairs that merged into a yellowing moustache. The sole of one shoe was detached, and papers stuck out from his beat-up leather satchel.

But the young priest who was with him... well, *this* one was a different story. She could regard this one with pleasure and think bright hopeful thoughts. He was so... clean. Clean and upright. And clearly quite sensitive. Just the kind of young man you would like your young priest to be...

Saint Sebastian

Yes this young priest was refreshing. In every place his companion was grizzled and frayed he was polished and clean. The black fabrics that cloaked him from neck to wrists to ankles were crisply pressed. His shoes had a gleamed shine. And his cheap briefcase of pebbly plastic still looked fresh off the shelf, from his nightly ministrations with a sponge. Few people have bodies as immaculate as his. He wore an infant's radiant flesh. His fair silken hair lay across a domed forehead of smooth and pink skin. His cheeks and nose, chin and lips, hands and fingers down to their white-mooned nails - the convolutions of his ears, even - all seemed scrubbed till they shone with a light all their own. He was fresh as a flower - except for his eyes. They were downcast and troubled behind bright gold-rimmed glasses.

Squeezing through a low arch in the stone wall at the top of the piazza, Bus 64 emerged at the edge of Saint Peter's colonnade. There it granted its passengers a last view of the cathedral, before heading down a back street on its way toward the Tiber. The young man pressed his face to the window and drew the scene in. The rows of noble columns cast black shadows alternating with shafts of bright light: the great organ keys of the Church, playing chords of Divine Music in this world full of tempests. Between the columns nearest him he could see clear across the *piazza*, to the columns on its far side. Each column was topped with a strong man of stone, all in fine changeless postures of piety and fervor.

How he loved this colonnade and how often he strolled here: to see these stone men of faith and borrow their strength when his young heart wavered. And how grateful he was for the faith they could lend him, which he needed so badly on days like today.

It was trying enough having to work with Giacomo, whose lapsed hygiene and waggishness made him seem more hobo than priest. It galled him how such a slack man could wear the collar, have a soft bed, a quiet room, and be served three balanced meals. Yes he knew this was just proof of the beauty of Christ's church, which opened its arms to the sick and oppressed, the homeless and ignorant, to villains and fools… so if it welcomed all these, it had room for a Giacomo. It was important, all the same, to keep high personal standards.

But Giacomo was the smaller peril on this weekly journey through temptation. Troubling thoughts would assail him; they always did on this bus-ride. "Sufficient unto the day is the evil thereof." But this rude bus furnished evil not just for one day but for the six days intervening. These few hours were sufficient to foul his prayers for the whole week, make his nights restive and loathsome, and stain his communion with his Lord.

Bus 64 set off down the back street toward *Castel St. Angleo*, passing souvenir shops full of ceramic cherubs and porcelain Marys, doe-eyed and contorted-faced Jesuses, plastic Pietàs, and postcards of a smiling masterful pope.

"First stop, Disneyland," said Giacomo with a throaty good-natured chuckle, relaxed and contented, hands folded across his paunch. The young man said nothing but his jaw visibly tightened. 'Disneyland' was Giacomo's quip for these blocks around the Vatican. He had a quip for most everything - but some things should not be laughed at, and Giacomo's good cheer had few limits. His laughter had a way of nibbling away at discourse till there were more holes than cheese, diluting and devaluing each subject it touched on. The spiritual quest seemed no more arduous for him than chuckling comfortably in his armchair. And most bothersome of all was how so many actually found him endearing.

Giacomo was not without qualities. He had ease and was good-natured. But what good were such qualities, such mere *human-ness*, unless first scoured clean by the flame of the Ideal? Giacomo enjoyed life at face value, took the low road of comfort. Always the wellspring of conversation and the font of good cheer. Let others be seduced by those animal good spirits, that led nowhere at all but the same tired circle of wine, smiles, friends and talk. And some whispered that he was wise! What nonsense! As if one could be pierced by the Spirit by just loafing in the easy chair of one's body, meeting everything with contentment. Let the others be diverted, taken in by soft roses. His own passion burned higher. He would always prefer Christ's thorn.

"Is it the silent treatment again today?" asked Giacomo, with a puckish, affectionate smile.

The young priest smiled wanly, but offered no answer. He tried to seem calm although snakes hissed within him. Turning to look back out the window, he could feel Giacomo's eyes searching and appraising him. He felt trapped and resentful as he imagined those bushy eyebrows cocked inquisitively above those tired twinkling eyes. He could feel their probe, their demand for… what was it?… which he never would give him. Giacomo's wide-bellied body radiated palpably, like a furnace. This too annoyed him, and oppressed him even further.

"It couldn't be… *me*… could it?" asked Giacomo with mock astonishment, as if shocked by the thought.

The young man knew he was being ribbed, and so gently and playfully he was tempted to banter back. But he mastered this wayward impulse.

"No it isn't you," he lied through pinched lips, though in part this was true. For Giacomo only compounded his problem on Thursdays.

Giacomo gave an extravagant sigh of relief that was ironic yet friendly.

"You had me worried there, young fellow." Then he chuckled again, taking such pleasure from their minimal exchange that his big belly quivered. This overflow of feeling seemed to need to be shared;

he placed one bear-like hand on the younger man's knee and gave it a good rattling shake.

The young man sat rigid, and endured this friendly touch. He would not stoop to such low poking, or let on that it pleased him slightly. Yes Giacomo was well intentioned, but once you got down on his level, there was no higher ground. So he set his heart against him and looked back out his window. But something in him forbade this, and tugged hard at his attention. He licked his dry lips. His bus troubles had begun.

Whose eyes were these, he wondered, with a will all their own, eyes darting and flashing among the passengers? They were his eyes, his own eyes, moving quite on their own, possessed by a hunger he was powerless to arrest. Impotent, he sat there, as avid furtive eyes, grasping greedy eyes, flickering feral eyes – all his eyes – kept scanning the passengers. They honed in first on a forearm, well muscled, matted thickly with coarse hairs black as coal. They then peered up a short sleeve to the side wall of chest, and the armpit beside it, with its dark sweated tangle. On and on roved his eyes, licked to sudden, restless flame.

He would later feel regret. This album of manly images that his eyes were collecting would revisit and torment him. So he summoned up his own images, to lead his mind back to safer realms. He thought first, quite by habit, of his Lord Jesus Christ. But found himself, for some reason, picturing Saint Sebastian, instead.

How he loved Saint Sebastian as portrayed by Guido Reni. How sweetly pitiful was the youthful saint, bound helpless to a tree with his flesh pierced with arrows. He could see the saint's youthful face with its moist parted lips, its flushed cheeks and dolorous eyes. And his full manly torso with its broad smooth man's breast. His bound arms extended languidly, his head turned toward Heaven. So lovely, so well formed, so vulnerable, unprotected – with just a loin cloth round his hips, concealing... He at once changed the channel...

He summoned up instead a chaste numbing Mary from some old Russian icon. Her face peered out solemnly from its oval cut hole.

Where a body should be, there was flat pounded silver. But this Mary was weak, could not quell what was inside him. On and on sought his eyes, finding first the fine swell of two strong athletic calves. Then the close-shaven cleft of a strong squared-off jaw. Then the twin prominences of tight buttocks. There he sat impassively, as his eyes roved relentless till they found what they sought: the great lopsided bulge, at long last. The great bulge so emergent, slung fat at the fork of two taut male thighs.

He stared and bit his lip. He implored Jesus to help him. But his body was deaf to prayer. And his eyes stoked the fires beneath his cauldron of sin till he boiled in the juices of his evil young body. The arrow-shaft of desire seared his priest's pulp-like loins, which clenched hard in a knot like a hot angry fist.

Giacomo's eyes opened slightly. He looked sidelong at his companion. He unfolded his hands and lifted an imaginary phone to his ear.

"*Salve*, hello there," he said gently. "Giacomo here. We can talk - if you'd like to."

He looked with concern at the troubled young man beside him.

"Talking helps sometimes. If you want."

With the phone still at his ear he waited a long moment for an answer. The young priest flashed a prim smile of refusal.

"Just trying to be friendly; can't help it sometimes. If you change your mind, ring me up. Any time… any time."

After another sidelong glance Giacomo wriggled in his seat, found a comfortable position, and within moments was dozing, his face smiling gently.

The young priest sat upright, much more spiritually vigilant, pricked hard to attention by his unchosen thorn.

The Tour

Today, *Castel St. Angelo* sits on the banks of the Tiber with the same squat stolidity it has sat with since medieval times. Long in disuse as fort, dungeon, and papal stronghold, it now receives tourists who come to see the chambers, passageways and armaments in its chilling interior. On its top, standing beside an empty cannon turret, Guido Boccamoto stewed in the grievance he would carry to his grave - or at least till he no longer had to give any more "culture" tours to these Philistines. It was an indignity to which a man his age should not need to submit. What for, after all? For a few measly *lire* to render his last years a shade more comfortable? Guido resented this, he resented it strongly. He resented having to recite the same lectures at the same places with the same dates and jokes, to these tourists, *deficienti*, who gawked at monuments just to punctuate their eating and drinking. It galled him too that his son-in-law, for having gotten him this humiliating job, expected his tail to be kissed gratefully at least once every day. On and on went Guido's grievance, quite as repetitively as his lectures.

Guido's eyes were now fixed on a thick oak door nearby, behind which lay the "Cell of the Dawnless Night". It was there, in 1593, that Pope Gregorius II was strangled to death by conspirators, at the bidding of Pope Gregorius III. Now converted to a charming *capuccino* bar, the cell was hosting members of the "Feelings '94 Tour", from Cedar Heights, Illinois. Having mounted the fort's six hundred twenty-three steps, they now refreshed themselves with coffee, which they hoped would jump-start their bowels, which nine days of pasta had reduced to a farinaceous swamp. Their spirits revived, they waddled out now to rejoin their guide, who for some reason was glaring at them angrily, as he stood beside an empty cannon turret.

Once assembled before him, they witnessed a remarkable trans-
formation. Guido's hostile eyes softened. His taut vinegary expression relaxed. And when his tightly pinched lips parted, out came the
first words of his lecture in the most mellow of baritones. Sonorous
phrases one after another poured forth effortlessly from his smiling
mouth, sounding less like lecture than song. By the time he had finished reciting the third paragraph from page 42 of "A Concise History
of Rome's Monuments", his view of the tour group was also transformed. No longer just a pack of bloated intestinal tracts, they were
his adoring admirers, gratefully attentive to their cultivated speaker.

The Feelings group, in truth, was a captive, if respectful audience.
And if the truth must be told further, Guido's main activity in life was
to assail people with words. At home he held forth to his wife, daughter, and galling son-in-law on every imaginable subject, to the point
of slammed doors, angry oaths, and tears. At church meetings he pon-
tificated endlessly. At political rallies he declaimed with passion. He
cornered the driver on his bus, the barman in his bar, the doorman
by his door, and drove each to desperation. No acquaintance was too
brief, no ordinary event too insignificant not to provoke his intermi-
nable monologue. What mattered was for him to be speaking, and it
was the lot of the Feelings group to have strayed within range.

With his back to the Tiber, Guido launched into an inventory of
the weight, number and variety of stone blocks that had been hand-
set to construct the fortress. At the front of the group, looking out
over the Tiber, stood Ted and Cindy from Cedar Heights. Try as he
might, Ted could not manage to give his attention to his guide. From
the moment he had stepped out on the top of this fort, even before
his *cappuccino*, some perception he could not formulate had been nagging at him continually, struggling to be born. It was a feeling of *deja
vu* that had yet to be clarified. It felt mysterious and significant - but
what could it be?

Then it struck him, all at once, in a flash. So *that* was it! How very
obvious! Yes, standing here on this parapet, looking across the Tiber to
the *centro storico*, felt just like standing on the ninth tee at the Cedar

Height's Country Club! Ho *yes*! What a remarkably similar sensation! The same elevation, and before him, a body of water he would bet was the same breadth, exactly. The only difference was that instead of the hoary Tiber he'd be face-to-face with "The Gobbler": the lake with the hungriest maw for a golf ball in northeast Illinois. Yes sir, thought Ted respectfully, you need your very best shot to get home free over "The Gobbler."

Across the Tiber below him was a stone bridge adorned with angels. On the other side of the bridge lay the *centro*, with its cobbled streets, antique shops, and Renaissance *palazzi*. Surveying this historic panorama, Ted pondered what would be the wise man's club of choice. A three-wood, he reckoned, might carry too far, putting him on the roof of that shop with the marble busts in its window. A two-iron, on the other hand, might well carry with a favorable wind, but might otherwise drop short, near that stone angel holding the crown of thorns, down on the bridge. The more he thought about this, the more Ted rather wished he were back home, instead of sweating here on this old fortress. How good it would be to be standing on the ninth tee with the green in the distance and the club-house just behind it, inside of which waited his all-time summer favorite: a sirloin char-broiled burger heaped high with crispy bacon, slathered wantonly with mayonnaise. He was sick to death of pasta.

Poor Cindy too, could not concentrate. She was mentally back in their room at the Hotel of the Emperors, which had all the conveniences the American traveler appreciates. No towel rack was certainly a convenience, as were bath towels the size of placemats, and enough clothes-hangers to please Mahatma Ghandi. Then there was the tiny table at bed-side. That too, was convenient, with the refrigerator on top of it with a radio on top of that and a lamp on top of that also. How many times had she gratefully awakened last night as this wall of appliances loomed buzzing, humming and throbbing above her? True, the refrigerator was well stocked, but at those prices the bottles might as well be radioactive. And though the hot water was *probably* abundant, as advertised, it dribbled out slowly from a shower-head you held like a phone receiver.

Guido had now come to the highlight of his tour - the sack of Rome by the barbarians, from the top of page 37. He launched mellifluously into his subject: "During the sack of Rome by the Visigoths, the placid Tiber you see flowing gently before you, was the scene of horrors from which our eyes would recoil with horror. Imagine, if you can, a Tiber so choked with bodies, of the suffering dying no less than the mercifully dead, that one could walk from one bank to the other without wetting one's boot-tops. Imagine the sacred papal seat to your right, transformed into a scene of bestial bloodshed and destruction. Imagine chapels burning like infernos then razed to the ground. Or holy fathers and sisters fleeing to vestibules and rectories, only to be hunted down, stabbed and strangled as they beseeched God for deliverance.

"And in those same *palazzi* you now see across the river, the aristocracy fared no better. Dukes and noblemen were run down in the corridors and cut down like dogs. Noble women, the fruit of centuries of breeding and refinement, were savagely raped in their elegant chambers." 'Raped?' ...hmmm...The word somehow glided into both Ted and Cindy's ears, where it managed to arrest both their wandering attentions. Retrieved momentarily from his golf course, and her hotel room, each set off at once on more succulent ruminations.

Ted rolled the word back and forth slowly in the fingers of his mind. Just yesterday in some gallery he'd seen two pictures on that very subject. The first was the Rape of the Sabines. It did not impress him. Some Ben-Hur-type soldiers who all had the same faces, same beards, and same statue-like bodies, were carrying off the Sabines, who looked pretty damn coy for women soon to be raped. The second picture was better. The Rape of Lucretia. It was easy to remember that title because everyone knew Lucretia. He wondered if she had started poisoning people because she was raped, or if she was raped because she was poisoning people. The soldier in that painting also came straight out of Hollywood, but at least his muscles and armor were done in excellent 3-D. He had a woman pinned to the bed in her fancy boudoir. Brandishing a long knife with one hand, he warned her not to scream with the other.

Unlike the Sabine women, this Lucretia looked reasonably scared. But it wasn't her expression he remembered so clearly. It was her body. That same plush languid body he'd seen everywhere since he got here - on sidewalks, in bars, even on girls in their teens. Those same broad ample hips, the same thick dark hair, and those big mascara'd eyes that were so frank, brown and open. This wasn't the blondes he knew from girly magazines or Las Vegas, voluptuous just in the requisite breasts and bottom. No, this body was plush everywhere, was plushness itself, in a way he had never seen back home. And in that painting of Lucretia it was all to be seen: the soldier had torn away her robe so her body was revealed in its sensual entirety. Broad undulous breasts with their black shadowed cleft. The fatted belly slung sinuously in womanly hips. The fleshy pit of the navel, the plump shaded mound down below. Seeing it in his mind now, Ted's blood swooned and his knees went weak. He closed his eyes for a long moment, to regain his composure. When he opened them he saw his Cindy, standing beside him, in her barn-sized plaid culottes. He looked away across the river, put his hands in his pockets, and felt wistful.

Cindy too felt moved to musings by that four-lettered word. Yes, she'd felt it all morning as they'd walked through the *centro*. She wasn't naive. She'd seen those black-and-white films from the 50's and 60's. You could feel it everywhere. Even the air here was steamy, corporeal, tumescent. And as they strolled among the old *palazzi* with their wide open shutters, you could not see into their shaded interiors - but you knew it. You just knew it. Out to the window would come one of those dark hairy men with that low oiled hairline. He'd lean against the windowsill in his sleeveless T-shirt, a cigarette hanging from his thick downturned lips. Or maybe it was a woman, also idle at mid-morning. She was still in her bathrobe, or slip - and again you just knew it. You knew a big iron bed was there, just out of view, and that stretched out on the sheets lay a nude hairy man, or nude fleshy woman, limbs negligently disposed, flush with satiation.

Cindy looked at her husband beside her, his hands in his pockets like a schoolboy. He was listening to more facts about this old pile of stones they were standing on. She looked across the river at the *palazzi* with their shuttered windows and darkened interiors. She turned back to their guide and tried hard to get interested, to divert herself somehow from what ached deep inside her.

Bocce At Sundown

B eside each of the front seats was a little chrome sign: *Posto riservato agli invalidi e mutilati di guerra e del lavoro:* many words to say "seats for the disabled." In one of those seats, with palms on thighs, spine erect, and the symmetry of a basalt pharaoh, sat Ignazio Bruno, his mahogany cane leaning against one leg. Notwithstanding his white hair, thick glasses, and the hearing aid that filled one ear, notable vigor still flowed through his body. Clad in the jacket and trousers of a bygone era, his over-wide tie formed a perfect knot at his starched collar. No color enlivened his unseasonable attire, save a gold pin on his lapel, testament to singular deeds in the Republic's dusty military past.

At the end of dark *Borgo St. Angelo*, the bus made a slow arcing turn. Sunlight flooded through the windows, illuminating the passengers and their view, up *Via della Conciliazione* to St. Peter's. What an expansive fine view, in a city dense with monuments that overwhelmed one at close quarters. How refreshing was this wide open boulevard that led straight to the Cathedral, like a carpet to a king's throne. And to none was this view more refreshing than to old Ignazio Bruno, in whom it provoked memories quite as warm as the sun's friendly rays.

He remembered the first impression of this same view had made on him fifty years ago, just back from his years in the army, in Africa. What a shock to see the old neighborhood cleared off and this broad boulevard in its place. Who could have imagined standing all the way back at the Tiber and seeing clear through to St. Peter's? How ceremonial! What an improvement! You could almost hear the sounding of strings or the fanfare of trumpets.

The neighborhood that used to be there might charitably be called 'picturesque'. 'Rundown' was more like it: rows of shabby ill-matched buildings that only detracted from the great cathedral. What a bold stroke to just raze them to the ground. And put nothing in their place and let the open space just breathe. This way, even back at the Tiber, the magnificent dome riveted your attention. And the closer you drew, the taller it grew, looming larger and finer the closer you came. This was fitting. This was fine. This was how a holy place ought to be presented - dominant, unobstructed - like a Parthenon or Sphinx.

There of course were sentimentalists. The carpers and critics of any new idea, who to this day lament those old ugly knocked-down tenements, full of people who could live elsewhere. And who should bear the brunt of their spitefulness but *Il Grande* - who it was so fashionable now to ridicule, as if things now were so much better.

Mussolini, that's right - who labored to promote a vision based on real patriotism, real integrity. And who died without a single *lira* of the citizens' money in his pocket. Of how many of *today's* leaders could the same thing be said? Yes, yes - he had his folly in those last years when he brought us into the big war - and are any of us still alive who didn't pay a dear price? But what about the many years before that? And who among us is without his own folly? And whose folly is mixed with such achievement, such rectitude, as was old Mussolini's? Or such spirit and such strength to turn words into action?

Ignazio looked out his window. Two nuns stepped deferentially into the gutter so a tourist group could go by. Two dumpsters at curbside overflowed onto the street. A man walking past threw an empty cigarette pack among the trash then stepped out to cross the street. A car swerved to avoid him. The driver leaned out his window, bared his teeth and hurled a curse. The man on foot slapped his palm on his bicep and jerked his forearm up, smiling fiercely. Where, wondered Ignazio Bruno, was the courtesy, the decorum, the orderliness that used to be part of the very air that one breathed? Where were the clean sidewalks, the safe streets, the punctual trains, the respectful citizens? Where was *fraternitas*, the civic bond that men needed if they were to live together like true men?

Looking across the aisle, he saw a lanky youth slouched down in his seat. The long hair that swooped low across his forehead was pinned down by a music headset. An insistent tinny rhythm could be heard, as the youth rocked his head in time with the music. On his t-shirt was the image of a monster with blood dripping from its mouth as it played an electric guitar. His jeans were torn open at both knees. He wore a dirty pair of those improbably large sneakers. And that earring – what did *that* mean – was it brigand or homosexual? A memory came back to Ignazio, from when he himself was a youth.

They were sitting round the lunch-table on a hot day just like this one. Father was in full uniform, as always, when that call came from the barracks. Two enlisted men had been seen walking in *Trastevere* with their caps in their pockets and their neckties undone; someone had called in to complain. Father finished his plate quickly, without saying a word, then left for the barracks, without even having his coffee. But why the hurry, asked Mother – not even time for coffee? Because those men were *his* men, said Father, and it was *his* duty to see that soldiers didn't go parading around half-dressed like that in public. The fault was the soldiers'. The responsibility though, was his. Could only be his. Yes – each man with his station and his duty to perform for the sake of the whole...

The responsible one, *il risponsabile*! This was not a word but a reality. Responsibility at the top, and at each step down the ladder. Each man with his duty, each answerable for his actions. People snigger now at the very thought – and just look where it's gotten them! A corrupt government gorged with the people's money, everyone ducking and pointing fingers so that no one ends up responsible for anything. And the private citizen was no better. Ducking, shirking and grabbing, always more desperately, for himself alone. Public rats and private rats. That was the whole story. A dumpster full of rats managing somehow to carry on. A dumpster that flatters itself as being a culture, a society, a civilization – just words!

He looked more closely now at the lanky youth. Were there actually parents sitting home somewhere, content, while an offspring like this circulated in public, bearing the family name? What could an educational system be, which was full to the brim with such young tramps as this one? And what kind of world could millions of such tramps create - for themselves even, let alone those to follow?

As such questions gripped his mind, Ignazio Bruno gripped at his cane, flexing and unflexing his strong bony fingers. There used to be an order - a meaning and duty to being a man. This was no fantasy. He had seen it. He had lived it. But it was gone now. Everything was in pieces, with no one to lead the way back

As for old ones like him who had seen that better day - they'd been washed up by the tide. Their time was now over. All they could do was just sit, watch and wait, with no change forthcoming. Tonight, like every night, Ignazio would walk to the park in his *quartiere*, where the grass was mostly sand, the trees were decrepit, the fountain was dry, and the statues had no arms or heads. There he would meet his friends, all old ones like himself who had nothing much left to do. And there they'd play *bocce*, to pass the time until sundown. Standing around on their sand-patch, they would roll the wooden balls back and forth, and vaunt, laugh and cheer when two balls clicked together. Nearby would be the young boys. They too would be playing. But they'd be kicking and chasing footballs on limber young legs, not just standing, smoking and talking, like Ignazio and the old ones.

Then the sun would go down. Both games would be over. The old players and young players would go to their homes and sit down at the tables their women had prepared. There, the young ones would gather strength to keep kicking, running and chasing, on into their naive hopeful tomorrows. And the old ones would gain strength to keep watching and waiting, and hoping as well, to play *bocce* again, tomorrow, before sundown.

Gypsies!

The 'Feelings' group waited expectantly for their bus to appear from around the bend. Beside them, at the perimeter of the old fort, were young Africans selling trinkets. These dozen or so listless, dispirited young men leaned against the wall or squatted on the sidewalk, beside blankets on which they all displayed the identical cheap wares: the same sunglasses, wooden elephants, fake alligator shirts and leather belts, which to Cindy's practical mind simply just was not common sense. Why were they all selling the very same things? Why standing all so close, one right next to the other? Why didn't they spread out, stake out new territories, develop individual markets? Where was their entrepreneurial spirit? Were they so depressed because business was bad, or was business bad because they were so depressed? And how passive they were too, so lank-limbed and subdued – not angry and scary-looking like the blacks she saw in Chicago. Their somnolent ways may have worked in some thatch-hutted village, but it sure wasn't working here.

Ted, meanwhile, was looking up the broad avenue at St. Peter's, whose dome loomed before him, indistinct and shimmery in the morning's bright haze. To be having such a direct, prolonged view of the great cathedral was, he knew, the kind of moment that is significant. But try as he might, he could summon forth not one fact from the guidebook that would make this experience edifying. He waited patiently, in good faith. And some edifying idea would most certainly have happened along, had he not been distracted by some bright motion nearby. Moving diagonally along the street at high speed and in his direction, was a pack of young street urchins swathed in strange mismatched clothes of all colors of the rainbow.

Gypsies!! These were gypsies! He knew it in a split-second. And not just because of that warning from their tour director, but because of the alarm that sounded throughout his body. There were about eight children around ten years old, and a skinny girl who was maybe twenty. Despite the infant tucked in a blanket slung round her shoulders, she ran right along with the others, all laughing and gabbing in some gobbledy-gook language.

These ragamuffin children looked dirty and amoral, and strange to say... free. Ted's body tensed all over.

"Gypsies, gypsies everyone! Battle-stations! Gypsies!" Ted called out to his companions.

His companions though, were slow to respond. They did not realize they were supposed to fall into formation, like a wagon-train preparing for attack by marauding Comanches.

"Shoulder-to-shoulder everyone, don't turn your backs to them. Tighten it up there, keep a grip on those handbags. C'mon ladies, tighten it up. Keep your eyes peeled!"

It was hardly a tight formation, but the Feelings Group managed to huddle together in a kind of herd. They fingered their purse clasps and cameras nervously as the gypsies came closer. The gypsies were carrying newspapers and flaps torn off cardboard boxes. Ted briefed his platoon quickly on the enemy's tactics.

"Whatever you do, don't be fooled by those papers; that's their trick: they come up and start waving some paper in your face. While you get caught up in the commotion they go straight for your wallet. Keep your eyes on their hands, not the paper. Everybody got that? The hands - not the paper."

The gypsies soon arrived. They stopped right beside the huddled group. For some reason or other though, they did not launch an attack. Nor did they even seem to intend to. Indeed, they seemed not to be interested in the Feelings Group at all, but fell to chatting and laughing quietly among themselves, while they waited for the bus. One, two and then three minutes passed uneventfully. The wary Americans began to feel foolish huddled so closely together in such a wide open space. Even Ted, vigilant and primed for defense, began to wonder. Could such motley, runty-looking kids really be the threat they'd been made out to be? A few more minutes passed in the same quiet way. And what had first seemed like war slowly wound down to a truce. The kids minded their own business. The tourists struck up conversations. A few more minutes passed, and the truce gave way to peace. After all, what could happen in broad day-light within sight of St. Peter's?

Then came a sudden cry from the group's fringe. It was Lillian McDermott.

"You little varmint, don't you dare! Get yer cotton-pickin' hands outta there!" she shouted, as the gypsies quickly surrounded her, waving and flailing their flaps and papers as they lunged at her purse. Lillian, however, was a poor choice as victim. Not only did she do light aerobics twice a week back in Cedar Heights, but she had bred Dobermans all her life, and was by no means a soft touch. Back-pedaling quickly away from them, she produced a folded umbrella from her handbag. She held it menacingly before her, daring the rascals to advance further. The children reformed a circle around her, wary of her unexpected strength, but prepared still, to strike.

But what was this? It was Ted! He charged straight into the pack of urchins, with a violence that surprised them all.

"You little fucks get the fuck outta here!" he shouted, slapping in all directions at their heads and kicking like a wild ass at their flanks. One of his kicks was a most satisfying bruiser: his toe connected solidly with one boy's sitz-bone. The boy pulled back at once, and for a split-second looked ready to burst into tears. Next, his face then showed a look of genuine surprise, as if he truly couldn't imagine what had provoked Ted so much. His face then settled in a sneer of derision.

Scattered by Ted's assault, the gypsies soon regathered in a pack about fifteen feet away. His martial spirit roused, Ted stood out in front of the group, both to vaunt of his victory and defend them from attack. Looking at the gypsies though, you would never guess they were wicked thieves who had just moments ago been thwarted. They relaxed at once, looking for all purposes like smiling school children. A few threw Ted looks of disdainful amusement. 'We tried our little game,' their faces seemed to say, 'and as you see, it was just a game to us, and meant not much at all. Just look at *yourself* though, still bound up in knots, still strangled on your violence. More shameful for *your* soul than a gypsy's little tricks, wouldn't you say?'

Ted, though, received no such moral instruction. He was thrown off-balance, as well, by their continued casual ease. In his view, they should have run off in terror, gathered force for a counter-attack, took knives from their pockets, *something* - not just stood there picking their teeth with those relaxed contemptuous smiles. After a few minutes watching Ted's war stance, the gypsy kids got bored. After a few jeering remarks they slowly ambled off. The boy who had caught Ted's surest kick stayed behind. Once sure of Ted's attention, he gripped his buttocks in both hands, ran his tongue back and forth across his lips, and made some lewd pelvic movements. He then turned and walked away with an exaggerated sashay.

It was not clear to Ted exactly what this meant, but it was clear enough to send the blood pounding hard at his temples.

"You damn well *better* be moving on you gypsy sons-of-bitches," he muttered fiercely, as they leisurely strolled away.

Only after they were out of sight around the corner did he turn back to his group. But what was this…? The young gypsy mother was still there, at the yellow line at the bus-stop! In her long multi-colored patchwork skirt, she was paying them no attention, as if nothing had happened. Completely absorbed in her baby, she was whispering sweet little nothings as she dandled it. One could imagine no more benign image of maternity.

It was just this that Ted found disconcerting. He could not see how this one skinny slip of a woman could pose a threat. But look what had happened with the younger ones: just when they've lulled you into letting your guard down, they mount an all-out attack. *Tactics, my friend, tactics.* He was sure this older one was being wily. He stood between her and the Feelings Group, still tense, still suspicious.

"Don't you all worry about it," Ted said to the group, waving his hand in the direction of the sights they should be savoring. "You enjoy yourselves. I've got this one covered. One false move and she'll get a taste of the same treatment I gave the others."

But if this gypsy mother was brewing some evil plot, her intentions were well concealed. And try as he might, Ted could find no sinister intent as she wiped a snot off her baby's upper lip.

"It's here! The 64!" came several voices chirping happily. The rectangular orange box loomed into view, towering above the Lilliputian vehicles all around it. It stopped at the light just short block away...

Maternitas

At each of Bus 64's stairwells was a humorous chrome sign: DO NOT GO DOWN THE STAIRS UNTIL THE DOORS OPEN.

The joke was that nobody waited till the bus had stopped safely. Not because it wasn't a sound suggestion, but because the stairwell was already packed full, always, with six or more bodies on its two steep narrow steps. True, passengers were packed tight everywhere, not just on the stairwell. But with the different elevation of these steps, togetherness took on charming new dimensions. Knees could gouge bellies, elbows could poke thighs, faces were introduced to breasts and backs, even buttocks. When a rail wasn't handy, one was held snugly vertical by the tight press of bodies as the bus bumped along.

The bus slowed to a stop with a loud squeal of brakes. As its doors opened with a loud hiss, the Feelings Group was faced with a sheer wall of elbows and chests, backs, legs and hands – a living cubist collage. Their first gasps of shock gave way to murmurs of defeat, as they resigned themselves to waiting for the next, hopefully less crowded bus.

"Skoo-zee, skoo-zee," though, came the surprising Italian of Lillian McDermott, as she firmly pushed and insinuated her body into the pliable human mass. "C'mon you guys, you just gotta get in the spirit of it," she called with a smile. "Try the front door, go to the middle, just give a push. There's space here for everyone; you just gotta *make* it for yourself!"

After brief hesitation the group warmed to their task. And after much pushing, many offended glares, and dozens of skoo-zees on all sides, the entire ton and a half of the Feelings Group had been absorbed into the stairwells. The pneumatic doors tried to close but they kept on reopening, their rubber flaps jammed by some wayward limb or lard. On the fifth try they finally closed. Bus 64 rolled on forward. Victory for the Feelings Group! Heady exhilaration seized these Americans, fueled by that secret thrill novices on this bus feel, at being pressed so tightly against strangers.

"Cheaper than a taxi," said Cindy. "Look Ma, no hands," chortled Thelma, raising her hefty arms above her head. "Surf's up," cried beefy Joanne, imitating the gesture. Even Ted offered a weak joke, as the stress of his recent battle wore away. But then, just as he began to feel the infectiousness of their cheery banter, he noticed with a start that one step above him, just two feet from his nose, was the gypsy mother with her baby. Batten down the hatches! Save that cheerfulness for later! Ted quickly checked the button on his back pocket and pinned his camera to his side with his elbow. He poked Cindy in the arm and with a hiss and the point of a finger, alerted her to the gypsy's treacherous presence.

The gypsy though, was still doing a good job of concealing her wicked designs. She was just humming little nothings as she dandled her baby fondly. But Ted kept his guard up. One could never be too sure. And indeed - Ted was right. For only moments after he had put her under the strictest surveillance, the cunning gypsy made her move. Reaching down the neckline of her blouse, she lifted out a slack breast and set her baby suckling at its broad nipple.

Ted and Cindy looked away instantly, each imagining that to witness this scene would violate the gypsy's modesty. By and by, though, they each looked back to steal rapt wide-eyed glimpses. Cindy at first felt all flustered. But once she'd settled down enough, she saw that this gypsy was serenely abstracted, off day-dreaming about whatever it is that a gypsy woman dreams about. The baby too, she noticed, was not the degraded illegitimate creature she had first made it out to be. It was a *human* baby and yes, a rather cute one at that. Its face was streaked and dirty, but babies often got that way, even in Cedar

Heights. And this baby was not cute in the way every baby is cute; it was genuinely so. With such a neat little bobbed nose, and squinted eyes that seemed to be smiling. Yes this baby seemed healthy, and happy enough too, slung in the blanket round its mother's shoulders. A flush of feeling came over Cindy, as some deep sense of kinship coursed warm through her blood. She saw this gypsy mother now as Mother, as all mothers. And she felt awe as she watched Nature hard at work in the infant, whose lips were sucking rapidly at the big distended nipple.

Ted also could not help but staring back, at that slack dirty teat she had slipped out... *just like that*! He couldn't believe it! In the middle of a city bus! Thievery, even sneak thievery, was at least something human. But this went beyond that - this went all the way to animal! Each time he peeked at the suckling baby he turned away hotly. An image came to mind from when their little Wendy had been nursing, of those boxes of formula Cindy kept stacked in the pantry. On the side of the box was a soft-focus picture of a beatific mother in a white nightgown buttoned to her neck, holding the bottle at her baby's mouth. Ted's anger flared to indignance. It was one thing to go around snatching handbags, but this was another thing altogether. Jesus Christ! This was disgusting!!

Ted and Cindy were not alone in regarding this gypsy. Rosanna Matita, a court stenographer at the nearby *Tribunale*, was observing closely also. She too, found the display distasteful, and appealed to the legitimized powers for its cessation. No need for emotionalism or anger, she reasoned. We must simply do to the gypsies what the Germans did last year. They don't belong where they are, so you just need to send them back where they came from. No need for ugly words like "deportation." It was repatriation, plain and simple. No World War II horrors; nothing the least bit unjust. Romania even signed the agreement - nobody forced them. And so? The legislative means aren't lacking; we Italians need courage to use them!

Beside Rosanna stood Angelo Grossi. On the scales in his butcher shop was a sugary picture of a praying madonna. In the back, where he cut meat, were pin-ups of naked women. Angelo knew meat and he knew money - and women of both kinds. He too had a solution to the burning problem posed this morning by this skinny gypsy and her nursing baby. His nostrils flared wide and his eyes glowed at the sight of her nude bosomed chest. The conflicted feelings she aroused in him were soon resolved into a single clear motive. Yes, the dirty woman needed a lesson. He knew just how to give it.

First thing he'd do is stride right into that camper or tent or whatever ramshackle thing she lived in, in that camp on the outskirts. He'd just stride right inside and make his first lesson plain as day: WHACK WHACK WHACK! - a few sound claps across the face and then BOK!: the haymaker, to cuff her down. Then he'd pounce down and grab up that big crazy-colored skirt. She'd be kicking and clawing like a wildcat - but no matter. She'd change that tune quick, like the *puttana* they all are in those crazy-colored skirts. Mmmm yes... that would teach her who's boss here.

As Ted, Cindy, Rosanna, Angelo and others watched and reflected, they too were being observed. Two sloped eyes peering out from a small tan face watched the thoughts mirrored on their faces. These sloped eyes displayed no feelings. They looked benign, inoffensive. This was a feigned mildness, though, the mask worn by the immigrant. Behind these mild eyes lay two other eyes, that were guarded and scowling and bulging with spite. 'That's right,' Imogena cheered to herself in her native Tagalog, 'that's right gypsy mother: just shove it back in their faces.... You keep on with your suckling and let them make themselves sick over it. They make me sick, these Italians – with their sweet talk lovey-dovey about babies... I'm not fooled when I'm pushing one of their fat babies down the street and they smile into the carriage and they smile at me pushing it. I'm not buying that smile. No I'm not.

'Twelve thousand *lire* an hour.' That's what they're smiling at. Twelve thousand and ought to be grateful. That's what they're thinking. That's all a *filippina* is to an Italian. Twelve thousand to boil them up another plateful of macaroni. Twelve thousand to wash their toilets and fancy clothes and take out their rubbish. Twelve thousand to keep some hag from tipping over when you take her shopping. I'm not fooled by their sweet talk and smiles. You keep suckling your baby, you dark little gypsy woman. Let them make themselves sick...'

Cindy, Ted, Rosanna, Marco, Imogena and others who were watching now, on all sides, all thinking... In the midst of this cross-fire of reflection, baby Lachlik sucked gratefully at his mother's gypsy nipple. The blanket around him felt snug. He felt warm and protected. The soft nipple filled his whole mouth. Warm milk flowed onto his tongue and coursed wet down his throat, then on down into his stomach. From there, it flowed out into every corner of his little gypsy body, bringing him new strength and energy to greet the great event of Life.

The Hospital Stop

Ever more loaded with bodies, Bus 64 struggled up the cobbled incline toward the hospital. Vinzo hated this stop - the place and the people and all that went with them. The hospital was a grey monolith that reminded him of the mausoleums in the cemetery where his parents were buried. It came right up to the sidewalk, where the leaves hung limp on exhaust-sickened trees whose bark was half peeled-off, leaving green, grey and brown patches that looked like army camouflage. Sticking out from the hospital wall was an enormous red cross, projecting out over the sidewalk, no different from the signs he saw everywhere, on gas stations and cinemas and billboards and stores. Buy gas here! signs like this said. Shop here! Eat here! Drink this! Smoke this! See this film! said such signs. But this sign was different. "Die here" said the red cross sticking out from the hospital wall. For what else did a red cross mean, but the end of the line? Or a bad time for those sitting for a spell, near the exit?

The hospital was gloomy and the passengers going there were no better. First there were the visitors, always hanging around the driver's cubicle asking him questions they knew the answers to. "This is the hospital stop, isn't it? My mother/brother/sister has been here for... he/she fell sick this past... we won't know if it's... until..." Or: "Is this where the hospital is? I'm coming all the way from ... my poor... you see... ever since last February. .." For these folks a straight answer was never good enough. They kept trying to wheedle something out of him: a smile or remark - what *was it* they wanted? And when they weren't trying to suck something out of him they spilled out their hard-luck story through the space in the glass partition.

Then there were the outpatients, the more obvious ones, that is - with their slings, their bandaged eyes, their neck braces and plastered limbs. Such a banged-up mess, the lot of them, that made shivers go up and down his legs. The others were not much better, those with no sling, cast or brace but whom he could spot just the same. They looked worried or gaunt or had punched-out eyes or ghost-like faces. They shook, they coughed, they tottered, and looked like hell generally. They were slow or decrepit, and needed help getting on or off.

Last came the hospital workers. Though they were the healthy ones, they spooked him as much as the clearly ailing. How normal they looked at curbside as they smoked, chatted or read the paper, looking natty in their white shoes and turquoise smocks. Once inside the mausoleum though, he knew they were up to no good. Draining out blood. Slicing muscle and organs. Punching needles through skin and veins. He could imagine what went on in there and had no wish to be reminded. All those natty-looking workers doing nasty tasks, nasty shift after nasty shift, day and night - like some factory in Torino, week after week, month after month, year in year out, *forever*... What's not to hate at this stop with its gruesome red cross?

The bus came to a stop. After the tides of people had moved on and gotten off, a frail old woman stood on the sidewalk, needing help getting on. But with a bamboo cane in one hand and a big manila envelope in her other, she just stood there, still and smiling. Two sturdy men went down. They crooked her elbows into a tight right angle, and with a one-two-three lifted her up to the top of the stairs.

Once she was inside, a stout woman all in black, in the front seat, rose laboriously to her feet. She had thick badly bowed legs and huge swollen ankles. "*Prego, signora,*" she said, indicating the seat she had risen from. "I'm not going very far at all, *prego...*"

"You'll do no such thing," came a strong voice from behind her. "Please sit right back down; this *giovanotto* here will give her his seat."

It was the voice of old Ignazio Bruno, sitting behind her, still in the pose of a basalt pharoah. As a witness to this scene he could not help but act. For how shameful this was - why just *think* of it! A swollen-ankled old *signora* having to give up her seat, when just across the aisle a perfectly healthy youngster sat by comfortably? Why just look at him, the good-for-nothing! The lanky youth with the long hair was still slouched in his seat, moving his head back and forth to the rhythms from his headset. It was not clear if he had even seen the two women, let alone felt his obligation. One baleful eye though, was peering out from beneath his hair, aware he'd been fixed in Ignazio Bruno's withering stare. But whatever he made of it, he showed no sign of movement.

"Yes, it's *you* he's talking about! You heard him, you young rotten spoiled slug. Get up there, get up off your duff!" barked a matron standing by, clear eyes fiercely blazing in her square powdered face.

"Don't waste your breath, *cara*," sighed the stout bowlegged woman. "These young ones today wouldn't move for their own mothers. Believe me, it's no problem, I can just..."

"Don't you dare move from that seat!" cried Ignazio Bruno with indignation. "You just sit right back down please." Then he rose to his feet and struck a valorous pose with his cane, like a youthful Garibaldi who had just captured a fort.

"No, no, don't bother..." continued the stout woman, rising heavily with resignation. "You can't expect these young ones nowadays...

"*SILENZIO!!*" cried Ignazio Bruno, now causing heads to turn everywhere. "You'll take your seat, and this young Turk will stand up yes he will - because *QUI COMANDO IO!!*"

QUI COMANDO IO. I'M IN COMMAND HERE! What strange words to resound through a bus on a nice summer morning. And so, tuning in now, what did the many newcomers to this drama see? Did they see the feeble old woman, so clearly in need of a seat? (no) Or the charitable stout woman, who so stoicly offered her own? (no) Or the lanky youth, who like a mule would not budge? No, they saw none of this. But what everyone *did* see was a wild-eyed Ignazio

Bruno valorously posed with his cane, his world war whatever-it-was pin bright on his lapel, declaring that he was in absolute command.

Comment was not slow in forthcoming.

"*Guarda, Il Duce*," snickered one man.

"Will you listen to Caesar!" chuckled a woman with shopping bags.

"*Stronzo fascista*! Fascist asshole!" came a loud guttural cry from the rear.

Stronzo fascista??!! It took a long moment for Bruno Ignazio to register these words, to realize that it was *he* who had become the object of scorn and amusement. But could this really be? Why just the thought of it was staggering! He, who was upholding the standards of a civilized people. He, who alone sought to secure these elderly women their rightful places. This was absolutely infuriating… and pushed the old man beyond all bounds of ordinary cantankerousness. He turned on the youth and began to thrash him with his mahogany cane, punctuating each blow with a wrathful cry.

Ah, what wonderful strength still flowed through his old weathered body! It cost two sturdy men nearby no small effort to restrain him.

Forcibly subdued finally, and wrestled back into his seat, Ignazio Bruno smoothed his lapels carefully. He adjusted the knot of his tie, and he pulled forward the crease on each pant leg. He noted with satisfaction that the stout woman was in her original seat. And that the ragged no-good youth had fled somewhere to the rear, with the frail white-haired lady settled peacefully into his place. His attire restored to correctness, he drew himself erect once again, like a basalt pharoah in his orange plastic seat.

"*Tutto a posto*, all in order," he said softly, to no one in particular, his chin jutting far forward. The bus rolled on forward…

54

Serena's Secret

Once settled in the lanky youth's seat, white-haired Serena Pedretti fell oblivious to the hubbub about her. Though the air was still aquiver from the valiant charge of Ignazio Bruno, the event coursed downstream into her past and disappeared. What was absorbing her now, wholly, were the two hands that were clasped atop the cane handle before her. *Her* hands these were, and remarkable hands at that. Such great knobby knuckles slung with tight tendonous cords. Such broad fans of bone in their loose wrap of skin, with cracked thickened nails on each big-jointed finger's tip. Yes these hands were remarkable - more marvelous than ever, more marvelous than what seemed just a moment ago, over sixty years past. Flawless china-shop hands they were then, with shaped lacquered nails and gem-studded rings. The hands of a lady, elegant and refined. But not nearly as fine as these gnarled talons now before her.

Who could understand it? wondered Serena. The same me, yet a different me, regarding my same hands, that yet were different hands. The same Serena who was yet a different Serena, absorbed in the same and yet different singularity of a moment. Two moments that were separated by sixty years, yet stood beside one another within her, as real as two passengers side-by-side in the aisle.

And what about the future? How many moments yet to come? The big question of the day, if indeed there had to be such a thing. She fingered the large manila envelope that was lying in her lap. Then she opened the flap and slid out its contents - but just a little. No need to pull them out more, or even think about them, for that matter. Just a short stack of x-rays, each imprinted with her name and the date, and the hour, minute and second of the exposure. It was the third shot that mattered. The shot with the gray blotch - the 'irregularity', as he had called it. This was the blotch the machine had so helpfully framed in white lines, as in the crosshairs of a rifle. This was the blotch that made the nice young doctor speak to her at such length. The blotch that kept his lowered eyes from meeting hers, that made his tone go so flat. The blotch that inspired him to such thickets of words, dense with discrete indirection, all to simply tell her, without having to say so, that she soon would be dead.

Silly, was it not, to think of all the ways she had imagined her end would first greet her. All those fears that had nagged or intruded at side moments: fears of accidents that never happened, dreams with frightful images that vanished with the alarm clock, the good citizen's fear of random attack, the dread that could fill the room from a newscast, unnamed torments she had anticipated, agonies too hard to endure… All of them so unlike this morning's banal event: a polite young man in a white coat in a clean quiet room, speaking of a four-syllable word growing on her transverse whatever, its dimensions measured precisely by his instruments, her survival probabilities worked out to their last permutation.

Death's time-worn road was well paved now, it seemed. Paved and well-charted, complete with road-map and time-table. It was not this way always. A ninety-year-old physician's daughter is no stranger to endings. Serena knew of another time – in which one died in a different way. How often she would wait up late, until dawn even, till Father came home from his vigil at some neighbor's parting drama. She could hear his voice even now, as he waxed reflective over brandy before going upstairs for some sleep. "Always the mystery," he would say, looking at the amber fluid as if studying it. "Always the mystery, always the unknown."

For days, weeks or months he would tell of some patient's worsening symptoms. He likened it to a chess game, move and counter-move. Doctor versus illness - the underworld - an opponent both wily and resourceful. Even when beaten, Father played out the end-game, and rigorously sustained treatment after hope was long gone. And when the game was played out, then the same sober sequence:

the call for the priest, the soul's brief emergence to profess its faith. The eyelids shut for good, and the sheet raised over head, while the snuffed candle's smoke drifted off into darkness.

Another image came to mind: it was Father once again, on the day of a surgery. First his ritual breakfast, neither too heavy nor too light. The carriage outside the door, the horse pawing impatiently at the gravel. Moments later it would be off trotting fast down the driveway, Father sitting erect on the rider's bench, immersed in its hooves' klip-klop rhythm. A meditation, he called it, this music of the hooves, which focused his attention.

What was it like, Serena wondered, for that young doctor today, driving to work in this traffic, beckoned to and fro by that beeping thing on his belt? What was he thinking as he gazed at the dials and meters of that machine that saw into her body? And what had he felt as he scrutinized her x-rays, clipped up before him in a neat row, like black laundry? "Always the mystery, always the unknown..." Did this young man have such thoughts such as these?

Serena looked at the backs of her hands again. Their slate-blue veins lay nearly entire, like worms, and she felt they were telling her some kind of secret. She saw how a vein disappeared beneath a knuckle only to resurface, wrapped round a finger joint - and she felt that was a secret also. Only of late had she discovered the secret - or maybe the secret had discovered her. But however it had happened, she now felt that *everything* was a secret - and a secret she could not share. Not because she didn't want to, but because she did not know how to say it. And who would believe her anyway? Who would believe a secret being whispered by a cane made of bamboo, by trees passing a bus window, or by an old withered hand?

Only now, at this late hour, did things press into her so sweetly and deeply. She had passed her whole life as does everyone, rushing and dreaming in blind, deaf refusal of the miracle of each moment. But what was this new solitariness, this strong *sense* of things she was now feeling? Was it some kind of initiation, some gift granted to the near-dying, that was uncommunicable, unintelligible, to those who believed life was for living alone?

Could she possibly explain this to her son Carlo and his wife Vanessa? How could she share with them this secret of living, while they insisted she was only dying? Without the secret, they would turn it all to tragedy, in their usual ways. With Carlo it would be his usual pretense of buoyancy and strength, which was all nervous movement and loud empty words. With Vanessa it would be that pathetic weepiness she always carried round inside herself. Only now it would seep out openly and proudly, with supposed good reason.

Moment after moment she would continue to live her secret - while they warded off their own deaths, which they feared seeing in hers. And that's how it would be – all the way till the end, pain included: moment after moment, secret after secret. Right now it was the secret of her bones rattling in this plastic seat, the trees along the Tiber passing by, with their lattice-work branches and sun-lit leaves. Then the secret of a short hobbled walk from the station to her flat. Then the great secret of lunch, with so many smaller secrets enfolded within it. First, Vanessa's gentle broth with *vermicelli*, which tickled your lips coming off the spoon. Then the soft potted chicken, with parsley carrots and crisped potatoes, salty and fragrant with rosemary. The secret of wine warm in her veins. The sawing knife and the fork's voyage to the mouth that could open. And the many secret ways that the tongue knew how to smile.

Then the best secret of all – her nap by the window. How good to be old, weak and sleepy, full of good food and wine. And to go to the wide chair with the plump cushions and set herself down in it. The window and shutters would be open. The courtyard would be still. And that reliable shaft of sunlight would fall across her chair for two hours, baking her to lusciousness in its warmth. She would give herself up to her food and the sun and the stillness and cushions, like the weary old white-hair which is all that she was, all happy and full, all curled up and cozy, like a sweet old gray cat!

Special Guests

Not just doctors, nurses and the sick and dying get on at the hospital stop. Many ordinary, temporarily healthy folks like us get on also. Today, two among them merit brief mention. Not because they are special, at least in any positive sense. But because they are *caratteristico*; no ride would be complete without them.

The first is a dapper gent who rides back and forth through the *centro storico* on a regular basis. In winter, he wears a camel topcoat and a nice Borsalino. When it rains, he wears a double-breasted trench coat with tortoise-shell buttons. On hot days like today, he wears a linen safari jacket with braided epaulets. But for all his fine clothes this man never looks quite right in them; he seems an imposter. Indeed, the only thing that truly suits him, which he wears all year round, is a port-wine-colored scar that runs from one ear to his chin. When this dapper gent comes on board, keep close watch on your valuables.

Vinzo watched him get on and knows just what he's up to. He even mutters something in disgust, for though Vinzo has his defects, he works for his money and is in no way dishonest. But don't rely on Vinzo's small virtue to protect you, for from his years of experience he has evolved wise rules of thumb:

1) Brakes on *tight*, while passengers get on and off.

2) Eyes straight ahead always, when the bus is in motion.

3) Pray you never hit anybody.

4) If you hit somebody, pray it was not your fault.

5) If it was your fault, pray you can weasel out of it.

6) When there's trouble aboard, let the passengers fight it out among themselves.

Sound advice - number six - when this man gets aboard with his port-wine-colored scar.

This fall, the papers trumpeted a new campaign that would rid the bus-lines of thieves. But in the many months since then, no results have been seen - just more new funny signs. Beside the center doors of each bus is a sign showing a stick figure passenger. Red arrows curve around from behind it, pointing at its shirt and its pockets, its camera and purse. Below the stick figure is written:

> *Attenti ai borsegiatori!*
> Beware of pickpockets!
> *Attention aux voleurs!*
> *Achtung taschendiebe!*
> *Cuidado con los carteristas!*

Working the center doors (in his preferred style), The Man with the Port-Wine-Colored Scar stood for hours beneath this very sign, successfully plying the trade it warned of. As women came on or got off, he would offer a hand or step aside to clear the way, which he indicated with a flourish. And to the elderly, he was solicitous, steadying them by the elbow, inquiring of their health - if only more people had such manners! Was a tourist lost? What a friendly fellow this was, who gave directions and advice, and with such clever quips also, in Spanish, French and English. And should mother and child get mired in mutual irritation, watch him restore harmony with a joke, a candy or kind word.

Against this succession of poses, such guile and calculation, what power indeed had one puny tin sign?

The Man with the Port-Wine-Colored Scar was not lazy, but on this sweltering morning his thoughts had already turned from work. He saw himself beneath the trees at *Porta Pia* sipping Camparis with his cousins, before sitting out the afternoon heat in a nearby *trattoria*. Like anyone who is self-employed, inertia sometimes got the best of him. It was a full hour before lunch-time, but something inside him had already switched off. It was with a vague sense of guilt then, that he withdrew his antennae, vowing to work a bit longer that evening, or some day.... If any fruit was to be picked on the rest of *this* ride, it would have to be *very* low-hanging.

Getting on behind The Man with the Port-Wine-Colored Scar was The Man with the *Mano Morta*. Now *mano morta* means "dead hand," but there's no point in looking; his two paws are quite alive and flexible. If you want to know why he is called "the dead hand," just ask a Roman woman – one who is neither very old, nor very young, nor decisively ugly. She will tell you. But don't expect her to maintain her good temper.

Like The Man with the Port-Wine-Colored Scar, The Man with the *Mano Morta* plays a game of stealth and dexterity, but one that requires a more meager kind of skill. It's a low stinky game really, but nonetheless popular. It's a game of molestation; here's how it's played.

Assuming the demeanor of an ordinary comatose commuter, he maneuvers himself so that his hand hangs beside some female bottom that he fancies greatly. Or he grasps a railing or seat-back so his arm or elbow will be near some breast he finds inspirational. Very casually then, and very gradually, he brings his hand or arm into contact. Not for him the ribald pinch, the gaffer's forthright squeeze, the lecher's lunging grasp. No, for him pleasure comes in the subtlest increases in pressure, finely adjusted to exploit the jostling bodies crammed so closely together. The aim of this game is to sustain and enjoy this insidious subtle contact.

Now the woman may know what is happening, but not so very well as you might imagine. With all this braking and jostling, with your knees, hips, thighs, back, shoulders and buttocks already jammed tight against others, it can be hard to be sure who's actually choosing to do what. And since bus etiquette suggests one ignore all this contact anyway, a woman's doubts can be strong. And even if she's sure, she is less sure what to do about it. Fight her way free through the crush? Confront the *bastardo*? And how: with a look or a gesture? Dare she actually speak out? Might this fellow get violent? And should she give the least sign of recognition, she learns how this hand earned its name. It goes dead in an instant - just another mitt minding its own business.

Today's player with the dead hand is a southpaw named Enrico. He takes the 64 cross-town each day to his fiancee's, for lunch. There, seated between her older sister and her mother, he enjoys an orderly sequence of well-prepared dishes, with all his favorites from the South. What comfort and solace, the oasis of lunch in this rude urban chaos. When he finally married, such pleasures would be all his. But with his fiancee's sister still unmarried, and himself still just thirty, things were fine as they were. No need to rush to the altar. But... after nine years of engagement, *beh*, a man can get bored. He needs some spice, a bit of sport, a bit of old-fashioned hanky-panky. And what better way to kill the hour cross-town, than some sly dog *mano morta*?

Vinzo's World

Pulling away from the hospital, Vinzo faced a tricky maneuver. He had to quickly cross over four lanes in order to turn at the bridge that crosses the Tiber. Lanes though, existed here but loosely, for the cars advanced as an irregular mass, like so many spermatozoons competing to nose out their brothers. To this difficulty was added the ungainliness of his bus. Could he manage to slide over without crunching the cars darting on all sides of him, ignoring his turn signal, thwarting him in the rudest ways possible? Worse still were the kids on *motorini*, who cut and weaved among cars recklessly, like drunken barracuda.

Inching forward and to his left, Vinzo surveyed the cars spread out before him. This inching soon stopped when the traffic light turned red. From both sides of the road, dark-skinned young men swarmed out among the motionless cars. A powerfully built Arab walked swiftly up and down, each upraised hand holding flowers that were wilting fast in the heat. Several open-shirted Sri Lankans walked a criss-cross pattern, selling Kleenex, Bic lighters, and those little trees that give your car the fake stink of fresh pine. A tall gaunt Tunisian hawked cardboards to cast shade on your dashboard. Two fleshy Morrocans with squeegies walked languidly from car to car, in slack search of dirty windshields.

This usual scene moved Vinzo to his usual reflections. 'Who the hell are all these people?' he wondered. 'And where the hell do they come from? And why the hell did they come here, and who the hell let them in? And what the hell are they good for, except crawling like insects all over our cars, pestering and nagging and begging like dogs, then holding up traffic when the light turns green?'

Directly beneath his windshield, one of these same troublesome insects was cleaning the windshield of a Fiat Croma Turbo 14X with a double exhaust pipe – a detail that caused Vinzo's eyes to bug out. 'Remarkable!' he thought. 'Could it actually be a 14X he was looking at, but with two exhaust pipes, not one? Now if it were a Turbo 23X and not the 14X – well, that would be understandable. Its extra cylinders made the double exhaust necessary, and was standard equipment. But a 14X with a double exhaust? He would look that one up just as soon as he got home. For on the shelf of an honored wall of his living room was every issue of *'Quattro Ruote'* for the last nineteen years.

Each month, with the concentration of a scholar, Vinzo pored over photos and lists of specifications of the latest cars being manufactured. He followed the automotive world as assiduously as others follow the stock market, sports or politics. He could tell you nothing about Germany, except that it had been infested with Nazis who'd became rabid, and that a big wall there had gone up and come down. But he knew rafts of information about the vicissitudes of Audi, of Opel, of Volkswagen, BMW, Porsche and Daimler Benz, and how their products had fared for decades.

Likewise, though he knew nothing about Japan – save that they were as stupid as the Italians in the war but had smartened up quick and gotten rich since then – he knew the dozens of new models launched by Nissan and Honda, Toyota and Mazda, Subaru and Mitsubishi. And though his knowledge of America was limited to TV and what he heard from his cousin Nuno, who visited New Jersey back in the seventies, his knowledge of Ford, Chrysler, and General Motors was downright encyclopaedic.

While the average person, seeing a Fiat, might see that it was a Croma and was white, Vinzo noticed if it was a Fiat Croma 1.6, or a 2.8 CHT, or a 2lO1E., or a 2.0 i.e 16V cat, or a 2.0 i.e. turbo, or a 215 diesel or a 119, 214, or 215 turbodiesel. And along with each model went a whole realm of specifications. Things like suspension systems, brake systems, fuel systems, engine sizes and types, compression ratios, body weight to engine power ratios, transmissions, climate control — not to mention performance factors such as top speed, rate of acceleration, gas consumption at different speeds and distances, and internal noise. Just as a gallery of dark old paintings, through knowledge, becomes a world of styles, schools and personalities, so too was the world of traffic transformed for our Vinzo. For him each car was a snowflake, endowed with its own automotive (so to speak) soul.

The light turned green. The mob of cars inched forward... except for the Fiat Croma Turbo l4X. The sluggish Moroccan was still wiping his suds off its back windshield. BEEEP!! went Bus 64's horn, with the sound of the squeezed nose of a frighteningly large clown. BEEEP BEEEEP!! BEEEEP!!! "*Sbrigati*, step on it, you little shit," hissed our Vinzo, pressing the horn with both palms till his biceps bulged out. BEEEP BEEEEEEEP! "I said move it!" BEEP! BEEP! BEEEEEP!! The Moroccan drew his squeegie hurriedly across the back windshield, leaving some dirty streaks in his haste. He then ran to the driver's window, throwing Vinzo a dirty look as he was being paid.

"*Ma vaffanculo*," Vinzo cursed into his windshield, adding an obscene gesture for emphasis. 'You move when I tell you, you black insect," he muttered. The Fiat Turbo Crome l4X with the double exhaust slowly moved forward. The Moroccan joined the others standing by on the sidewalk.

It is of course understandable that Vinzo should have such an extensive set of criteria for regarding cars, for not only is he surrounded by them all day, but they present an almost infinite variety. This is hardly the case for humans, that most stagnant of creations, who come in such a limited number of models, and whose smallest alteration calls for cycles lasting eons. No wonder, then, that his criteria for classifying people should be more modest. Perhaps more could be said about different aspects of our Vinzo's perceptions, but there's no time now. The light's green! We're actually moving!

Across the Tiber

We may be dismayed by our driver but not by our bus. Bus 64 emerged from the Fiat Coach Division in Torino on May 5, 1986, a robust orange toddler of nineteen tons. But unlike living newborns, which must mature first in many ways, Bus 64 was born fully operational. After a normal gestation period of 512 man-hours, it rolled off the assembly line and was towed to a parking lot at 3:15 that day. Just six short days later it was in a bus depot in Rome, and was at once put in service, shoulder-to-shoulder with adult buses, all veterans of the road.

Among mammals, gestation results from the briefest of exertions. Mitosis then takes over to fulfill nature's destiny. But how different was the birth of our Bus 64.

The brightest men on several continents studied metallurgy and chemistry, physics and engineering, to make this lumbering bus we take so much for granted, and even complain about. But what an achievement is a tire, what a feat a pneumatic door! And this molded plastic seat, and this red electric call-button! At no point in this process was anything automatic. Advances came only through experiment and industry. This uncomfortable box in which we now roll is one of the humbler triumphs of technology, that pride of our age.

If we swam across the Tiber, it would take two to five minutes (but don't try it; the last person who did went belly-up from the toxins). If we walked across any of its bridges, it would take one to three minutes, depending on our vigor or distraction by the sights. But this morning, aboard this powerful exemplar of modern technology, Bus 64, it will take five to nine minutes from one side to the other.

So long just to cross such a short bridge? Yes that's right, but no impatience please, for after all: many others must travel along both sides of this river. They too must keep moving. The lights are slow but they're needed. Rome wasn't built for cars anyway - so just try to think of it this way: imagine you are one tiny blood cell in a tiny capillary somewhere in an old bloated voluptuary - one who is overfed, drinks too much, keeps bad hours and debauches. We should be grateful things move at all then, albeit pokily. And they sometimes *don't* move, as you no doubt have seen. So - if *this* charm doesn't work, just remember: it's the Eternal City that we're crawling through. So what possible difference can five minutes make, this way or that?

No griping or whining then. Let's try to divert ourselves; it's easy enough to do here. Look, for instance, at those two bridges, just a short way upstream. The further one is called *Ponte Sant'Angelo.* That's pontih-sant-angelo - a pretty sounding name. The words are nicely musical though their meaning often gets lost: that is, bridge, saint, and angel. It's like 'Los Angeles', which also means 'angels', but to no one at all, but instead suggests Hollywood and freeways, earthquakes and lifestyles, black men and gangs, and shooting and fires. This makes sense in Los Angeles, for look where you will you will not see an angel. It makes less sense on this bridge, where ten tall angels stand at intervals, wearing large feathered wings and air-blown stone robes.

Tourists and pilgrims admire these angels. They're tickled by the props in which Catholics rigged up religion. But it's 1994 now. This angel-saint motif has long passed out of vogue. These themes still survive though they're long tuckered out. The bones of the Catholic carcass, though, are still being burnished here. The guidebooks repeat in fine creaky phrases that the torch still burns bright in this crucible of Western values. That's hokum of course; it's a sideshow of fossils, profound though they be. They're nice relics for some folks but nothing to most. The times have raced forward and left all this behind - though where we have raced to, is hardly clear. But wherever we've gone to, saints and angels mean little.

But even in old times things were no doubt quite like today. Life was the same old rounds still, of sitting and hauling, and chewing and sleeping, and wishing and fearing and straining and dreaming. It was wrapped up, though, in a much prettier package. The big money went into pictures and churches and statues. Thus this marvelous old city with this marvelous old bridge. While we with our lights, phones and TVs, our cars, planes and penicillin, have scant need for angels save as images in old artworks, or a skirt to grasp at, in desperate moments.

You can see this bridge on foot later, if you wish to, and get from these statues what you will. The angels still speak in their mute passionate language, standing high on their pedestals against the blue summer sky. One holds a shroud, another a crown of thorns, a third offers a handful of nails up to heaven. All three wear a piteous expression, and ask the same question: 'why?' Along with them stand other angels: one with a cross, one with a column, another with a pike and sponge. These angels are smiling though. They're tranquil, beatific. They've found something sublime in the same cruel deed. Walking this bridge is an alternation of extremes: angels of misery, angels of joy, angels of misery, angels of joy. A strong experience to whoever still bothers with such things as angels and saviors and teachers of men.

At one end of the bridge stand two saints cut from stone. One holds open a book; it must be the Bible. He looks dead serious as he reads it. The other holds a sword upright. He too looks serious. But since saints are not violent and don't carry swords, we must figure out for ourselves why he's got one, and why he's so stern, and what that might mean to us - if anything. There are many ways to approach this, but no great need to bother, since these two fellows make such a fine snapshot. These statues form a perfect frame for the angel-studded bridge with the old fort right behind it. It's a perfect composition you can line up in an instant. You may have to wait a few moments till some tourists move on, but it's well worth the wait since your shot's a sure winner. When your picture is developed, write the name on the back while it's fresh in your mind. That's *Ponte Sant' Angelo*, or bridge, saint and angel.

The next bridge, nearer to us, is *Ponte Vittorio Emanuelle II*. Little effort, as you can see, has been spared in its decoration. Its arches are bordered in garlands and cornucopia, floral wreathes and palms. Lion's heads, eagles, curlicued scrolls, and quivers of arrows are tastefully distributed in the cornice-work. An ornamented balustrade girds its sidewalks on both sides. Statuary compositions are set at intervals along its top. These statues are more complex than those single angels we just saw two hundred yards, and three hundred years upstream. From the bus we can't see them well, but their writhing forms speak clearly. They say 'ponderous', 'melodramatic', 'rhetorical', 'exaggerated'.

If you cross *that* bridge on foot you can see what we mean. Soldiers strike heroic postures while protecting distraught women clutching crying infants. Brawny nude men built like comic-book heroes hold their fallen comrades-in-arms. Some of these statues wear helmets with the old Roman crest, to convince moderns that they too, bore within themselves the greatness of Empire. They all swear allegiance to a block-jawed man who stands impassively above them. But ...with those two hemispheres on his chest, he must be a woman. His/her name is probably Justice: there's a scales in one hand.

This bridge is excellent too, in its own grandiose way. It's particularly lovely at dawn and at dusk. The forms take on a classic simplicity in the half-light, and are beautiful against the timeless sky, across this timeless river with its angelic bridge and ancient fortress. Looking at this bridge through the half-blind eyes of aestheticism, we forgive it the stupidities of the age that produced it. We ignore its brutish soldiers and maudlin mothers, its angels weighted down with sharp weapons and chains - naughty counterparts to their pious breathren just a short bit upstream. We enjoy just their beauty, which is all we choose to see.

The first bridge came from a time that liked images of men who were inspired by celestial beings. On the second bridge these same symbols were demoted, to vaunt the vanities of the motherland. Both bridges reflect their age, as does this third one we now ride on. You can't see it of course, but don't worry, you aren't missing much. The only thing pretty about it is its name: *Ponte Principe Amadeo Savoia-Aosta*.

This bridge looks as if it were drawn from a high school science book: Chapter 12 – Elements of a Bridge. Or from one of those line drawings they put in the dictionary, so you will not confuse a 'bridge' with, say, a 'breechloader', an archaic rifle, or with a 'brig', a square-rigged ship with two masts. This bridge is quite plain. Its rude concrete base supports three graceless arches with no decoration. Its plain balustrade offers nothing to the eye, and serves just to keep us from driving off the edge into the river. This bridge was conceived just to bear vehicles. It's got no ornament and makes no bow to any muse or ideal.

Leap-frogging from one bridge to another makes us wonder - about the next bridge that will span the Tiber. We can't, after all, imagine a Rome that stops building. What might it be like, then? One of those mono-rails we keep reading about, that slides swiftly on super-magnets? Or a hydrofoil that whisks crowds across on a cushion of air?

These are sunny speculations. They may well come to pass. But as we look at these bridges from one age to another, we see things are clearly declining. Getting worse, only worse. And things don't look too rosy anywhere. Look around. What do *you* see? Is there any light *you* can see, shining bright, on the horizon? Terrible forces have been loosed and are growing only stronger. Maybe the next bridge will be a step backwards: a pile of boulders, a ramp of felled trees, or a swaying structure made of vines. Hardly nice thoughts to be having on a nice day like this one. But things sure can get bad and god-awfully destructive, as we drift further downstream from those saints and those angels.

A Fish Out of Water

The poor Tiber is now toxic. Modern lore has it that just one drop of its water, in either of your ears, will dispatch you as quickly as any potion of Lucretia Borgia. From whence comes this befoulment? The usual story - you know how it goes: corporate incontinence and civic neglect. But there's one special element you may not have suspected...

Rome's cats are beloved. They lounge in droves around monuments and in parks. They live three and four generations strong, beside familial dumpsters. Old women set out food for them. Books, pictures and calendars celebrate them. But these cats aren't loved just for their furry cuteness or noble mein. They're loved also for their fanged vigilance. For modern lore has it also, that for each man and woman, Rome hosts thirty-three rats. We see them so seldom because they keep a prudent low profile. Now the rat, did you know? is at home when in water. The Tiber provides them a congenial and safe concourse. They swim in it routinely in thousands and thousands, rendering it a dilute viral broth.

This river scene's not refreshing. See those grey-green turbid waters, those sparse reeds sticking out like scraggly hairs? It's hard to believe that this river was once called *pupo biondo*, 'the blonde child', in praise of the charm it so naturally exuded. That old Tiber flowed down from pure green Umbrian heights. Wise ancients chose to settle here, where the earth smiled so warmly and Fate blessed their big dreams. It was by *that* Tiber's banks that Michelangelo set his river god, whose strong noble repose was symbolic of its waters. Just one century ago, these banks were walled up with tall travertine slabs; thus the scene we see now: a kind of drainage ditch by Praxiteles. Poor yesteryear's blonde child is today's ailing mortal.

See that fellow down there fishing, on the banks by the bridge side? In him we sense the calm that this river once transmitted. But why is he fishing, you ask, since the river is so toxic? Certain fish, it turns out, are more hardy than we are. Not delicate or small fish (they too can't survive here), but big fish, big nasty fish, all scavengers and bottom feeders – the aquatic equivalents of those dogs that guard junk-yards. Such fish can survive but their flesh pays a price. Before you can eat them they must first go through detox: kept alive in fresh water till they cast out their feces and more sewerish elements. After three days, at most, you can then eat them with pleasure. Of course, you can bypass all this with a trip to the market. You walk out in five minutes with clean boned fresh filets. But such logic is repugnant to the spirit of fishermen. Where there are fish there are fishermen. Fishermen fish because they like fishing. Why they eat what they catch should need no explanation.

Franco is the name of this fisherman on the riverbank. He comes down here each day when he's free for a few hours. His friends invite him to play cards, to watch the soccer match, to sip coffee and smoke cigarettes. Franco at first goes along, but within minutes he goes quiet and gets restless, uncomfortable. The next thing you know, you look for Franco - and he's gone... He's fled to the Tiber with his tackle box, rod and bucket. 'What's the matter with you, Franco?' 'What's the problem?' 'Why can't you mix in?' 'Why always down to the river when you hardly catch a thing?' Franco's heard these same questions innumerable times. "I don't know," he responds with a shrug and shy smile. "I guess I just feel like a fish out of water."

He's caught nothing today, nor a fish in three weeks. Though he's pleased when they bite he's still pleased if they don't. He most of all just likes watching the river move by. And even if he never caught another fish - ever - he'd die grateful, still smiling - because of the fish that he'd caught right here, last year, for Good Friday.

It was the Tuesday before Good Friday. He'd come down to the river with his older boy, Gino. His bucket was empty; they'd passed three lovely hours. And then... late afternoon, just when he was ready to call it quits, a fish took his bait, and with such suddenness and force he was near pulled into the water. He fought with this fish a full ten sinewy minutes. He'd pulled many fish out of water - but none as big as this one. Its head emerged gaping-mouthed, wild-eyed and massive. Then out came its body; it kept coming and coming, and coming and coming, and coming and coming like some fish-limousine. The moment he saw it he thought of Good Friday.

As soon it was landed, Franco jammed its head down in their bucket of water. Thank God he'd brought Gino. And that the car was nearby. With Franco holding the bucket while Gino kept the fish's head jammed down in it, father and son carefully mounted the travertine steps up from the river. The fish was thrashing wildly. Precious water was splashing out. Finally, they reached the car. Franco, of course, took the wheel. It fell to Gino then, in the back seat, to wrestle with this fish to keep it from dying. This was no easy task. The fish was strong and belligerent. The street's bumpy cobblestones made the water slosh dangerously. Off they drove.

"*O Dio*! Papa look! The bucket's tipped over!!"

Franco turned round and looked back. There sat little Gino leaning forward over his thighs, with the fish's head and tail sticking out on both sides, slapping hard at the seat.

Franco screeched to a halt. Leaving the car triple-parked, he rushed into a bar and went straight to the pay-phone.

"*Pronto?*"

"*Cara*, it's me. Don't talk please, just listen. Fill the bathtub to the top. All the way. Keep it full till I get home. No time for questions. Trust me. Love you. Ciao."

A moment later Franco emerged from the bar lugging a caseful of *acqua minerale*.

"Quick!" he said, sliding the case onto the back seat before rushing back to the wheel. The drivers behind him were honking angrily.

Gino quickly poured all twelve bottles into the bucket and jammed the fish's head back under. Franco's pounding heartbeat eased up as they moved slowly along with the rush-hour traffic.

"Papa look quick!!" Franco wheeled round. The fish had thrashed free. Its mouth was sputtering. Its gills were heaving open and shut violently. Its fins were flapping fast as hummingbird's wings. Franco looked at the empty green bottles piled up on the back seat. *Acqua gassata*! Those bubbles! The poor fish couldn't take it.

Down a side street Franco saw a fountain in the middle of the *piazza*. He set off at top speed and drove recklessly half up onto the curbside beside it. Without a word of instruction, Gino dashed out and heaved the flailing fish up over the basin walls of the fountain. Seconds later it was gliding along serenely, beneath three well-chiseled cherubs and the crossed keys of the Papal crest.

Franco's heartbeat eased up again. He took the jack out of the trunk and hiked up his car so it would look like he had trouble. Then he and Gino sat to wait till the traffic died down - after rush-hour it would take them ten minutes instead of fifty. Father and son sat quietly on the fountain wall, admiring their fish swimming laps. It was the biggest fish he had ever seen pulled from the Tiber - maybe the biggest that had ever lived there! It was nearly four feet long and robust and full-bodied. Franco saw himself at the head of the table, after church on Good Friday, serving steaming filets to his wife, his two sons, the four grandparents and two aunts.

The traffic died down. They took off their shoes, rolled up their pant-legs and climbed into the fountain. But the fish swam as fast as they could wade, and had a canny way of shifting speeds and changing depth, of feigning stillness and then accelerating. Only with their nets and great effort were they finally able to trap it. They were soaked top to bottom.

The shrill doorbell rang insistently. Maria Assunta looked through the peephole, but no one was to be seen. She opened the door tentatively, and found Franco and Gino huddled over a big bucket, the tail of a fish sticking up in the air from between them. Her protests about her clean floors were in vain as they rushed through the living-room down the hallway. In an instant she saw it all: three days with no baths. But seeing Franco's set chin and little Gino's happy eyes, her complaint died at her lips. She knew when a grievance was best kept to herself.

Franco slept fitfully that night and he rose before dawn. He went straight to the bathroom. His fish was alive, although not very convincingly. Its scales were dull grey. Its eyes were clouded and sullen, as if it knew it was dying in a human's bathtub, and felt humiliated and resentful. Its gills hung open flaccidly, giving occasional listless movements. The tissue inside them was pallid. The fish would drift half a foot forward till its nose hit the front tub-wall, then drift back again slowly till its tail hit the back. Every hour on the hour, Franco let water drain out slowly while he added fresh water from the faucet. Old *nonna* came by regularly, and watched disapprovingly from the doorway. Maria Assunta didn't come near and kept her thoughts to herself.

Thursday morning, she rose early to a bed that was empty. She found Franco and Gino in the bathroom, tending their fish. She of course didn't notice, but its eyes were less clouded. There were a few bright glints among its scales. The tissue inside its gills was not putty-colored but pale pink, and the gills themselves waved weakly, but steadily. It made slight wriggling motions that rippled the water, as if beginning to remember that it wished to be swimming. Franco had to work on Thursdays, so he carefully trained Gino how to let out the dirty water while adding clean water from the faucet.

At dawn on Good Friday, Franco's last slumbering moments were disturbed by a dream. In his dream he was bringing out the kitchen trash to the dumpster in front of his apartment. He stepped on the foot pedal. The dumpster lid went up. And there, atop the mixed refuse all heaped up inside, lay his limousine-fish, blanched to whiteness, stiff and dead. The scene then changed quickly, to a neon-lit market. There stood Maria Assunta at the counter, happily fingering a wad of cash, while a white-coated man cut filets from a fish. Franco awoke in a sweat, short of breath, in a panic. It was not even seven o'clock – and Maria Assunta wasn't in bed! He leapt out of bed and rushed straight for the bathroom. God help that woman if his fish wasn't there!

Sure enough – the bathroom light was on! Franco's top lip curled up. His adrenalin surged. He was wild-eyed and panting. He rushed down the hall and banged open the door. There, lined up beside the bathtub, on chairs brought from the kitchen, sat Gino and Taddeo, Maria Assunta and *nonna*, all gazing down into the bathtub, their eyes filled with wonder. A great splash came from the tub. Franco looked down too.

O la Madonna!! How his fish was transformed! Its eyes were like glass and had piercing dark pupils. It seemed to be thinking, and looked intelligent, even wise. The insides of its gills were suffused with red blood and they opened and closed powerfully. It was thrashing and splashing, trying to turn round in the tub. Best of all were its scales. They were sparkly silver like mica, iridescent like a rainbow. "Papa!" cried out Taddeo, clapping his little hands together, "Look at your fish! It's a fish made of diamonds!"

What a memorable feast they had, on that best of Good Fridays! All nine had kept eating and eating, and eating and eating – till all that remained was head, skin, and clean bones. Franco thought of that Good Friday each time he went fishing. And when troubling thoughts came and would try to disturb him, he'd dissolve them at once by just thinking of his fish made of diamonds.

Sitting down now on the riverbank, he gave a few tugs at his line. Though he hadn't felt a bite in two weeks, he liked to give a tug now and then anyway. The stone bridge loomed up over him, filled with traffic at its usual standstill. Nearest to him, at the rail, was an orange bus packed with people. At the windows, some were pointing down at him. He couldn't hear them, but he didn't have to. He knew what they were saying: Why is that man fishing? He can't possibly catch much. This river's polluted. Why does he even bother?'

Franco gazed down into the grey-green water and the current lazing past him. Small eddies swirled around rocks that nosed up through the surface. The sun overhead made a blinding circle on the water, which radiated out hypnotically into undulating waves of light. In the water he could see a car tire ringed with seaweed that waved gently with the current, and the silver glint of shopping cart, further down in the murky depths. He looked up, then, at the orange bus and the people pointing down at him.

No, he could not explain it. Not to himself, let alone to others. He'd been asked many times and had yet to find an answer. Away from the river, he felt like a fish out of water.

Trolling

The bridge behind us, we now pass into the heart of the city, through narrow streets never meant to be corridors for cars. It's a wonderful place that can sometimes oppress us. Too many monumental structures that are too close together, too heavily embellished, constructed too ambitiously for forever. They boast and exhort, pontificate and command. All is opera and symphony, oration and drama. There's a quiet voice here too though, that these buildings also speak in. It's a voice that's much gentler, with its own excellent message, often overpowered by the rhetorical din of the structures. This quiet voice is color.

On all sides of us pass statues, mighty columns and sheer walls made of granite, stone and marble. These aren't just forms though, but colors as well: whites, slates and grays sing a chorus in august measured tones. These walls we see also, made of slim Roman brick: how high they loom over us, stacked ponderously in so many thousands. And they speak intensely too, through their colors as well. From vealish beiges to the darkness of dried blood: it is thus that we understand them, in our organs, in our bones. Then the broad stucco'd sides of buildings with their friendly water color washes. Such are these restful umbers and ochres, shell-toned pinks and siennas, burnt oranges and muddy reds, that we recognize earth as their paint box, earth as their song.

The earth provides these colors and consents to their employment. They remind us as well, that these buildings we see are but earthen stuff rearranged, on brief loan for some centuries. You will not surpass the earth, say these colors, through your feats of construction. For even as these buildings please us, their colors gaze past us, asserting in silence the supremacy of *terra*. *Terra* terrestrial, *terra* impersonal, implacable and primitive. *Terra* prior to artistry, *terra* prior to Empire, *terra* prior to the human face. Such is the sane message of the colors of these buildings, and what endows them with such elemental charm.

These buildings endure but their surfaces fade. The city, *per fortuna*, attends to their coloration. It still regulates the painting of each *quartiere* - a small touching gesture in this age of obliteration. Romans hence, then, will enjoy this same palette as did their counterparts long ago - just as we now enjoy it as we pass through these corridors.

There's a wrong note in this harmony, though. It's that squat cube-like structure on each third or fourth corner: the news kiosks, each gaudily shingled with magazine covers in screaming reds, acid greens, acrylic turquoise and the like, each box a shrill, discordant collage. While the buildings on all sides chant of earth's timeless constancy, these kiosks cry frantically, and breathlessly, of *today*. And it was for the news of *this* day that we see a man approach this kiosk, before taking the bus home for a well-deserved rest.

A minor official for his ministry of agriculture, Ahmed spent two weeks here each month, administrating the movement of the foodstuffs his country imported. On the strength of his signature, thousands of cans of tomatoes, peas, carrots, artichokes and beans, and bottles of olives, pickled onions, anchovies and oils, and sacks of flour, corn and animal feed, and huge wheels of cheese were flown or shipped home. Though these business channels were well oiled, the custom's work was onerous. How fatiguing were those many offices with their byzantine regulations, endless forms, mulish employees, and long lines. Having stood in lines since seven this morning, Ahmed was tired and hungry, and more homesick than usual. Only back at the *pensione*, with his feet propped up as he read his Arabic paper, might he call Shazi preparing dinner in the kitchen, and speak to little Faiz playing beside her.

Approaching from behind, he had to go around the kiosk's right side, to the rack of international papers. And passing this right side, what a panorama he would pass! There were magazines on how to make your body healthy, by feeding it vegetables and light cheeses. And others to tell you how to make it just happy, by swallowing buttered pastas, dressed meats, and fine wines. There was a magazine devoted to banishing cellulite, and another to building muscles like a comic book hero. Here were magazines on how to arrange the hairs on your head, how to powder and color your face, shellac your nails, paint your eyelids. Here was a magazine just on jewelry. And five others just on clothes. Here was a magazine on sewing, one on embroidery, one on knitting.

Feeling sluggish? Here were magazines on how to exercise, one for at home and one for the gym. Not inclined to action? Here were the planet's best sportsmen, performing in photos you can hold in your hands: separate magazines of men kicking soccer balls, hitting tennis balls, throwing basket-balls, whacking golf balls, spiking volleyballs, lifting weights. Here was a magazine on race cars driven at breakneck speeds, and others on motorcycles, on trail bikes, on surfboards and windsurfers.

Here was a journal devoted to speed-boating on the water's surface. And a journal on scuba-diving below it, and one to yanking hooked fish out of it. A landlubber, you say? Well here was a journal on lovable land critters, their habits and habitats. And another on how to shoot them. And another on how to shoot at concentric circles on paper, or at villains on the streets, or intruders in your home. Here was a journal on mercenaries: their weapons and kill-tactics. Here was a special on the handguns of World War II. And a review of fighter aircraft since Vietnam. And a commemorative on the Battle of Britain, and on Rommel the Desert Fox, and on tank technology in Kuwait.

Your interests are more sedentary? Here was a magazine for coin collectors, another for stamp collectors, another for cat owners, another for dogs. Here was one on computers, on how to take photos, how to draw still lifes, how to look at paintings, how to collect antiques. Here was a magazine on how rich men made their money. And another that showed the houses they share with their rich women, and where they take vacations.

Content with your own humble sphere? Here was a magazine showing how to decorate your apartment. And a magazine on house plants. And one on babies, how they think, feel and grow. And here were comics for the older tykes, one with ghosts, one with monsters, one with cowboys, one with spies. What could not one find, on this kiosk's right side?

And so why did Ahmed turn left, when his news rack was right? And why did he slow down till he was just barely moving, placing his left foot so slowly before his right foot, then his right foot so slowly before his left? Ahmed knew why, for it happened here every time. The beast gave the orders, and Ahmed obeyed. As he turned left around the kiosk, he kept his head facing forward as his eyes strained far right, keen for the lively impressions that were soon to arrive.

L.A. ACTION NIGHTS screamed the yellow block letters on a bright purple cover. And there, before his very eyes, stood a six-inch-tall redhead, topless and smiling, with one spike-heeled shoe on the bumper of a sports car, and a micro-skirt hiked high on her buttocks.

SHANGHAI SECRETS purred the next one. A petite Oriental was clad in black bangs alone. Her left hand pinched one nipple between her thumb and her forefinger. Her right hand held a bamboo fan before her exotic pudendum.

WILD STALLIONS OF AFRICA cried the third cover. A white woman faced front on all fours, her painted lids closed, her tongue lolled out like a hog after the slaughterhouse stun-gun. Behind her knelt a pudgy black in the role of the Stallion, who bemusedly thrust at her high proffered rump.

Ahmed's eyes roved these covers, but saw none that were new. He would never actually buy one. He didn't really even want to look. Yet here he was again, looking as always - he could not seem to help it.

When he had first come to Rome he had found it incredible. How could it be that at kiosks to be found on every corner, which men, women and children passed together on their daily rounds, such things were displayed openly? Such things existed back home, but they had to be sought out from unsavory types in low districts. Back home vice existed, but in stagnant pools cut off from the main stream. Here the main stream was polluted, all was sanctioned and blessed. These lewdest of images were displayed in the most public of places, where everyone went for the most routine of purchases.

How strange to him how all walked by so blithely: men with briefcases, children with school knapsacks, women with their groceries and babies. All filed past or made purchases, immune even to curiosity. Only Ahmed, it seemed, was intrigued, an iron speck beside the magnet. Only Ahmed had lapsed virtue, for try as he might he could not pass without pausing. A strong force rose up within him, stronger than any counter-thought he set against it. He was drawn irresistibly to these stark carnal images.

Next came the cheap comics that seemed like they never were bought, but just yellowed in the display window. He wondered if they were yellowed when they were first printed. Wherever he went they all had the same themes. One was women in public places being pleased while men fondled them. Sometimes it was a nurse with her uniform top open, her impossibly huge breasts being grasped by a patient or doctor. Or a secretary taking dictation while her boss pawed her bare bottom. Or a waitress whose mammaries hung down near the soup, or a pantyless shop-girl reaching up to a high shelf.

The second theme was men being surprised in mid-coitus. Someone was peeping through the keyhole, or through the window, or from under the bed, or from inside the closet. Or there was a shadowed figure at the window with a knife, or a detective with a flash camera, or a soldier with a pistol bursting in on the forbidden tryst. The third type was the weirdest. These showed women being strangled, women gagged and strapped to chairs, women being slashed, shot or mutilated, with open-mouthed terror. Then there were those he could never understand, like the woman doing strip-tease before her nervous young son, or with her face in the soccer player's crotch in the middle of the stadium.

Shame and fascination rose up in him in turns. The shame was because he should not be curious, and should purposefully walk on like everyone around him, wholesome and content with the clean sunlit day. The fascination was that this side of life was forbidden - but was real and existed. It exerted the same captivation as did photos of war, crime or starvation, whose terrible graphicness one stared at, as if some secret were being confided. Back home, the beast was well-known and confined by tradition to its appropriate place. Here the beast was untethered and indulged in a thousand forms of titillation, calibrated minutely to the desires of the citizens.

How strange were these streets here. Wherever you walked - past the shoe shop, the perfume shop, the bookstore, the gas station, the pharmacy, the grocery, the travel agency - you were met by large color photos of bare leg, bosom and buttock. On TV it was the same all around the dial: women selling products with their breasts and their legs, or show hostesses dressed like whores filled with school-girl good cheer. What was strangest of all was the decorum and propriety. The conflict that drove him to this kiosk's right wall, seemed quite neatly resolved by all those around him.

Next came the magazines of men, with muscular arms held behind their heads in the poses of women. Here were square-jawed men in leather vests, in cowboy hats, or police caps. He knew what they were up to. It was not to his liking. Yet even these too, command-ed his repelled fascination. There were lithe youths in bathing suits, or in gym shorts, or...

What the... ??!!

Who the... ??!!

Yee-OUCH!!! !!!

Poor Ahmed. A young boy was trolling here too. And was not looking where he was going, either. They smacked right into each other, face-first.

"*Mi scusi*," quick-mumbled the boy.

"*Mi scusi,*" quick-mumbled the man, as they bounced to each other's sides and sped off in opposite directions. Ahmed restrained his grimace and the impulse to rub his stinging kneecap. He marched straight to the news rack with a decisiveness that would make it clear - to whoever might be watching - that this had been his sole intention all the while. Taking his newspaper with its Arabic characters, he strode forthright to the cashier.

Once there though, what was he doing? He slowed down *again* to a sloth's speed. Poor Ahmed. He just could not help it. Slowly, he slid his hand into his pocket, and then slowly slid out his wallet. And then slowly he brought it before him, before slowly parting its leather sides. Slowly, he extracted a one-thousand *lire* bill, then a second one, and then a third one. And as he manipulated his cash slowly, his eyes darted quick and nimble among the gossip magazines.

Look! A famous movie star striding into a film premier - in a gown you could see through!

Look! The wife of a prime minister on the deck of their yacht, swabbing sun-tan lotion on her stretch-marked breasts!

Look! The Princess of Monaco getting out of her limousine, her errant left nipple visible - in its entirety!

Eventually eventually, many milliseconds later, he had to pay. Handing his money to the cashier, he looked up expectantly. If it was a man he could linger, flush with the respectability of having bought a newspaper, and leaf for some moments through these magazines.

"*Tremila,*" said the cow-eyed woman inside the kiosk.

"*Grazie, buon giorno,*" said Ahmed softly, as he folded his paper and gave a nervous bow.

"*Buon giorno,*" said the cashier, with a smile for the polite gentleman. But Ahmed had already fled guiltily to the bus-stop, to wait for the 64.

Who Still Prays to the Madonna?

There are countless remarkable walls in this city – but this is not one of them. A block from the news kiosk, it has escaped restoration and the demolition ball, though it cries out for either. Bridging the gap between two old *palazzi*, it stands at the sidewalk and tamps off the alley between them: a darkened slot at whose bottom lay rusted boxsprings, *motorini* carcasses, rotted planks and assorted trash. This fragment of wall is attached to nothing and supports nothing. No plaque declares it noteworthy, no guide will suggest you see it. It's old, but not so very old, and has none of the charm or gravity that old things can have. Its surface is a patchwork of dirty stucco, gouged-out stone and crumbly brick. It looks decayed and that's all. On a busy street such as this, why has this wall been left standing? Could it be on account of the Madonna?

Yes. Look: six feet off the ground is a small rude mosaic. Hundreds of stone chips set long ago depict a haloed mother with a haloed child. They are rendered with scant artistry. Their faces convey no feelings. The outlines have no rhythmic movement, the masses no geometric harmony. Even the stone chips, probably once bright and cheerful, are now dull browns and grays. Indeed, this forlorn Madonna is well suited to the wall she is set in.

Embedded in the wall all around her are dozens of small blocks. The mason's rough strokes are still visible, never smoothed over or blended in. Into each block are carved the words *per grazia ricevuta*, with a date and some initials. These blocks offer thanks for old prayers that were answered. But that was a different time then, when a different rhythm ruled this street, frantic now with pedestrians rushing nowhere, drivers carried by in vehicles, everyone tuned to modern thoughts, modern dreams, and... modern prayers? A good question – for who still prays to the Madonna?

But look! Beside the Madonna, a glass vase in a rusted holder stands out from the wall. Last night it held wilted flowers, its water was brown with algae. This morning there's no algae, the vase has been scrubbed clean, and fresh water has been poured in by an unknown hand. A woman emerges from a side street, a pocketbook in one hand, a single gladiola in the other. She bends head and knee before the mosaic. She places the point of a high-heeled shoe in a chink in the wall, then boosts herself up to set her flower in the vase. Another quick genuflection. She wipes her scuffed shoe-top with her palm and is off at a half-run to the bus-stop.

Who is this woman who has prayed to the Madonna? Black skirt and white blouse. Red handbag, red shoes, red belt. Gold chains on each shoe, a gold buckle on her belt, a gold chain on her handbag. Gold rings on four fingers. Not one speaks of marriage. A silk scarf draped across her shoulders completes the display, which is all undermined by the body beneath it. Yes, it's trim and at a glance seems attractive in smart clothes. But all ease and well-being have long been squeezed out of it. What remains is a clenched body locked in defeat, her soul seeming fled from this unfriendly world.

Though her face looks in bloom it's all liquids and powders. Near the ears and the jaw-line, the skin's doughlike and flaccid. Her hair rises in lively waves on both sides and in front, but in back it's matted flat, unrevived from the pillow. Her front teeth stand out at an unfortunate angle, and are crooked, like crossed fingers. Sunglasses hide her eyes - a wall of dark plastic that goes half around round her head. But the grooves in her forehead swing so anxiously upward, that one sees her pained eyes even though one can't see them.

When the doors hissed open she pushed herself up into the mass of packed bodies - just another body wedged into just another crowded bus. But in one way she was different, for she yearned with the prayer of her one gladiola.

Inside, she looked at the man who had gotten on behind her. He was well-built and well-dressed and was holding a newspaper in

Arabic. He had open guileless features. He also looked kind. His skin was darker than that of most Italians, but he could easily be from Bari or Calabria. She would not mind having two nice dark-skinned children by this nice dark-skinned man. Though he surely was not Catholic, Mother could in time be persuaded. At first she'd resist - that was only to be expected. But with Father now gone she would finally give in, and want only what was best for her one daughter's heart. The Arab man turned. He wore a gold band on one finger. She at once turned away.

CHANGE OF LIFE screamed the ad that she found herself facing. She shuddered and turned away, only to face the same ad across the aisle. But this ad was different. It said CHANGE YOUR LIFE, not CHANGE OF LIFE. She'd read the first one too quickly. She squinted to read the text.

CHANGE YOUR LIFE

In a rut? Life passing by? Wondering if it's too late
to create the new life you've always wanted? If
your answer is 'yes' that's no cause for despair. Do as
thousands have done: Call *Istituto Informatica* - and
enter the exciting world of computer programming.
You *can* recover lost time...

She looked at the ads on both sides of the aisle. CHANGE YOUR LIFE, said the second one. CHANGE YOUR LIFE, now agreed the first one. Okay, then: change your life. She was more than willing. But how, she did not know.

There were some things you could do to make certain things change. Others were just out of your hands. Here she was again - another day in circulation - surrounded by men on all sides. Men streaming forth out of buildings in the fine morning sun. Men standing at bus-stops with brief-cases in their firm grasp. Men striding on sidewalks and whizzing by in taxis. Men talking in bars with their white teeth all smiling. Men all around her wherever she looked. Men

were a full half of everyone. No corner without one. So why why,
Mother Mary, not one man for Anna?

A teen-aged girl came alongside her. No older than sixteen, but
well-versed already in the arts of allurement. Lips: deep rose-red gloss.
Lashes: awnings stiff with mascara. Cheeks: buffed, rouged and blended. Brows: plucked, shaped, and blackened. Her hair was drawn up
to a cheap rhinestone tiara, and cascaded down her back in unruly
extravagance. A butt-clinging skirt. Legs with white fish-net stockings. Pert breasts forced together and the sharp cleavage bared proudly.
Her shoes, belt and handbag - all three were bright red – which sent
a pang straight to Anna's heart.

The girl turned to whisper something to the woman beside her,
who had the same forehead and hairline, same hips, calves and carriage. It was clearly her mother. The mother though, wore no make-
up and was plainly dressed. Her simply cut hair had been let turn half-
gray. Anna felt like a hybrid of this mother and daughter. She too was
arrayed in full mating plumage, but without this effort, she'd look just
like this mother. Neither one nor the other, she unsuccessfully combined both. Her heart ached at the thought of her poor muddled life.

What would she not give to be this drab simply dressed woman,
set peacefully in the fullness of motherhood, arm-in-arm with her
growing daughter? To what end were her own woman's arms and her
woman's legs if she passed through life solo, like a ghost or a phan-
tom. Why all this bother, the so-earnest routine? Tinting each hair that
sprouts white and wiry. The smoothing of legs and the glossing of lips.
Her ears hung with bangles. Her neck dabbed with scent. Why her
woman's red river that was now running dry? Why her secret chamber that grew older, and would soon close forever?

She would soon be at work, with men working beside her at the
counter. Men sitting at desks in a phalanx behind her. Men lined up to
see her, to hear the exchange rate. Good worldly men, educated men.
Responsible men, kind men. Men with shined shoes and silk ties, and
airplane tickets and credit cards. Men whom she fell in love with. Men

whom she married. Men she bore sons to, at the start of each day. But by mid-morning her jaws ached from too much hard smiling. She was soon in no mood for children, or for husbands or fathers. All she would see then was hands grasping for banknotes and forms to fill out. All she would hear would be voices that were serious, about lire and dollars, and sterling, yen and marks. Transaction transaction transaction transaction, numbered consecutively by her computer, on and on, and on and on into her manless tomorrows.

Behind the Arab was yet another man. He looked like an Italian, but then maybe he was not. Though he might not be Italian, he sure knew how to dress. He wore a sharp summer suit. The kerchief in his breast pocket picked up perfectly on his tie. She sidled a step closer. He was fresh from the shower and wore spicy cologne. In his hand was a roll of papers that said 'Antique Prints' on the wrapper. She bent forward as if to brush her skirt. In pencil was written the name Aldo Margutti. His name then, was Aldo. And her name was Anna. Aldo and Anna. They went together quite well, no, this Aldo and this Anna? Quite rhythmic, quite right. Yes, Aldo and Anna. Or Anna and Aldo. Whichever way you put it, it sounded good, it sounded right. What do you say, Mother Mary? Don't you think it's a match?

This Aldo turned away; something had caught his attention up front. And though she knew it was pathetic, she could not help but feel rebuffed. Such anguish, over nothing!

But little did Anna know, that just two steps behind her, a man with brown eyes was admiring her deeply...

Aldo's Old World Return

None found the press of the crowd more agreeable than Aldo. To be back in Rome, to have strolled the neighborhood he grew up in, and after so many years to be healthy, well-dressed and carrying gifts – who could be bothered then, by the discomfort of a bus? Especially this bus, the same bus he had taken daily, as a boy. As a boy it had been Bus 27, and though now it was Bus 64, it was just as wonderful, packed and smelly as ever! Nostalgia stirred within him, as he regarded the passengers, all hot, harried and wilted. Things were much as he remembered them, but were different as well. He was a six-foot-tall man now, not a four-foot-tall schoolboy.

How much he had detested this bus! It was miserable at all times, but especially so in winter. One moment he'd be snuggled warmly in sweet dreams under wool covers. Moments later he was thrust among strangers shrouded in coats, hats, gloves, and scarves, all wordless and still, like a roomful of mummies. One morning he had been surprised to see Father Rosario, his headmaster, on the bus. Father was humorless and stern. The boys hated and feared him. But wrapped in his heavy coat and scarf and curled up against the window, he looked like a big unhappy baby. His lips were pursed tight. His eyes were squinched shut in misery against the new budding day. Aldo's fear drained away forever then, along with his hate.

How odd now to be a tourist now in his old *quartiere*, near *Piazza Navona*. As a child he had been indifferent to the tourists as they swarmed through the neighborhood in packs, each seeming the same as the other. Only now could he catalog their many species. The troops of retired Germans who marched from *piazza* to *piazza*, still spry on aging legs, in their neatly pressed quality clothes. The packs of East Europeans, bulky rumpled country bumpkins lumbering about in cheap department store clothes, out of place in this city of *la bella figura*. Then the Japanese, all in black suits, ties dispensed with on account of the heat. They stayed huddled close together looking closely at everything, earnestly looking, earnestly looking. There were art tourists and food tourists, God tourists and clothes tourists. Tourists who roved boldly, wide-eyed with adventure. Tourists clutching maps who walked stiff-limbed with fear. Tourists walking dead on their hooves as the guide's narrative drones on. The child Aldo had seen none of this.

As Aldo the American, he now felt how he was an intruder. In the bar, he got the arrogant treatment reserved for the tourist, whom the barman secretly blames for his Sisyphean ordeal of dirty cups, spoons and glasses. The proprietors in the antique shops were obsequious and condescending. At one shop he had bought five old engravings. He moved them from hand to hand now, to protect them from the shifting crush of the bus. When he was little, old prints were everywhere: in the living room, the parlor, the bank and restaurant, the barber shop, at school and at church. But like tourists, to him they had meant nothing; they were old black-and-white things people hung up on walls. Only after growing up in the New World had he come to see prints for what they really were. And had found it easy to love them greatly.

In 1994, in California, he could forget the Old World had ever existed. Speaking into his cell phone as he sped along the freeway, he could see himself as riding the crest of the future in a world that began with himself. In the Old World, it was impossible to sustain such illusions. The buildings reminded one, everywhere, that one is but the latest to walk earth's very old stage. Even as a boy, these buildings had sent him messages. Laying in bed at night, he could feel the thick walls of the *palazzo* exert a palpable force into his room. The surrounding buildings added their pressure, too; he could feel all Rome arrayed around him like a tight, dense range of mountains. Lying in bed he felt he lay into the securest of vaults, safe from time or attack or the whims of hostile Nature. And however terribly it might thunder and storm, all stayed muffled, distant, and tamed.

How different was his bedroom in San Francisco, whose walls felt so porous to the world all around him. There too, lying in bed, he could feel beyond the confines of his built room. But there was no solid Rome there, just sky, wind and stars. He could feel, without seeing them, the fog's vapors that rolled in, as the gulls traced curved arcs in the moonlight. The New World could seem to obliterate this Old World completely. And only then had his love for antique prints been born.

He loved those old images of a world undefaced by machines: of harbors with swaying forests of wood-masted boats, sailors at the lanyards, stevedores on the docks, the goods stacked up on shore. Hunters with dead deer slung between poles borne on their shoulders. Women waiting in kitchens filled with feathered and furred creatures being prepared for the flames. Soldiers in armor with swords, pikes and bows. Massive castles built of stone blocks. Rustic cottages with thatched roofs, grazing animals in the front yard, a wood-pile by the side, where a maid draws water from a well. The four winds in the Old World were not charted by TV weathermen, but whistled out capriciously from the pursed lips of gods. Saints dwelled in caves where horned demons could torment them. Shepherds lazed by sheep as days passed that had no hours. Fishermen on riverbanks coaxed fish out of water. Huntsmen rode horses through woods thick with game, faithful dogs bounding alongside them. How he loved this Old World shown in pictures. To him it was the real world. Though he never had seen it, he yet felt this in his heart.

These antique shops in Rome affirmed what the New World denied. Here he could see a real suit of armor, an old helmet or sword. Or a wood and leather bellows, or a doorbell that was a bell. Or pens with nibs and inkwells, the mounted head of a deer or wild boar. Or a much labored upon, poorly done portrait, better than any photo's perfect likeness. These old things were strangely compelling, and at times seemed almost to speak.

To little Aldo, this old stage and its props had scant meaning. What mattered to the child were the people: his family, friends, and neighbors. A person meant more than the finest of works of art. Take Tinto, who worked with wrought iron. What a character for a young boy to enjoy! His workshop was cool in the summer; he let Aldo and his friends play there as he worked. In return for this favor, Tinto acquired an audience for his far-from-bad tenor. He'd sing song after song as he forced iron into curves which he then welded together. He sang Verdi and patriotic anthems, liturgical chants and Neopolitan love songs, all with unabashed sentiment and an exaggerated *vibrato*. When not singing and working he'd be smoking or drinking: short black twisted cigars that smelled like garbage and had to constantly be relit, and white wine that he poured from a jug through a funnel into an empty beer can. "Keeps the germs out," he would say, pointing to the small opening at the top of the can, then waving his hand at the dangerous air all around them.

What impressed young Aldo best was Tinto's belching and farting. In his own family both were suppressed. Tinto quite made up for them, with belches he extended a rich snorkly five seconds each. He would extend them into musical phrases, or work them seamlessly into songs that were already in progress. His farts too were expressive in a way Aldo had not dreamed could exist. Before a blast he would stop what he was doing, and assume an expression that was strangely earnest and sincere. He would put his hand to his ear as if straining to hear some distant sound. Then after he had blasted, he would say to the boys with great seriousness: "Young fellows, I hope you know… they heard that one all the way at the Vatican." Then peering into space as if into a crystal ball: "Yes they have indeed; the Swiss Guard have just snapped to attention." Aldo had repeated Tinto's remark in like seriousness to his grandmother, expecting her likewise to be impressed. But she had only pinched his cheek viciously till he fell to his knees bawling.

This morning he had passed Tinto's workshop. Tinto was now gone, his place taken by another man who worked wrought iron. Aldo was stopped short at the workshop, nonetheless, for some long magic moments. The door itself was a small marvel: three thick unfinished planks that looked like they came from a shipwreck, held together by broad rusted iron slats with enormous brass rivets. Securing this door to the thick wall of stone were five slide-bolts, a great chain, and a padlock big as his hand with a huge key-hole.

The workshop floor was bare earth. Faint light came through the door, but the workshop was unlit. On all its walls, piled to the ceiling, were the dark forms of bed frames and head-boards, fences and railings, trellises and gratings, like black tangly plants in some overgrown jungle. In the midst of this darkness, a light blazed up suddenly, blinding white, incandescent - the torch head of the workman. Bent over and intent in his windowed metal visor, his torch hurled sparks madly through the vast darkened room. He was no longer a mere artisan. He was Thor now, or Hephaestus, forging not railings or gratings but new planets and stars. How blind, here again, had that little boy been!

And so it had been everywhere, on this long-put-off visit home. For the child there was Tinto, who worked in iron. And Pepe, who ran the bar. And Salvatore, who had the *tipografia*. And the old Mirabella's, who sold antiques. Today, he saw such characters as wonderful - but only as types - as barman, as printer, as artisan or art dealer. As individuals they now looked ordinary, indifferent to this place that only visitors thought extraordinary. In antique shops filled with wonders, the owners played cards, or read the paper, or slouched in chairs doing nothing - bored idle custodians of these things that survived them.

Most moving of all had been the shop of Signora Bargello. For the six-year-old, nine-year-old and twelve-year-old Aldo, her shop was just one among all others. But when Aldo turned thirteen he'd grown new eyes with which to see. Surrounded by candelabra, framed mirrors, polished tables and silver service, the Signora sat at a curvy-legged rococo desk, on a curvy-legged chair with a pin-cushion bottom. There she would lounge all day, smoking cigarette after cigarette in a long ivory holder. How feverishly had he been attracted to her shop window, as to some primitive idol of female concupiscence. In a skirt wriggled high up on her hips, her fleshy legs were plumply set, one across the other. Her massive breasts fell in mounds on both sides of her chest, their inner slopes on display in her deep decolletage. Her soft boneless arms even, were compelling to the ardent boy. He would jog back and forth past her shop, kicking the soccer ball like a boy – while the man growing within him stole hot glances.

Aldo had passed the same shop today. The Signora was still there! sitting now in a sturdy-legged desk chair at a large roll-top desk. All around her still glistened polished furniture, silver tea-sets and gilded frames. But the Signora was no idol — she was all age now, and grossness. Her now-mountainous body was consigned to a sack dress, save her stout pasty legs with her feet in flat slippers. Her ashtray was still full, though she held her cigarette now in her bare fingers. Looking in through the window, he'd watched the labored rise and fall of her bulky chest and shoulders, as she drew the smoke deep into a body that looked soon to give out.

As he looked at the living ruins of old Signora Bargello, surrounded by the fine furnishings in her centuries-old shop, he saw that in some strange way, this legacy of objects survived – while we did not. And this was what rendered them precious and lovely. Looking up out the bus window, Aldo watched this legacy move on past, on the tops of the *palazzi*. Scroll, plinth, and column. Entablature. Caduceus. Griffin. Oak wreath. Gargoyle. Muscular nudes straining to hold up an archway. Goddesses perched on roof-tops, the boundless sky as their backdrop.

At the front of the bus now, a ruckus broke out. Two old pensioners were cursing each other with great abandon. Their tiff was clearly comical. The passengers around them were smiling broadly. Their good feelings rippled back to Aldo and he found himself grinning. To his side was a dowager with a pinched mouth, a sharp nose, and accusatory eagle eyes.

"Nothing like a good wrangle to spice up the ride," she said.

Aldo nodded and smiled weakly, which was sufficient encouragement for her to launch into a story. He could understand her only in patches. She said something about a holiday and a party and family and friends. She said something about a *cotoletta*, a cut of veal, and a *coltello*, a knife. But these words were so similar and she kept using them so quickly... The knife, she said, was here, or it was the veal perhaps, that was there. Something happened suddenly on account of the veal, or the knife, then something else happened with the knife, or the veal. Whatever it was, the police came in a hurry, and some poor fellow died before they made it to the hospital. "So you see how very little it can take..." said the dowager, motioning to the fight up in front.

Aldo again smiled weakly. Having found an audience, her eagle's eyes were now robin's. She launched at once into her next story... "She'd lost her husband and both sons to the Fascists. She took a cat in as a companion. But she was so terrified something might happen to it that she couldn't bear to be apart from it. So she took it with her everywhere - to the grocery, the post office, the bar, even to Mass on Sunday. Now cats don't go for collars, but this cat had no say. So there'd be the two of them, walking together down the street: she in her black shoes, black stockings, black dress and black babushka, the cat crouched and skulking, scowling and hissing on its chain..."

Aldo stopped listening; the dowager chattered on. He kept smiling and nodding as he took in the larger scene. The tiff between the oldsters up front had become an uproar. There was much smiling and trading of quips. Faces all around him beamed with hilarity and high spirits. Pressed tightly among so many warm loud smiling people, he felt suddenly giddy. Indeed, the bus now felt like those peak moments at a party, when wine, blood, friends and music merge into joyful feelings out of time. Out of the corner of his eye, he saw the building tops move past with their grand stately figures. But that classical Old World now seemed distant, irrelevant, beside the impromptu festivity of this packed raucous bus. Yes, that little boy was quite right also: life was the people one lived with. He felt cheered, all the same though, by these statues on the sidelines, on this triumphant parade of his Old World return.

The Tiff of the Dinosaur *Pensionati*

Up front on the aisle, Gianni Manelli is reading about the latest corruption scandal in Parliament. The lead article is giving him the big picture. Later, he'll savor the small article in the corner. It's about the suicide of one of the ministers. He's saving it till the end, like a sweet after dinner. Across from Gianni is Roberta Pirelli, her nose poked in a paper also. She's scrutinizing a grainy photo of the latest corpse found in Palermo. She's staring at the open mouth, the stained sheet and the big pool of blood as if awaiting some revelation. Nearby, Federico Magnani is scanning the news also - some Arabs or Jews in Israel or Lebanon blew up some synagogue or mosque because some Arabs or Jews shot some Jewish or Muslim leader. Yes, a bus-ride can be stressful, but how soothing is the daily paper. As reassuring as an old pair of slippers!

Portly Renato Ortondo was reading his paper, as well. After all, being on pension was no excuse to withdraw into the seclusion of your living room. Though it was nine years now since he had closed the doors of his small grocery, he still tackled the dense text of *Corriere della Serra*, despite the strain that it put on his old weakened eyes. Others could read *La Repubblica*, with its blaring headlines and big photos for the *illetterati*. But a man like himself - well - even sitting on a bus one should keep one's mind nimble, stay up-to-date on the issues that really mattered. Take for example this analysis of German unification...

Ouch! Who's the blockhead stepped on my foot?!... Anyway - a piece such as this, written not from the usual perspective of economics, but rather... *Damn it! Again! And right on my corns!... now where were we?...* but rather, to examine unification more as a clash of cultural values. Now that was an interesting slant, subtle stuff. He could imagine how

La Repubblica would handle it: more tired shots of bare-chested youths sledge-hammering the Wall, or skin-heads on rampage with swastika'd pates. No - for the thinking man there was one paper and one paper only - *Corriere della Sera* - no ifs, ands, or *CRISTO!! Yee-OWW!! On my corns again! That's the last straw!!*

"*Mi scusi, signore,* but would you please mind watching out. You've just stepped on my foot here, you know."

Standing above Renato was portly Enrico Amendola, a retired high school geography teacher. He moved the offending right foot a wee bit to one side, then silently reassumed the role of statue-like passenger. This wordless response was not entirely to Renato's satisfaction.

"*Mi scusi, signore,*" began Renato, fixing the eyeless statue in his reproving stare. "It would be a common courtesy, you might know, to at least say *mi scusi* when you step on another person's foot. Just the minimum sign of courtesy to extend in such a circumstance - wouldn't you think?"

"*Mi scusi then,*" came the clipped reply - and not just with annoyance, but with a damnable trace of sarcasm! This didn't sit well with Renato Ortondo. It didn't sit well with him at all.

"*Mi scusi, signore,*" he began, in condescending tones. "You may think I'm pointing this out only to bother you, but perhaps you don't realize that this was the *third* time you've stepped on my toes. It's not just one accidental slip I was talking about..."

"Get off it! You think I stepped on your foot on purpose? This is a city bus. You're not in your living room. You wanted me to say I'm sorry I said I'm sorry. *Basta!* That's the end of it!"

"*Mi scusi,*" shot back Renato, anger rising. "I am not so stupid as to think this is my living room, nor am I so stupid not to know what I am doing with my own two feet. You do take your feet to be your responsibility, yes? They're at the end of your own two legs, no? Or did you think that perhaps they were the responsibility of another, of..."

This lame attempt at shaming was not even clever. But it had been made publicly. People around them were watching. Enrico rose manfully to the challenge.

"Listen you," he cried out, using the familiar form *tu* of the pronoun 'you'. "I've had it with you and your goddamn foot." And he used the familiar form of 'your' also! "Why don't you just stick your fat face back in your paper and stop acting like such a *stronzo*."

Stronzo!! and the familiar forms of address as well!!! Renato's blood boiled over - this was beyond all limits of propriety. He leapt to his feet, his own portly belly flush against Enrico's portly belly, jaws snapping like a tortoise as he let loose his rancor.

"Just who do you think you are gives you the right to call me *tu*? You don't even know me and I don't know you, and there's no way I would ever want to know you - and you think you can insult me in public? You... *burino*!"

"*Burino*?!!" roared Enrico. "You're the *burino* who hasn't got the courtesy to accept a simple apology and needs to throw a tantrum over absolutely nothing. It's you who's the *burino*! Not me fella, but you!! You're a ball-breaker of the first order, you know that...?"

As their volleys escalated, the passengers were hugely amused. Teeth bared, portly belly to portly belly, neck veins bulging, hands cutting the air for emphasis, they looked like two dinosaurs fighting it out in a B-film from the 50's.

"*Stronzo, maleducato*," hissed Tyrannasaurus Rex, incisors flashing, fists pounding away at the air.

"*Scemo, vigliacco*," screamed Triceratops, head thrashing back and forth, his stout index finger flailing the air.

Both men's tempers were now incandescent. This was the point in the movie when one dinosaur finally moves in for the kill, sinks its fangs deep into the neck of the other, from whose wide open jaws issue its deafening death-bellows. Indeed, who knows how far things might have gone, had not an unexpected third character been written into this script. Into the heat of this battle, a plump matron now came forward. She placed her hand gently on the forearm of T-Rex.

"There there now," said the matron in slow soothing tones. Her father was as old as these two fellows. She knew an old codger can get riled when it's hot. "We don't want to be getting ourselves all excited on such a hot day, such a very hot day, do we? We can just sit down now then, don't you think? and forget all this excitement. Such a *very* hot day. We don't want to get ourselves all worked up."

Her touch and her soothing tone had a dramatic effect on Tyrannosaurus Rex. The terrible tension that had gripped him began to visibly drain away. Till little by little, this dinosaur came to resemble a portly retired grocer named Renato Ortondo.

"But he... ," began Renato, protesting weakly. . . "he. .."

"Yes yes, I know," said the matron, putting her hand on his shoulder, "but we just want to be relaxing now and forgetting all about that. It's not good for our health. I'm sure this gentleman didn't mean to offend you. *You* know that. I *know* that you do." By 'this gentleman' she meant Triceratops, whose ire, likewise, was now fast fading. Indeed, with each passing moment he looked less and less animate, more like the statue-like passenger of before.

The matron now guided Renato gently back into his seat. He sat there looking confused by the sudden and mysterious disappearance of his anger. "But he... called me *tu*," he protested feebly, like a petulant child.

"Yes, yes, there's been a big misunderstanding, but that's over now," said the matron, her mouth right beside his ear, a hand placed on each of his shoulders. "And we've got just one thing we want to do now - and that's to relax."

"*Scemo*," cursed Enrico, barely audibly, in his final parting shot, before returning to one hundred percent statue.

"*Burino*," came Renato's last weak whimpering jab, as he turned back to his paper, to learn more about the promising changes taking place up in Germany.

Emilio's Lament

There's a quiet street just off the heavily tramped tourist routes. No more boutiques or souvenir shops, no bright signs for *gelato* or *pizza*. But on the sidewalk half-way down the street, a table with a checkered cloth beckons: yes you've strayed, says this table, but come closer: there's food here. Beside the table is a short walk-down, then a door flanked by display cases. In the left one are curled black-and-white photos, autographed by singers, boxers and race car drivers you have never heard of. In the right case is a hand-written menu and a yellowed magazine clipping, which claims that here you'll find hand-made pasta and fresh seafood, with generous portions at good prices. The sign above the door says '*da Emilio*'. This is Emilio's place. Let's step inside.

Inside are ten tables like the one on the sidewalk. Sitting at three of them were Emilio and his wife and son, who were finishing the morning's prep work. They worked out front to give their legs a break, and because the fluorescent light in the kitchen gave them headaches. They could also watch the TV that was on a shelf behind the cash register.

"Rain today," said his wife as she plucked *rughetta* leaves from their stems.

"I didn't see a single cloud," said her son, as he stuffed sausage into hollowed zucchini. "Did you hear it on the news?"

"No, I didn't hear the news. I saw the same sky you did. But when your father gets into this mood I can tell you: it means rain. You just wait and see."

"Aaach-ch," came Emilio's low guttural comment. And to

emphasize his point, he turned his lips down in a pout, and tossed his head to one side like a horse.

"Say what you will, dear," said his wife. "I've seen this mood of yours before, and it always means rain."

"Aa-ach," muttered Emilio again, with much less *brio*, but just so as not to leave her unanswered. It was true he was in a black mood. He had been in it all morning. And he had been in it before and he knew where it came from. It was *not* from the weather. How often he had tried to explain it, and in how many different ways. But she seemed never to understand, or to think about it, or take him seriously. Yes that was it, she didn't take him seriously, but just carried on in that contented way women have, which was too accepting to understand how a man could be troubled.

On the wall beside him hung a cheap reproduction of an old engraving. For two decades he had worked alongside it. It had always brought him pleasure. Yet in moods like today's even this print seemed to mock him and make him go sour. It showed a rustic tavern on a bluff in a gentle Roman landscape. Out front were gaily dressed peasant men and women, celebrating another carefree day of friendly sunshine. The women were smiling as they danced and beat tambourines. Or they gazed dreamily into the eyes of the men in broad-brimmed hats, who strummed guitars, toasted each other heartily, or simply enjoyed being alive in their Michelangelesque physiques.

In the midst of this merry-making, behind a table heavy with food, stood the inn's jovial proprietor. His right hand rested on a wine jug, his left on a loaf of bread. And there he stood beaming, like the sun surrounded by its planets, providing and blessing these revelries. This proprietor, of course, was Emilio. This print smiled at him as he hustled to tend to his guests' ceaseless needs. Like an icon it affirmed him as he rolled pasta, cut vegetables, or worked the books for long hours.

Emilio enjoyed cooking and serving. He really did. But with each passing year and now each passing week (so it seemed), it was fast being

110

drained of all pleasure. He used to have a sun-lit place on the outskirts, just around the corner from his flat. He could lock up after lunch and go home to snooze, work with his plants on the balcony, or leaf through a magazine. Work used to be fun. His customers were mostly regulars. He could join them at their tables for a smoke, drink or laugh.

When the building was razed to make way for a new subway, he had jumped here, to the *centro*. But with no sunlight, a kitchen window that opened to an airshaft, and no chance to go home, he felt reduced to just tired hands and legs. And his customers were now tourists – and so who, now, was Emilio? Just another effusive Latin, a specimen, a side-show. He was good for his mustache, his repartee, his bits and pieces of foreign languages – but only in the intervals between courses, when there was no food or wine. His day used to have an easy rhythm, but now it did not. And what was life anyway, that had no easy rhythm?

Beside the old print hung another icon: a piece of fabric stretched across a rude wooden frame. Embroidered in bright crewel-work were the words that had hung in his father's house and his grandfather's house, and who know how much further back?

The Ten Commandments of the Roman
1) Work is depletion.
2) We are born tired and we live in order to rest.
3) No one has ever died from too much rest.
4) If work is health then praised be sickness.
5) If you see someone resting, join him.
6) Rest all day so as to sleep well at night.
7) When you feel the urge to work, sit down. It will pass.
8) Don't do today what you can do tomorrow.
9) Seek to do little in life, and what little you must do get someone else to do for you.
10) He who invented exertion died from it long ago.

As Emilio sat brooding, an ad was unfolding on the TV. He had seen it at least fifty times already. A svelte blonde housewife was in the kitchen with her perfect blonde son. Standing at the stove, she was pouring *ravioli* from a plastic pouch into a pot. Down they tumbled into the boiling water in dreamy slow-motion splashes. The window behind her opened to a landscape that was green clear to the horizon. Her clever son knew this wasn't fresh pasta. It was a supermarket imitation. His smiled like a conspirator with his white perfect teeth.

"*Che stronzate!*" cursed Emilio, without even looking up. His son suppressed a giggle. He and his mother rolled their eyeballs, and continued to work serenely. They did not know the exact source of Emilio's displeasure, but they always soon enough found out.

The advertisement rolled on. In the dining room, the housewife placed the last bowl of *ravioli* before her guests. A tense silence. First forkfuls raised to mouths. *Ravioli* thoughtfully chewed. Another long moment of silence ... and then... '*Che Buona Pasta*!!!' The table erupts in a frenzy of compliments and mastication. Such a great success! And just think, all agree - she made it by hand! The housewife smiled modestly as the accolades poured in. She winked at her son. He winked back. And his perfect teeth smiled.

"Yes," said Emilio, to his squat dark-haired mate. "We should all do so well. All we need is a few more trees outside our window and a son who takes better care of his teeth." His son smiled. His teeth were indeed yellow. But for Emilio this was no joke. He was staring down now, glowering. This was the calm. Then came the storm: "Will someone please tell me," he asked loudly, "just what is the point?" With a sweep of his hand he indicated himself, the *trattoria*, and the whole created world beyond them. "You have to ask yourself, at some point: *why bother*? What for? Why keep slaving, in this *dungeon*? For what? To keep up with the taxes? To keep a tourist's gut lined? To keep this *culo* in motion so it doesn't run down?"

He squeezed a blob of *gnocchi* flat between his thumb and forefinger, and regarded it with hostility. "Let me tell you something: the slaves in Egypt had it better than we do. Much better, I assure you.

They worked in the open air, in the sunshine. They worked hard. They slept well. And when they were finished, they knew they had done something. They could look up at a pyramid… *a pyramid*! – and be proud of their efforts. What have *I* got to be proud of? You tell me. A pyramid of *gnocchi*? Some slave I am. Some pyramid mine is: it never adds up so you can stand back and see anything. It just walks out the door in a hundred different gizzards to get shit out in hotel toilets the next day. You call that accomplishment? You call that living? Maybe you do but I don't. I don't think so at all."

Emilio's wife and son calmly kept plucking and stuffing. A vituperative Emilio was no cause for alarm. His wife smiled at her brooding husband with twinkling brown eyes.

"Emilio…" she began, in kindly musical tones.

"What?!" he snapped back, still glowering at his *gnocchi*.

She looked at him for a long moment. Go on, said her calm bearing, and her bushy eyebrows set in a mock frown. Rant all you want, you bad teddy-bear of a husband, but don't expect me to take you seriously. "E—mee-lee-o," she said in a sing-song, inviting him to step aside from his rancor.

"I heard you the first time. If you've got something to say then just say it," he said gruffly.

"You're so naughty, *amore mio*," she chuckled, finding his churlishness adorable.

Emilio gave a grumbly growl. It was bad to be upset, and worse, still, not to be able to get others upset along with you. But by far worst of all was to be harassed by affection!

"Why don't you go out for a bit," said his wife. "Go to *Campo dei Fiori*. Get a change of scene. Get us some fish. You feel better after you go there; you always say so yourself."

"Fish enough in the cooler," grouched Emilio, still hunched over his *gnocchi*.

"Enough fish? We're low on *vongole* and *scampi*, and we need at least a few pieces of *spada* since it's still on the menu. *Vai. Vai.* Hop the bus, take a little stroll, breathe some fresh air, pick up the fish then hop back. We're almost done here now anyway, so *vai! Vai vai vai!*"

With a heavy sigh, a defeated Emilio slid back his chair. He took off his apron, wiped his hands on a towel, gave his wife a peck on the forehead, then shuffled up the stairs to the street. All right then, he thought, as he stood at the bus-stop. He would do as he'd been told. He would take the bus. He would go to the market. He would breathe. He would walk around. He would buy some fish. He would do each thing she had told him. But of one thing he was certain: there was no way on earth this would make him feel better...

The Ambulance

Ooh-WAH! ooh-WAH! ooh-WAH! Long before anyone else, observant dying Serena heard the approach of the ambulance. She had heard it long before it appeared, following it as it turned corners, its shrill sound echoing off *palazzi* at different angles with increasing volume. Starting out as a faint sound, its siren was blaring now just ten meters before the bus. It was trapped at the intersection which all blocked up with traffic.

ooh-WAH! ooh-WAH! ooh-WAH!

The siren invaded the bus through its open windows, driving deep into ear canals and pummeling their drums. Ignazio Bruno simply switched off his hearing aid. But for everyone else there was nowhere to flee.

ooh-WAH! ooh-WAH! ooh-WAH! went the trapped ambulance.

"There's a sound bodes no good for someone," said an old woman, shaking her head ruefully.

"At least it's heading towards the hospital," said a woman beside her. "What if it got stuck on its way to the patient?"

"What's the difference?" said a third woman. "Whoever heard of such a thing as a good direction in an ambulance?"

"God help you if you ever have to ride in one!" added another woman emphatically. "It's like an empty van that you rent for the weekend. Just an oxygen tank. If you're lucky."

"She's right," said the first woman. "It's not like America. One ambulance there is like one of our whole hospitals."

"It's a crime," said the third woman, "with all the taxes that we pay. Why even the *Egyptians* in my building go home when they get a real health problem."

"Crime? Where's the crime?" challenged a gruff codger with a white mustache. "We Italians make our own bed then can't believe we've got to lie in it. You want to see a real crime, take a look out the window."

This gruff man had a point. As the ambulance had sped along, the cars ahead of it were supposed to pull to one side. The cars at the intersection should have done likewise. What had happened though, was this: Instead of pulling to one side, those ahead of the ambulance had speeded up, hoping to dash through the open swath that would be created by the more stupid drivers who deferred to the siren. But there was a shortage today of stupid drivers. Those racing forward had jammed an intersection, which was further jammed by traffic from two side streets that squeezed in, also hoping to exploit the situation. The intersection was choked now and no one could get through. Including, of course, the ambulance, which stood stuck in the impasse, its driver glaring disgustedly at the cars all around him.

ooh-WAH! ooh-WAH! ooh-WAH! went the siren relentlessly.

The drivers in the front cars, on all sides, leaned out of their windows. They waved angrily and righteously to command those opposite them to yield. The drivers in the second ranks, on all sides, began honking, to show their solidarity with the front cars, and to urge them not to yield but to bull on through. On the periphery were those dumb drivers who had pulled aside to let the ambulance pass. Victimized by this jam, as well, they too leaned on their horns to express their displeasure.

ooh-WAH! ooh-WAH! ooh-WAH! went the ambulance.

HONNNK! HONNNK! HOOONNNK! went the car horns.

Inside the bus, a stout woman clutched her shopping bag against her body, and closed her eyes as if in pain.

ooh-WAH! ooh-WAH! ooh-WAH!

Two teen-aged girls stuck their fingers in their ears, rolled their eyeballs, and made exaggerated expressions of distress.

ooh-WAH! ooh-WAH! ooh-WAH!

A mother with a look of alarm on her face stroked her little girl's hair robotically, and imagined this was comforting.

ooh-WAH! ooh-WAH! ooh-WAH! went the ambulance.

"ooh-WAH! ooh-WAH! ooh-WAH!" sang out the little girl, delighted as she mimicked the sound of siren. "ooh-WAH! ooh-WAH! ooh WA!!!" she sang with glee, looking around happily, to share her pleasure with those around her.

Why what a naughty young girl this was, not to know that a siren is not musical, that it is irritating, and portends death. On all sides, adult faces turned on her disapprovingly, or glared at her mother to demand she chastise her. Holding her forefinger to her lips, the mother leaned over and shushed her.

ooh-WAH! ooh-WAH! ooh-WAH! went the ambulance. "ooh-WAH! ooh-WAH! ooh-WAH!" sang the little girl with her winningest smile, sure she could charm away mother's bad mood. Mother, however, was in no mood to be won over. Grasping her daughter's shoulder, she shook her hard to make her quiet.

"Wooo-aaaaaaahh!!" came the wail now from the little girl's throat, as tears ran down her cheeks.

ooh-WAH! ooh-WAH! ooh-WAH! went the ambulance, still locked in on all sides.

HOOONNNK! HOOONNNK! HOOONNNK! went the cars in frustration.

"W-AAAHHH! W-AAAHHH! W-AAAHHH!!" wailed the girl ever louder, heartsick that mommy had turned against her and sided with strangers. Glaring eyes bore down more heavily on the girl's mother. Mommy could not take the pressure. SMACK! SMACK! SMACK! went her hand, giving three whopping whacks to her little girl's bottom.

"ooooOOOOAAAAHHHHH!!!" cried the little girl, her cries now full-throated. Tears poured down her cheeks. Drool flowed from her quavering mouth. With the little girl now wretched, some women who had moments ago been glaring, now displayed smiles full of sympathy and adult magnanimity. You know how little girls are, they said, clucking and cooing at her. Ah, the foibles of youngsters! How well we all know it; we once raised them ourselves!

Refusing their smiles, the little girl stamped her feet and refused consolation. "OOOOAAAAHHHHH!!" she screamed out, even louder now, if that was possible.

Watching the little girl, Serena tried to send her an encouraging smile. But she was crying too desperately to notice, so Serena closed her old eyes and just listened. The horns and the siren and the little girl's cries all merged into a lattice-work pattern somewhere in her neurons, a Persian design made of sound all around her. The rumbling of the bus made her plastic seat vibrate, and it felt as if her frail body was being shaken to pieces, as if she were being dispersed into the atmosphere as part of this dancing Persian pattern. She sat this way for some time, feeling buoyed by the sound. When she opened her eyes she saw the little girl still crying, and the passengers still looking besieged, and the *piazza* still mobbed with vehicles. Serena closed her old eyes and was again dispersed into space. How much more openly or loudly could a secret be told?

And so more moments passed. The stopped ambulance held its

patient, whose heart had just failed. The little girl kept on wailing, whose heart had been broken. Scores of angry-hearted drivers traded blasts from their horns. Some pedestrians walking by paused and chuckled at the comedy, feeling cheerful to be mobile. Behind them, the paint on a church-front slowly peeled. From a building nearby, a red, white and green flag hung down listless in the heat.

Ikabona's Lullaby

Ikabona was tired. So tired that it felt like the marrow in his bones was sore, and the bones were crying dry tears. The yellowed rheumy eyes in his wide black young face looked unutterably sad. On this bus if you were old, you got a seat. If you were pregnant, you got a seat. If you had a crutch, you got a seat. If you were lucky, you got a seat. But if you were only so tired that your bone marrow hurt and your bones cried you did not deserve a thing. Ikabona's head slumped to one side and his forehead hit a pole, snapping him back to wakefulness.

Why was it unthinkable for him to just go up to some passenger who looked strong and well-rested, and simply ask if they would mind giving up their seat? He knew the word for 'tired'; it was *stanco*. "*Mi scusi, signor or signora*," he would say, "*sono stanco. Sono molto molto stanco.*" And what would prevent someone from doing him a good turn then? It was no big deal, after all.

He knew though, that a flat "I am tired," spoken from his black face with his yellowed eyes was no winning approach. There were better ways it could be put, such as: "Scuse me (smile smile), but I find myself feeling suddenly overcome, terribly weak - dear me - has that ever happened to you? — terrible, isn't it? heh-heh - well I was wondering if you wouldn't mind, and etc. and etc." But Ikabona lacked the courage for such boldness, and the vocabulary to even do so. And he was black, in the end. So it wouldn't work anyway.

Ikabona was on his way to the free lunch they dished out at a church near the station. Today was soup day. '*Mee-neh-stroh-neh*', they called it. It was really quite good: a tomatoey broth filled with vegetables, potatoes and macaroni. It was the best dish they served there - but only if you got in line early enough. The fools who did the serving didn't have the brains to keep on with their stirring, to keep the potatoes and vegetables in proper suspension. They dug all the good stuff off the bottom and were too generous at the beginning. So by the time the pot was half-finished, they were serving just broth with a few floating scraps. This bus was so slow that he'd get just such a bowl - with the usual roll and apple - not a lunch you could go far on.

'Why can't you keep stirring?' Ikabona whined testily, at these soup ladlers cross-town. 'Why can't you keep stirring, save some good stuff for Ikabono?'

Ikabona felt faint now; he needed a seat badly. But the only way he'd get one was to jockey for it as usual. He surveyed those sitting near him, all dead-fixed in their places. He saw no roving eyes, no muscles poised to move, no looks of anticipation. Two people had luggage; they'd stay on all the way to the station. But even if one got up, he could not claim their seat. First rights went to the old matron with the *filippina* holding her shopping bags beside her. No matter that she was well-fed and well-rested, and definitely quite strong - boy, how she'd muscled him aside getting on at the Vatican! But white hair spoke louder than a tired black face, or black bones that were aching so much he could cry.

Ikabona sidled onward, appraising the seated passengers for their potential. A young woman was straining to look forward out the window; this was promising. Then here were two priests. Could they be going as far as the station? Why would they stray so far from their fine *Vaticano*? The young priest repelled him; he looked pinched in and pissy. But the older one looked friendly, and generous and kind. These Catholics were funny, how they turned away from women and tried to do good deeds. Maybe if he leaned against the pole near the older priest, and let his head droop and let his face show how wretched he felt - maybe this nice priest would notice and offer him his seat, happy to do a good deed. This was self-pity; Ikabona knew that; he had his pride. It would be nice, all the same, if he could wangle himself a seat *somehow*.

Just then, the man sitting at the window right near him folded his newspaper, straightened his tie, looked out the window, then down at his watch. Ikabona's eyes flashed about quickly. He saw no white hair, no crutches, no babies, no women. The man rose to his feet and moved off toward the exit. Ikabona stared, incredulous, at the empty orange seat. He just stood there, though, and did not move – expecting some old crone who could smell empty seats to appear now, out of nowhere. But a long moment passed. And no crone could be seen. This was too good to be true. A window seat till the end of the line!

Bending his knees slowly, Ikabona lowered himself into the seat as if into a tub of hot water. Aaaahhh-yes! The seat's plastic surface felt like a featherbed, soft and delicious. His bone marrow felt sweet and his bones began to smile. He leaned his head against the window and let his eyelids drop down. The bus rumbled rhythmically over the cobbled street - biddy bim bom bom, biddy bim bom bom - soothing, so soothing, like drums beating at sundown. Biddy bim bom bom - day's labor ending - Biddy bim bom bom - time to relax. The sun beat down on his head like the hot hand of God giving blessing, pressing warm peace within him as he eased into slumber.

TOK. . . TOK TOK! Ikabona's head snapped upright. What was this? TOK... TOK TOK! A child in the seat behind him was kicking his seat bottom rhythmically with both feet. TOK… TOK TOK! But what could he do? A black face could not tell an Italian mother to tell her child to stop kicking. And then there was the problem of words, always that same problem of words! TOK… TOK TOK! Ikabona thrust his head back against the window, determined to sleep.

Scr-EEEECH! The brake linings cried out as the bus came to a stop. Ooh-wah!! Ooh-Wah!! OOOH-WAH!! The siren of an ambulance drew nearer and nearer. And did not move off into the distance but stopped right outside his window, where it shrieked in his ears. He opened his eyes. The bus was jammed in a sea of cars, along with this ambulance. Soon the cars all around it were honking as well.

Ikabona's head now throbbed as it baked in the sun, as the child kicked his seat, as the ambulance siren screamed, and the cars were all honking. And on top of this all, a little girl now began wailing.

He could not see the girl well, but she must have gotten smacked; they don't cry *that* hard just in vain tantrums. How old might she be? Five, or six at the most. He knew this from his own girl, little Talulu back home. Girls were cute when they cried at that age. First their little body gets all tight: they hold their chest up and their head high and tuck their chin down to the point of bursting. When they finally can't hold it, then the tears start to fly.

Ikabona thought now of Talulu. Such a sassy devil of a little girl! Pushy and bossy like she owned the whole world. Always testing his limits - he would even forget he was the grown-up, so caught up could he get in the battle of wills she so loved to set up. He of course always won; he was stronger, after all. And when her sass finally failed, then out came her cries, just like the ones he now heard. The monster would then shrink to her true size: just a five-year-old girl who was upset. She'd throw her arms round his neck, so helpless now, and trusting, and he'd scoop her off the ground with his heart filled with love.

His thoughts turned toward home now, to his Kimba and Talulu, living their lives without Ikabona. He saw the two of them alone spending long quiet nights together. As it grew late, he saw Kimba carry their dozing daughter off to bed. He could see her limbs, which were long, brown and graceful. And as he saw her bend over, he could see her slender breasts hanging to dark tapering points. As he looked at her breasts with his tired closed eyes, a pleasing warm swelling now took place in his lap. The hot sun baked him sweeter and sweeter, till he swelled up completely. A honeyed warmth spread down his legs and up into his chest, and out both arms and into his head. The little boy's kicking now felt gentler. The girl's crying now grew fainter. The siren and car horns faded off in the distance. The hard seat was again feathered, as he leaned his head back against the window. Biddy bim bom bom - the bus was again moving. Biddy bim bom bom – hot soup was waiting. Biddy bim bom bom - drumbeats at sundown. In his curved plastic seat Ikabona now slept at peace, his broad dark lips curved in a gentle crescent smile.

The Boot

The siren of the ambulance faded off in the distance. Four cube-shaped matrons cluck-clucked as an epilogue.

"Terrible. A real sin," said the first one, shaking her head side to side.

"It seemed like an awfully long time," said the second, "but it was only six minutes. Six and a little bit. I looked at my watch."

"Just listen to you!" said the third. "Only six minutes - imagine! - just minutes indeed! Easy to say when you're standing here healthy on two feet. But on your way to the hospital, your life's gone just like that..." She snapped two sausage-like fingers soundlessly together.

"Just pray to God it made no life-or-death difference," said the third woman, as she swiftly traced a cross upon her shelf-bosomed chest.

"Amen," murmured another, crossing herself also.

"The sin," continued the first one," is that something as precious as life should be decided by something as stupid as a traffic jam. But that's how life goes. I've seen worse even, and recently. It was right outside my window. Let me tell you what happened..."

The three cube-shaped matrons leaned forward to listen.

"I live in *Trastevere* - on a narrow vicolo near *Santa Maria della Scala* - wonderful church - you've heard of it I'm sure. Well - for the last year at least, the *vigili* have been waging war with the boot. I don't drive myself - never have - but I hear everyone complaining. If you park wrong they clap the boot on your car wheel and you can't move till you pay the fine.

"Well – this big car was parked badly on my street, which was just stupid. The vicolo's so narrow that only the smaller cars can squeeze through it. The *vigili* came by but for some reason didn't tow it; they just clamped on the boot. Then they just left it like that, so no cars could get by. Now this was at sundown, and that night, as I sat out on my balcony, one car after another came up, honked till the driver got out and saw the boot, then backed up the whole block and went back out on the *Lungotevere*. There's never much traffic at night, so this wasn't much of a problem.

"Well – next morning the car was still there, half sticking out with the boot on. And what should come heading down the street, the very first thing, but a funeral procession, going to *Santa Maria della Scala* at the end of the block. The hearse rolled along slowly, maybe thirty mourners walking right behind it. From my balcony it was obvious; I could see it all coming: the hearse reached the boot and there was no room to get by.

"Well – the driver got out and just stood there staring at the boot, as if it would melt or disappear if he only stood there long enough. Meanwhile, the widow and her grown sons and daughters were all standing behind the hearse, all long-faced and sniffly, waiting for whatever the problem was to be cleared up.

"Well – more cars started turning into the *vicolo* – so that soon a dozen at least were backed up. The ones further back, of course, didn't know a thing about the boot or the hearse up in front. Next thing you know, the street was jammed to the far end of the block, and of course everyone was honking.

"Well – the mourners were still standing in place with their heads hanging down, but it was starting to dawn on them that something was wrong. One of the grown sons went forward and looked at the boot and started talking to the driver, and soon the two of them were shouting and cursing - you know how that goes. Now when the widow heard all this she started forward herself, but her daughters held her back, told her to stay put and keep her long face, which was of course only right. So she stayed there in back but it wasn't easy. I could see steam coming out both sides of her veil.

"Well - next the *motorini* started coming through, squeezing by on all sides. They'd pull long faces too, when they got to the hearse, but as soon as they'd squeezed by on the sidewalk, they'd buzz off beeping their horn, doing zig-zags, standing up on their back wheel and all the rest of it. This didn't improve the widow's mood one bit.

"Well - there was no point in calling the *vigili* then waiting god-knows-how-long till someone comes to tow the car off. The only thing to do then, was to slide out the coffin, squeeze by on the sidewalk, then carry it to the church, just half a block away. This was no pretty choice but at least it made sense. What else could they do? Just wait there all morning?

"Well - they slid out the coffin - a beautiful piece of work: polished wood, shiny brass, piled two feet deep with the most gorgeous of flowers. The sons and their friends tried to pass the coffin front-wards, but with the big car there they couldn't get good support under it, and they scratched the hearse twice, which started the driver shouting again.

"Well - who should happen to come sauntering along just then, la-dee-dah from the *piazza*, but two *vigili* in their white uniforms and sunglasses, looking just like they were on vacation. They came over to see what was the matter. Now as soon as the widow saw them, she'd had it with mourning. She lit right into them, pointing at the boot, cursing and stamping her feet. The poor *vigili* tried to calm her but the more they tried to reason with her, the crazier the poor woman got, shouting louder and louder and pounding on the hood of the hearse.

"Well - just when it looked like she was going to snap off into hysterics - Poooff! - she just lost it. Something inside her gave out and she collapsed on the hood wailing these terrible high thin wails. It was pitiful... like she was already at the graveside.

"Well - just when her crying got to the point it was absolutely *heart-breaking*, what should happen next... but the flowers on the coffin top started rustling... and shaking... and rustling... and shaking... and then this deep heavy pounding sound... THOOMP. THOOMP. THOOMP... started coming up from inside the coffin. . . and then... a deep voice spoke out.. ."

"Get out of here!" cried out one of the listening matrons, her porcelain teeth smiling broadly beneath her considerable moustache.

"Not bad!" said another, her belly shaking with laughter. "You really had us going there!"

All four women now chortled together merrily, loudest of all, the woman who had told the story.

"Well — It was *almost* all true," she said, wiping a tear from one eye. "All of it until the last part, with the THOOMP THOOMP THOOMP. But I'll tell you one thing, in all seriousness: I wouldn't surprised if one day, for real..."

"Wouldn't surprise me at all either," snapped the first one, no longer laughing now, or smiling. "There's no peace for the living in this city, so *you* tell me: why any special breaks for the dead?"

"Amen," said the second one, her smile now gone also. She was careful though, this time, to trace no crosses upon her chest.

Emilio's Change of Heart

Campo di Fiori. A disgruntled Emilio surveyed the shoppers and produce stalls in the open-air market. It was hard to imagine how a stroll in this confusion could do much to improve his mood. What kind of a 'stroll' could one possibly enjoy, hemmed in on all sides by these wide plodding women with shopping bags in both hands, all weighted down like pack mules? And as you plodded along with them, what was there to look at but puddles from the fountains strewn with rotten artichoke and lettuce leaves, crushed oranges and smashed tomatoes? Or blood-spattered animal limbs hung in butcher stalls with dubious refrigeration. This was relaxing? Refreshing? A nice change of scene? And what a din there was also. The clipped tones of price haggling and loud boorish vendors crying *MILLE LIRE MILLE LIRE MILLE LIRE*!!! at the top of their lungs, just to tell you that potatoes were for sale at the same ordinary price.

Should he lift his eyes for relief from this maggot-like food-grasping, what did he see looming over him, but that statue of Giordano Bruno. Poor Bruno. Burnt at the stake in 1600 in this very *piazza* for having the gall to suggest that the earth revolves round the sun. Not a happy exit, which this statue seems designed to avenge. His dark grim figure towers above the *piazza* full of grave malevolence, shrouded in a hood that makes him look more like an executioner than a martyr. Emilio plodded on dutifully as his wife had instructed. But how useless this was - as he'd predicted. He had been happier by far being unhappy in his own *trattoria*.

But as onward he trudged, something slowly began to happen. Passing stand after stand of fresh fruits, flowers and vegetables all twinkling in the sunlight, the first glimmerings of good cheer started rising up within him. And why not? He had nature for good company.

Why just look at those celeries piled high, a miniature tree each one of them, each stalk vertically ribbed, all a refreshing pale green. And these eggplants as well: one hundred twin brothers all the same teardrop shape, each fiercely agleam with its shiny black skin, and a small green beret with its hacked-off stem tassel. What a pleasure to walk in this wonderful market, greeted by straw-bound necklaces of garlic, verdant piles of spinach, furry kiwis and spotted bananas, and red, yellow and green peppers. Who wouldn't feel cheered by this bounty of nature, who tirelessly generated such marvelous forms?

Emilio was now whistling bits from Rossini as he strolled the market in enchantment. *Che cavolo!* Could it have taken just ten minutes for his spirits to have lifted so thoroughly? Did his dark mood really vanish so quickly, like walking pigeons sent a-scatter in the blue summer sky? Amazing how the right setting will change a man's mood! And how smart his good wife had been to know this! And how lucky *he* was, to have such a smart, fine, loyal mate! Even Giordano Bruno now seemed transformed. He no longer looked malignant, cursing the food foragers round his statue, all indifferent to his cruel fate. He seemed instead now to be blessing them, wise and compassionate, from beyond the grave.

Emilio cheerfully made his way through the market to where the fish vendors plied their briny wares. There, on rude planks laid across sawhorses, lay rows of shelled, finned, gilled, scaled and pucker-lipped creatures, eyes wide-open in shock at this alien world of air. *Cozze, alici, merluzzi, vongole, calamari, spada, sogliola, gamberi*: sea creatures in profusion, spread out on fern leaves and sprinkled with chipped ice, tended by leather-faced men and squat aproned women who abstractedly waved papers to shoo away flies.

"*CIAO BELLO!!*" With a thump on the back and a hearty loud laugh, Emilio, now the herald of good cheer, greeted Stefano, his fishman.

"*Ciao,*" said Stefano quietly, "*come va?*"

"*BE-NISSIMO!!!*" boomed Emilio, sticking his chest out like a bantam, smiling for the whole world to take note of, as he unleashed a torrent of expansive banter.

Moments later, as he waited for Stefano to wrap up his purchase, he studied the head of a swordfish propped upright on the table. What a remarkable piece of construction! Its body was as wide as Emilio's ample waist. Judging from the size of the fluked tail that lay severed on the cobblestones, this fish would need to bend to get through one of our human-sized doors. And such eyes! Each one as big as his palm, endowed with wizardly optics that could see through the ocean's depths. Now dried out by the sun, each was a flat shrunken disk, smaller than the socket that held it, clouded and useless. And then finally... the great sword-like beak. It was parted as if smiling, with pink tissue down its throat as far down as he could see. Just yesterday this fish was spreading terror in the waters off of Naples. But yesterday's bully was today's poor *bastardo*, displayed clown-like, with a lemon spiked on his beak.

A thought struck Emilio that sent his already high spirits soaring. An outstanding idea! And why not? It was possible, it was definitely possible...

"*Senta*, Stefano. How much for me to take the *spada's* head off your hands. Put it to work at my place instead of yours...?"

"No way. You must be kidding. You gonna haul that big smelly thing back with you? It's heavy as hell and stinks like a toilet. They won't let you on board."

Emilio was undaunted. He had already solved these minor problems. He waved away Stefano's objections with a big toothy smile.

Minutes later, Emilio was at the bus-stop. His basset-hound eyes were fixed on Bus 64, stopped a block away at the light. At his side was a big black plastic garbage bag with the fish head inside it. Only the final three inches of its beak stuck out discretely beyond the twisted tie-wire. Emilio reviewed his strategy: as the bus approached, he would stand directly in front of the bag so as to block it from the driver's view. As the bus came nearer and the angle changed, with mincing side-steps he would keep it hidden. Once the driver had passed he would grab up his fish head, hop on at the rear entrance, and five short blocks later: Tah dah! He'd be home free, with the remarkable head of a *spada*!

Green light. The bus rolled forward. Emilio hulked with studied nonchalance before his catch. As the bus came up closer, his little side-steps kept him between the fish and the driver. Then came the dramatic moment, when the broad windshield was right upon him. He looked cooly at the driver, the adversary he was outsmarting at this very moment. But this foe was an oaf! A moronic ape! Beneath a Cro-Magnon brow both his eyes were as blank as marbles. It was a marvel that this fellow could guide a bus through city streets, let alone spot contraband being smuggled aboard, and so cleverly at that. The bus came to a stop with the screech of its worn brake linings.

After letting the others get on ahead of him, Emilio hoisted the garbage bag up onto his hip, and embraced its turgid heaviness close against him with both arms. He took care to enter the stairwell backwards, so as not to lead with the *spada's* point. 'Bravo, bravo', he congratulated himself, as the doors hissed shut, missing the point by a hair's breadth. '*Bravo bravo BRAVO*!!' He was safely aboard now, as good as home free. He could already see the hungry tourists as they looked down his street, and instead of that ordinary checkered tablecloth, they'd see this proud king of the deep, its spear pointed skyward, with a lemon spiked on its tip! Kept on a tray of ice, popped in the cooler between meals, it would keep... who could say? It might keep for two weeks!

On the Road to *Largo Argentina*

After absorbing Emilio and the others, Bus 64 moved on but briefly. After a block and a half it stopped flush up against Bus 173, which was stopped behind Bus 44, which was stopped behind three buses and five taxis that had likewise been halted. Craning his head out the window, Vinzo looked down the *Corso* to see what was the problem. There was nothing to be seen. He slouched down, set to wait. The passengers gazed around blankly, looking off into empty space, without expression. Call it the strap-hangers sleep of the dead.

Two minutes passed. A fat fly kept thudding lazily against the inside of the windshield.

Two more minutes passed. Still no sign of movement, except for the fat fly.

At this point a switch seemed to have been tripped among the passengers. Veterans though they were of such turtle-paced rides, they reserved the right to get cranky. Like a den of beasts waking up ornery from hibernation, they expressed their frustration. Men looked up testily from newspapers they could no longer concentrate on in the quiet, still bus. Wrists were cocked upwards, and watch-faces provoked oaths, grievous frowns, dramatic sighs, grumblings of missed appointments, squandered lives, civic ruin. Indignance, contempt and distress were expressed with word, face and gesture as the herd lowed in solidarity. The only abstentions were a dusky thick-lipped woman drawn straight from Gaugin who sat still and expressionless, and the gypsy with her baby, still off thinking distant gypsy thoughts.

Vinzo craned his head out again. A-ha! So there was something! A police car up the street was parked crosswise, blocking traffic. The whirling light on its roof sent out brilliant blue flashes that were gobbled up by the bright sun.

"*Incidente*," muttered Vinzo, slouching down further. "*Testa di cazzo.*"

A few passengers stuck their heads out the window. Soon everyone knew. Many who were going just a short distance thought they might as well just walk. And others who were going further, thought to walk a few blocks past the accident, and catch the buses that merged into the *Corso* further on. A reasonable enough wish, which they relayed to their civil servant.

"*Apri, per favore*," called polite voices from the center doors.

"*Back doors, per favore*," echoed others at the rear door, all cheerful at their imminent release. Five seconds passed. Then ten... The doors did not open. Was this driver deaf? Best to make themselves clearer then.

"Middle doors! Open up!" boomed the same voices, in demanding, menacing tones.

"Back doors! Open up you!" cried their comrades in the rear, angry prisoners demanding freedom.

And still no response! What was wrong with this driver?! Here they were, absolutely motionless, against the curb, on a straightaway, in broad daylight, with an accident that could take forever. And here was a driver who went by the book and would only open the doors at the designated stops! How arbitrary! How rigid! How arrogant. Just think: to be actually following rules! This was *Roma*!

"Open up, you *cretino*!" cried a woman with a bouffant hairdo, the wings of her powdered nose arching up as she snarled.

"Don't play the jackass!" shouted a businessman, in a voice that was half-exasperation, half-command.

"You're here to serve *us*!" called out a matron with an old-fashioned pocketbook. "If it wasn't for us you'd be in the unemployment line tomorrow!"

A volley of insults and demands pelted Vinzo's thick hide. 'To the devil with all of you.' he thought first, slouching down even further. 'Not one ass gets off till I let it get off," he thought next, with a joyless smile.

Now these passengers were well aware of the species they were dealing with. Not a thing could be done. A sullen air of mutiny filled the bus, while its evil captain yawned, then scratched his belly.

Four more minutes passed. The road remained blocked. It must have been a bad one. Though there was no sound of an ambulance, people were streaming along the sidewalk toward the scene. Blue-coated shop-girls came out of their stores. Faces appeared at fourth and fifth floor windows. People came hurrying out from *Piazza Navona*, which made no sense at all, since it was half a block behind them on the far side of the street. You would think someone had stood atop a statue in the middle of the *piazza* and announced through a bull-horn:

> *"Attention please, all strollers and idlers! There has just been a terrible accident, nearby on the Corso. If you stop lounging and are quick about it, you might get there in time for a most interesting eyeful."*

But then... what was this…? How wonderful! The front-most buses were finally moving out into the center of the road, where one of the white-helmeted *vigili* was waving them on, past the scene of the accident. Bus 173 rolled forward slowly. Bus 64 rolled close behind.

All our bored exasperation disappeared in an instant. Not only were we moving onward to our important destinations, but we would get to see an accident, as well. And it might be a bad one! A less sturdy vehicle might have tipped over, but the well-designed Bus 64 stayed upright as everyone massed to the side facing the scene of the accident. Sitting passengers pressed their faces to the windows. Standees leaned across sitting ones. And the standees behind them leaned on their backs and their shoulders, so as not to miss out. Newspapers were folded. Books were shut. Eyeglasses came out from purses and pockets. The bus inched along slowly. All would soon be rewarded.

Finally, finally: we arrived at the scene. Beside the police car with its flashing blue light, lay a *motorino* twisted into scrap. Beyond it lay a blue-jeaned body, its limbs skewed at improbable angles. A jacket was draped over the rider's head and shoulders. A girl sat on the curb with her face in her hands, crying. The crowd that had gathered stood motionless and watched.

A hushed silence fell over the passengers as the bus rolled past.

Two old women began crossing themselves.

"*Dio mio dio mio dio mio,*" whispered one of them, shaking her old head from side to side.

"*Che poverini,*" said the other one, her head hung to her chest.

Two teen-aged girls clutched each other's arms and bit their lips, their eyes brimming with tears.

Two teen-aged boys simply stared, wide-eyed and sober, temporarily mature.

Two men touched their balls, a reassuring gesture reserved for seeing hearses and nuns, and scenes such as this one.

A middle-aged man shook his head as he tsk-tsked disapprovingly. "Driving like *pazzi*. What do they expect? What do they think is supposed to happen when they drive everywhere like such *pazzi*?"

"Should have been wearing his helmet," said his companion, nodding in agreement with this logic.

"Looks like he was," said a third man, pointing out the window. And indeed – he was right. The spherical form of a helmet could be seen beneath the jacket draped over the body.

The first man was not impressed. "So big deal. He was wearing a helmet. What of it? You want a miracle? You can't expect a helmet to do everything when you ride like these kids do, driving crazy like *pazzi*."

"You got a point there," agreed the second man. The third one nodded thoughtfully.

Vinzo too, had caught his eyeful. Hot bile rose up his throat quickly, with the taste of sour coffee and tobacco, and surprisingly, yesterday's *melenzane parmigiana*. A cold clammy sweat broke out over his body. His shirt and his T-shirt clung to his back. But soon the traffic moved more briskly and the breeze brought relief.

Just as he was feeling some relief, a *motorino* swerved out from a sidestreet, driven by a boy with a bin filled with sandwich rolls wedged between his chest and the handlebars. At any other time Vinzo would have handled this with ease. But with the dead boy fresh in mind, he swerved sharply and slammed down the brake pedal.

Screee...VOOOM!!!

Who could possibly keep his balance? Everyone crashed forward into seat-backs or went toppling down on top of each another. One heard sounds such as one never heard, save in rare moments like this: surprised squeaks, shocked squeals, desperate gasps, fearful moans.

Once the first shock had passed, though, people quickly recovered their bearings. And in chorus they let loose with an extravaganza of cursing. The greatest glories of malediction were hissed, thought, yelled, breathed, muttered and grumbled at our Vinzo. Vinzo hunkered down on the wheel. His thick hide thickened perceptibly.

Because of the sobering scene all had just witnessed, an unusual solicitude and courtesy prevailed as people helped their neighbors to their feet. Many had bruised elbows, shins or shoulders, which they rubbed with grimaces or rueful smiles. One man handed a pair of eyeglasses to a woman, who smiled wryly when she saw a lens missing. Another looked angrily at his watch, whose crystal was criss-crossed with cracks. One man looked particularly crestfallen. He held a bent, crushed roll of antique prints. An old woman all in black, with a white bun, had been thrown flat on her back. She didn't move. Could it really be...? Was she... dead? But then her eyes opened and a big smile split her lined brown leathery face. She was hoisted to her feet amid cheers and laughter.

As everyone readjusted themselves, an unrepentant Vinzo drove on. He did not even turn round. The bus soon settled down. But this calm was short-lived. A single cry from the rear sent an unmistakable message: someone had been really hurt.

"Jesus Christ oh my god, call a doctor, somebody call a *doctor!*" It was Ted from the Feelings Group, shouting in English. Slumped on the floor against the ticket-validating machine was Cindy from Cedar Heights. Her ample right buttock was clutched in one hand. A red stain spread slowly on her barn-sized plaid culottes. On the floor beside her lay a big black garbage bag. Some kind of pointy thing was sticking out of it.

"Stop the bus!" shouted Ted, bulling his way to the call button. He pushed at it frantically, but after the first ding it made only clicks. And the bell only told Vinzo to stop at the next stop, where he had to stop anyway. People called out to Vinzo, from the back, to alert him.

"Stop the bus!"

Aprite le porte! Open the doors!!"

"...*in dietro!!* In the back!!"

They may as well have saved their breath. Knowing he was just a half block from the next stop, Vinzo invoked his last rule, #6: 'Let the passengers fight it out among themselves.'

Seconds later the bus pulled up to the traffic island at *Largo Argentina*. A crowd clamored close, to get on. But when the doors opened with their loud hiss, passengers came rushing out with unusual urgency.

"Make way! Call a doctor! Let us through!"

At the back of the bus, Cindy lay on her side against the ticket-validating machine. She looked wide-eyed and dumb - a scared creature in shock. One woman held her hand and fanned her. Another patted her forehead with a handkerchief. It cost several strong men no small effort to carry her down to the traffic island, where they leaned her against a trash barrel. A small crowd gathered around her.

A small crowd never stays small for long, and like a magnet, this one drew forth from around the *piazza*. People came out from the bank across the street and the bookstore beside it. They flocked from the bus-stops on the other side, and emerged from bars still holding cups and sandwiches. Others, who could not be bothered with just another urban distraction, simply got on board, eager to move on.

With Bus 64 now stopped, newly arriving buses were backed up, blocking circulation around the whole *piazza*. As the honking built to its usual crescendo, a white-helmeted *vigile* went to the front of the bus. He took Vinzo's name and bus number on a small notepad, then waved him onward toward *Piazza Venezia*.

As the bus chugged away, a small throng was still clamoring around poor Cindy from Cedar Heights. A disconsolate Emilio sat on the low wall nearby, which encircled ancient ruins. He was shrugging to a *vigile* taking notes on a clipboard. Beside him sat the plastic bag with its fish tip, now bloodied, pointing proudly upward still, to the open sky. Two stray cats that had come up from the ruins nosed the bag with great passion and rubbed back and forth against it. A calico kitten pranced up daintily. It was keen to explore.

Pantheon Rose

Yes, the guidebook crooned and prepared us for magic, when we first saw this temple, stoic heart of Rome's ancient soul. But no magic exists here. How can there be? The *piazza* teems with strollers and skaters. The teens round the fountain are all movement and noise. And all these serve as sport for still others, the body-trollers, seated in swarms at cafe tables with beach-bright umbrellas. Amidst all this, what possible place has this grave old gray temple?

Inside the temple, things seem no better, just cooler. It feels too much like a script: We see the great vaulted dome and we wonder at the ancient feat. We see the hole in the *cupola's* center, and duly find it odd that rain, no less than the sun and the stars, was invited to pour through. We see Raphael's tomb, and sigh on cue at his early demise - like the crowd all around us that wanders about with cameras. Or listens as the smart tape machine tells what this shrine's all about.

We touch just the surface. The old gods that preside here elude us, completely. They won't disclose themselves to strollers, or be captured by cameras, and are mute while we sit here, spinning words and more words. Maybe if we closed the guidebook and shunned the guide, and looked not to where any finger pointed... Or if we bent a knee, or bowed our head to some wise granite block...

But it's no use, let's move on... out through the towering iron doors, which open at the push of a fingertip - and are remarkable, as all agree. Before we leave though, let's pause beneath the great-columned portico, in whose shade we can linger in this temple's embrace, however faint.

But who is *that*? Over there. That hag with her lap full of flowers? What a strange looking creature! With her whole wardrobe on her back! Blouses one over another over another. Shawl upon shawl on her shoulders. Layers of skirts around her waist hanging down to her ankles, with beat-up laceless hiking boots, their tongues sticking forward, on her feet.

She's a street tramp of course, but she's definitely distinctive. White hair pulled back, piled high beneath a baboushka. A pointed chin whose upward curve meets her hooked beakish nose. She looks like a witch - but not the wicked screecher in cartoons. She's the witch of times yore, of legend, of the Brothers Grimm. The shrewd witch, the hoary wise one, who knows animals and the forest, the wind, moon and tides, and the hidden ways of men.

Sitting on a column's pedestal, she's hunched over a pile of roses in her lap. One by one she cuts their stems short with a knife, nicks off the lowermost thorns, then wraps the stem up in foil. Her bony hands are well-practiced. Cut, nick thorns, wrap. Cut, nick thorns, wrap. She works intently, with real force - you wouldn't dare interrupt her. When she's finished, she'll take a bus to a church where they know her. While the roses rest in a tub of water, she'll doze through the afternoon's heat on a shaded pew She's been going there for years. The priest doesn't mind. But he still doesn't know who she is or where she comes from, or where she sleeps or what her name is. And neither does anyone else. Let's call her Pantheon Rose.

Later today, the sun will go down and the sky will go black and the stars will come out to shine. And the lamps will cast their mellow light on the Pantheon and its *piazza*, which will look like a stage-set, quite romantic. And the lovers will come out to promenade. And into this night will come Pantheon Rose, with her flowers cradled in the crook of an arm. Beswathed in her blouses, skirts and shawls she'll shuffle slowly down these streets, her body stooped like a question mark - a world unto herself. Gypsy women and children rove these streets also, they too selling flowers. But a gypsy can be wheedling or pathetic, or grasping or snide. We'll see their roses in the gutters at dawn, in fives and tens, limp and unsold. But not so the roses of Pantheon Rose.

Approaching a couple at her slow inexorable pace, she turns on no pathos, and also no charm. As her bony hand rises crane-like to extend forth a flower, she seems not to be selling, but rather, to be offering something. She is offering a rose, but offering more than a rose also. And we don't know what that is till we look into her eyes, which are flashing, black and alive, and faintly ironic, like a fox. There's a sparkle there too, but it's hers, hers alone. It's not asking for any smiles in return. When her gaze penetrates, we're caught unawares - and it's only then that we begin to see...

Till now, all this has existed for us, and for us alone: the ancient temple's grandeur, its lamp-lit stage, the night sky with its smiling stars. All props in the little theaters of our own little lives, in which we stroll puffed up and serene, basking comfortably in their reflected luster. And never moreso than when we saw this quaint hag, a throwback to another time - such superb *divertimento*. But as her black eyes probe ours, we feel that somehow, we've been punctured. We know nothing about this old woman, while her twinkling fox-eyes seem to know very much about us. They know about our car and our flat with its lock and its furniture. About our refrigerator humming, stocked and waiting. Our paychecks and savings, our pillowed bed and television, our vacations and insurance, our watch, thermostat and wardrobe. As we take the rose from her hand, we see her wizened face against the starry sky. And she sees us. And she is watching, closely watching.

Some who sense these watching eyes hide from them instinctive-ly. Up she will shuffle to some couple strolling arm-in-arm. And no sooner does she extend a flower than the young Romeo digs for his wallet. He's nervous, over-eager; and he does not know why. Other Romeos sense nothing but they buy just the same. For what a bargain a rose is anyway: perfect pretext for stealing a kiss, or snaking an arm round a lovely waist. And Pantheon Rose just watches. And pockets her money. And with never a thank you, shuffles on down the street.

Her roses for tonight are all clipped, wrapped and ready. With thrust and counter-thrust of her aged limbs, she manages, like a camel, to rise up to her feet. And off she goes - step step step - bent like a walking question-mark, through the colonnade. As she moves slowly through the throng, a strange feeling steals over us. But what can it be, this sweet confusion that we feel? The teeming tourists seem to fall away now, into silence and insignificance. The *piazza* fades away too, becomes distant and dim. As this hag picks along, things get infused with strange and new clarity. What a moment ago seemed banal, now seems gripping, portentous.

We are struck dumb to staring: at unfathomable stones and unfathomable columns, and at numberless bricks, them too, incomprehensible. The word 'pantheon' drifts into mind, but it's just a sound now, and drifts away, meaningless beside what we see now, all so strange and unknowable. Strange, these old blocks we stand upon. And strange, our being here to stand on them. Everything seems so old – and we ourselves perhaps, oldest of all.

But just as mysteriously as this feeling came over us, so too does it vanish. And we again feel burdened by the close noisy milling crowd. This temple is again a carnival, banal and displeasing. Out from the portico shuffles Pantheon Rose, through the crowd, and down a side-street. And it strikes us, with certainty, that it was through her that we stepped somehow, for brief moments, out of time.

Who is that woman? How has she spent her life? Did she ever marry? What does she think about? So many questions spring to mind, but they're all trivial, except for one, which we must ask her, when next we see her: 'Pantheon Rose: who are we?'

In the Palm of His Hand

Piazza Largo Argentina. In the midst of this bustling *centro* lies a striking oasis: a full square block of ruins, the once-hallowed site of four pre-Christian temples. More than two millennia past, men gathered here to conduct rites of which we know nothing, to gods about whom we know just as little. All that remains is this charming glimpse of the antique. Broad staircases lead to the foundations of half-intact temples. Stately columns, now truncated, reach up like the stony fingers of some ancient hand, expressing some unknown message into our contemporary air. Fallen pediments, plinths and columns lie strewn among the grass and lush moss. Gauzy-topped umbrella pines lean this way and that.

Alas – these temples are largely ignored now, by both tourist and native. The ruins are sunk below street level and the surrounding glass walls are dirty. The stairways that lead down have padlocked gates. Should we try to contemplate the scene nonetheless, the din of traffic grates intolerably. Indeed, though thousands utter the name '*Largo Argentina*' daily, they refer not to these ruins, but to the thoroughfare that swirls around them. This sacred site is now little more than a traffic rotary. The only ones who seem to appreciate it are its resident cats, perched on walls, stones and pedestals in serene contemplation.

No such reflections, however, clouded the mind of Cesare Massimiliano as he surveyed *Largo Argentina* from the window of his penthouse office. Antiquities had little to say to this practical man, despite the classical splendor of the room he worked in. All around him marble busts sat in their niches, decorative moldings played musically at the junctures of wall, floor and ceiling, while gods, nymphs and satyrs romped through glades in the old frescos overhead. But to him these were mere accoutrements - the things men like himself surround themselves with, but without knowing why. Each person has their muse, be it art or history, philosophy or science, that whispers sweet things in their ear. Cesare too, had his muse – a muse as timeless as any. His muse was money. But this muse did not whisper. In excited hoarse commands it urged him to tactics and strategy, calculation and competition – and above all else, to profit.

For Cesare, today was yet another day of accumulation. In less than an hour he had a meeting at the Ministry, where three years of negotiations would give birth to a new nationwide consortium. Not only would Italian products be put on a solid new footing throughout Europe, but Cesare's family business and investments would be strengthened as well. All that remained was for six very important men to sign twelve sheets of paper, an event for which his lacquered pen had been clipped to his breast pocket since sunrise. Though triumphs such at this were no longer unusual for Cesare, each was preceded still by its own keen anticipation, and had its own separate savor.

Looking down at the *piazza*, he watched the listless commuters huddled on the traffic island waiting for their buses. Groups of people such as this were a source of great reassurance to Cesare, such as others might get from mountains, bodies of water, or expanses of soil. It didn't matter if it were a football stadium, a papal mass, a combat battalion, or these heat-fagged commuters. What mattered was that groups of people meant consumers, consumers meant markets, markets meant transactions, and transactions meant profit.

Did he know any of these people, who inspired in him such comfort, such tranquility? Not a one. All that mattered was that they were many. That they rose up from their beds and reported to work. That they labored and fed. That they consumed resources needing constant replenishment. That their car parts wore out, like the fabrics on their backs and the shoes on their feet. Such a wonderful logic ruled life's myriad apparatus. Everyone bound to the turning wheel they had no choice but to keep turning, the whole clockwork giving bounty to men like himself – who were strong enough to harness it to their indomitable will.

In moods such as this one, Cesare saw not the same Rome everyone else saw, but a kind of toy Rome - a miniature city in a wind-up-doll world. Here were charming toy buildings set on white-striped toy streets, with toy lamp-posts, toy streetlights, and toy cars and toy taxis and orange toy buses. And moving about among all this were the toy people, feeling purposefully propelled on their preordained rounds. A tinker-toy world that was quaint and adorable. He felt easeful and buoyant. A warm benevolence spread through him like brandy, suffusing him with the happy feeling of his own life so agreeably superimposed on this world that lay beneath him. What a fine life and world! He felt he could hold it in the palm of his hand.

Cesare's prim secretary Rita appeared in the doorway in her prim suit and prim glasses.

"Your meeting at the Ministry is still on for twelve-thirty?" she half-asked half-reminded him, with wrinkled brow. "Shall I call the cab for you now?"

"No, it's o.k., that's all right," said Cesare with a wink and a smile and a wave of the hand. "The Ministry's just up the street. I'll just slip down into the *piazza* and hop a bus, thanks just the same."

"As you like," said Rita with a short bow, closing the polished walnut door quietly behind her.

Moments later Cesare emerged from the elevator and descended the marble staircase to the street. Strolling shoulder-to-shoulder among the crowd, he felt lightly whisked along by his expansive feelings. Like a monk among lay people, with pleased detachment he observed the foibles of these folk on all sides. Here were men with briefcases and newspapers, their minds stirred to turbulence with fresh worries about office politics, new taxations, market fluctuations, money devaluation, imagined privations. Cesare smiled inwardly. What a maudlin affair, the financial world of the common man! The monthly check chewed by portioned payments at one end, and portioned pleasures at the other. A sinking ship kept afloat by anxious bailing-out, alone. How absurd to not move forward, but to struggle and struggle just so as not to go under!

There was another side to this coin, though: the splendid Italian spender! Say what you will about this Latin creature: say he's slovenly and disorganized. Say he's vain, selfish and over-emotional... whatever his faults they were easily outweighed by his restless acquisitiveness, his admirable wanton willingness to let money fly free from his hand. Why just look at these shoppers!

Here were eager eyes scanning for possessions, both practical and capricious. Here were covetous eyes stealing glimpses of costly inaccessibles. Here were children's eyes, in adult heads, roving restless from one novelty to another, sick for stimulation. Here were ten people hypnotized by a display of wrist-watches, with a hundred variations on the same basic product. Here were ten others pressed up against a window full of shoes, studying the ten thousandth way leather had been cut, shaped and fashioned. With what fine dedication they attended to their shopping!

Cesare's revery would have continued. But as he came near to the bus-stop he sensed something was wrong. Crowds were swelling now around the traffic island. All traffic had stopped. Buses bumper-to-bumper formed an orange wall leading out the *piazza*. On the side streets, stopped cars were honking. His muscles went tense and his solar plexus knotted. This was not supposed to be happening. Things like this happened - but they happened to others, not to him. Not to Cesare Massimiliano, on his way to a meeting that would impact the whole nation! What possible place was there in plans as important as his, for a run-of-the-mill grid-locking Roman traffic jam?

What should he do, though? Dash a few blocks and hope to find a cab that would carry him round this bottleneck? No, that was too risky; he might come up dry. Should he head off on foot, then hop a bus when they started moving again? That too was risky, for how long might *that* take? And if he walked he'd be quite late. He'd be soaked through his suit and would no doubt be stinking.

In the budding throes of panic, he was ambushed by a sudden savage gnawing of hunger. So fierce was this onslaught that he felt weak, void and wobbly. Curse the selfish wanting bag, with its bad sense of timing! So overwhelmed did he so suddenly feel, that he needed to dash to the nearest bar. For he needed, not later - but *now* - many mouthfuls of something, of anything, to go slithering down to his stomach. And some mighty glugs of beer, all frosty in his throat, to chase it down. Chuck the traffic. Chuck the cab question. Chuck the ministry. Chuck the consortium! When this gaping hole shouted, one's priorities changed fast!

It wasn't until he had half-crossed the street to the bar that he realized what he was doing. 'Get a grip, fella! You've a big meeting to get to!' But with pedestrians jostling him on all sides, sweat pouring down his back, and fiendish acids gnawing in his belly without mercy, Cesare's tinker-toy world was now distressingly real.

Why oh why hadn't he taken the cab, as prim Rita had suggested? But then why hadn't she been more insistent? She *knew* time was running short. She *knew* buses were unreliable. She rode them herself, every day. So if she knew all of this and had offered to call a cab, why then had she gone soft? Why hadn't she insisted? She knew damn well that this meeting was crucial. So why hadn't she *said* something, or better, *done* something, instead of just giving that dumb 'as you like', then leaving him stranded in a rotten fix like this one? Some secretary, his prim Rita! Probably flown out of the office and down in the bar already, where the secretaries all gossiped like birdbrains.

Cesare would have castigated Rita further - as she deserved - but reason briefly intervened to suggest that this would get him to the Ministry no faster. He'd take up with her later. In the meantime, he needed action. What about that policeman who was holding up the lead bus, just standing there like a scarecrow, doing nothing?

"Hey you listen," barked Cesare, striding up to him face-to-face. "What's going on here?" he demanded, in imperious tones.

"*Bo,*" grunted the policeman with a shrug. "Some woman just got carried off the bus. Someone said she'd been stabbed."

"Can't you get things moving?" challenged Cesare. "This lead bus is ready to go."

The policeman nodded as if in agreement, but then there it was again: that damnable gesture Cesare knew only too well. The lips turned downward into a pout. The jaw rose defiantly, like a baby refusing its bottle. Then again came that shrug and that ignorant word "*Bo*." Cesare looked with disgust at this creature before him. Hell, this city was becoming more Arab every year.

"Who's the ranking officer, who's in charge here?" he demanded.

The policeman gave a horse-toss of his head toward a *vigile* in the distance, in his white-domed helmet. Cesare stalked off toward him at once, exasperated to bursting...

No Need to Bother

Nothing much to look at on *this* dark corridor of a block. No shops and few pedestrians. Just exhaust-blackened brick walls covered with tatters of old posters. But... what's that over there? That big plaque on the corner, held by two blockish stone angels? Maybe if we squint we can read the inscription...

Al GLORIOSI CADUTI...

"To the glorious fallen in battle." Oh. So it's *that* kind of monument. Well then. No need to bother. Just another war monument with its long list of long-dead soldiers. You'll find such lists of war-dead almost anywhere you travel, so if you've seen one, as they say, you've seen them all. But that's putting it too crassly, of course. Some sentiment is definitely, is always in order here: that choked muffled cry, that awe, horror, incomprehension that any war monument, anywhere, can stir up inside us.

But why indulge in such feelings? Just look, after all: angels are holding the plaque on either side. They're not very well done, but art isn't the point here, but rather, that they represent angels. Real angels, who shimmer in eternal reality, like compassionate rays of sun, watching over us from beyond ourselves, from beyond time, from beyond death itself. Or are these only words, and are angels just an artist's fancy? Well, they must have believed in angels - no? - whoever put up this monument. So if these war-dead are now in the excellent custody of angels, why be teary? Angels wafted these soldiers up into much ampler spheres. We can rest peacefully then, in the presence of this, or any war monument for that matter - no?

What? You'd like to look closer now, at this dark ugly plaque?

No problem – all are present and accounted for. The two hundred or so dead men have been carefully listed, and even sub-listed by rank, with the members of each rank alphabetized. Under 'First Lieutenant' we find Antonio Bagelli, followed by Stefano Maggio, who just managed to nose out Vincenzo Martini. Under 'Second Lieutenant', we find six other dead officers: Sebastiano Castelli, Giovanni D'Ambrosio, Giancarlo Grossi, Arturo Pittoni, Ernesto Tonarelli, Fabio Trezzi. Then, under 'Corporals', we find 19 alphabetically-listed dead First Corporals, followed by 24 alphabetically-listed dead Second Corporals, followed by 8 alphabetically-listed dead Third Corporals. Finally, we come to dead Privates: a real horde: well over a hundred. Their names have been carved in much smaller letters. They too, have been alphabetized, but the sub-ranks have been dispensed with: First-, Second- and Third-class Privates have been all thrown together. Maybe someone decided that once you got down to Private, distinctions of status did not matter. Or maybe the stone-cutter miscalculated, and had to dispense with extra headings so that everyone would fit in.

This chiseled list once consoled someone, but hey... let's not get sentimental. Rome can give us far better war memorabilia than this blackened plaque of nonentities from some minor campaign in a forgotten contest. After all, near the Colosseum we can thrill to the mighty campaigns of Caesar. And at the Forum we can contemplate the vicissitudes of Empire. Just imagine their war councils, as Hannibal's elephants trudged South, braving snow-filled Alpine passes! Yes, this city is simply *filled* with epic celebration of the sword and its victims.

And didn't Plato say, long ago, that war is man's constant state? And has he been proved wrong since then? Of course not. So in today's peaceful Rome, why dwell on unpleasantness?

After all, the grandfather of teen-aged Yoko Kokimura and the grandfathers of her three giggly friends may have been killed by Americans in 1944. But it's 1994 now, and cute Yoko and her friends are on their way to the Gucci store near *Piazza di Spagna*. They're planning to buy a key-ring, a wallet, and maybe maybe maybe, an evening handbag.

And here's Mustafah Nazar, going to rehearse with his jazz group. His body is vibrating with rhythms he can't wait to express on his string bass. What difference does it make how good his father and uncles were at killing Frenchmen, when war's hot breath passed over Algeria? And here's Manuela, who does translations from Italian into Spanish, whose two uncles... in Catalonia. And Enrico, whose father... at Trieste, in '39... and Nigel, whose father... in a spitfire over the Channel in '42... and whose grandfather on the Somme in '16...

Why even our gypsy mother takes her place now alongside us civilized folks all around her. Her grandparents were bulldozed into the earth somewhere in Poland, in '44... One could easily go on. But whatever for? Take any busful of ordinary people like us, and their roots will be steeped in the blood spilled in war. So - as we said when we first saw this monument: there's no need to bother. To what end, after all?

Today, after all, is today. And it's a good day. Granted, it's beastly hot, but it's still a *good* day, not a *bad* day. Let's look no more then, at this war monument with its poorly done angels. This is *Roma*, after all; and that's *amore* spelled backwards. The afternoon still lies before us, to be enjoyed, filled with *pizza* and *gelato* and shiny new shoes. And for dinner we can try *pasta primavera*, with soft *mozzarella* that's made from buffalo milk. And have you ever tried iced *Sambuca*, with a coffee bean floating at the top?

One Spilled Grapefruit

Anna knew these things happened on the bus. All the time in fact – but not to her. Not once, in all these years. But now it *was* happening. What should she do?

And what a dumb question that was! What should a grown woman do on a bus in broad daylight when a man's got his hand on your bottom? And he's pressing and fondling while you stand there and do nothing, listening to your own voice as it asks what to do!

She should move of course. That much was obvious. She should move, get away, but more than this – she should speak. She should speak to this hand loudly. She should go off like an alarm, like a shrieking mad siren, to spotlight this hand and its dirty deed. She should confront and accuse and then smite this bad hand. In her mind flashed a severed hand on a battlefield.

This much seemed clear, but she just stood there, still thinking. And as she thought, the hand began to seem more distant. She could still feel the ring on one finger, impressed on her buttock. But as for herself, she was floating elsewhere, like under gas at the dentist's. She was up near the roof, or floating above the traffic, like a balloon. She felt strangely dislocated, anchored only by this hand that pressed firmly, where it shouldn't. Between her mind up above and this hand down below, her head sat in between, face to face with an ad.

Side by side were two photos of the same man. In the left one he looked stressed and disconsolate. The hair on his head was a thinned scraggly mess, the skin of his skull showing through in patches. In the right photo he looked relaxed, with a confident smile. His thick mat of hair was swept up in a pompadour. She read the text also:

Have you been robbed of the assurance a rich head of hair can bring you? In the past you had but one choice: to suffer and be silent. But now, with computer-assisted techniques from the clinics of Switzerland, available in Italy now for the first time...

Anna wondered what a computer could have to do with the growth of real hairs, real follicles, and actual glands. Was this fellow in the picture wearing a wig, or had he actually had treatments? In either case he looked ridiculous. She remembered the story of the man with three wigs: one short, one medium, one long. As the weeks passed he would switch from one to the other, until after some weeks with the long one, he would march off to the barber-shop, from which he would return having switched back to the short one....

And yet... it was her heart, was it not, that throbbed hard in her throat, so her tongue seemed to fill her mouth? And her bowels churned with some cold unnamed fear. Not fear of this hand she had tried to make peace with. But fear of her own pounding heart and her own throbbing throat, and something deep down inside her on the verge of eruption. And then suddenly, out of nowhere, a voice shrieked out:

"GET YOUR HANDS OFF ME!!"

The whole bus went silent. Everyone turned. It was Anna who had shrieked. In her fine clothes with her silk scarf draped fashionably on her shoulders, she stood by the rail, fists clenched by her side. Her well-coiffed head was thrust forward. Cords bulged out on her neck. She was breathing like she'd run a mile. Hidden behind dark glasses, her rage-filled eyes could yet be seen.

The dark-skinned man she was facing stood tensed for defense. His face meanwhile, strained to appear relaxed and composed. But his nostrils betrayed this - they flared open and closed and then open and closed. His brown Mediterranean eyes were quite beautiful but lizard-like. They shone with contempt and bemused derision. His sensuous lips drew back till his fine teeth formed a smile, inviting all to smile along with him, at this deranged high-strung woman.

Two men in neckties smiled broadly at this cue from the dark man. Others became lively and alert, glad for a drama. Several women grew stern. Their brows knitted and their eyes sharpened. But one and all were noncommittal, waiting to see what developed.

"Don't give me that smile," hissed Anna. "You know exactly what dirty business you've been up to."

The dark-skinned man's teeth disappeared and his lips twisted to a sneer. He raised his shoulders and thrust his hands away from his sides, displaying the innocence of his open palms. The sneer left his face as his lips opened again to a smile.

"Don't play dumb with me. You – had – your - hands - all - over - me," she declared, in hammer-like tones that went fact-fact-fact-fact. Her seriousness galvanized the crowd. This dark man had to produce more than smiles and mime now.

"Pfff-t," he said, giving his chin a quick upward jerk. "You're a crazy woman. Full of imagining." With his index finger he made quick jabs at his temple, to make the source of her problem clear to everyone.

He leaned back against the rail with a panther's tense ease. The crowd remained passive. The bus rumbled on. Twice she'd accused him and twice been repulsed. The crowd's interest was waning. He followed through now, vaunting in dialect.

"I may be a dark man, from the South, but I have my honor," he said, thumping his chest with his thumb. "You have your fancy clothes and your big sunglasses, but you're rotten and a liar *inside*." He pinched his nose with his fingers, as if to a bad smell. And spat down on the stairwell and ground it in laboriously with his shoe.

This was nasty and arrogant. It was also bold and clever, for at this insult, two men in neckties folded their arms masterfully across their chests. And the faces of two other men cracked into smiles they were quick to restrain. This Southerner and molester was bold, cunning and male.

The faces of some women, though, now glowered with smoldering anger. Others just burned inwardly, over this woman who had been abandoned.

Moments passed. And then surprisingly, Anna lashed out with fresh fury.

"Nobody is fooled here," she said scornfully. "*They* all know that you're lying, and *you* know it too. When we get to *Piazza Venezia* I'm calling the *carabinieri*. We'll see what *they* think about this your-word-against-mine."

Her strength and control lent authority to her words. And with the word *carabinieri*, fright flashed across the dark man's eyes, before he again took up his sneer.

"You don't scare me with your *carabinieri*," he said, with a manufactured chuckle. "Bring on your *carabinieri*. Bring on an army; see if I care. I never did one single thing to you. You just keep it up. Just keep it up and I'll take *you* to the *carabinieri*; I'll take *you* to the *carabinieri* instead."

The dark man now exuded a menacing hostility. "She thinks she takes me to the *carabinieri*," he muttered angrily to himself. "Just you watch. I'll take *her* to the *carabinieri*, crazy bitch of a woman." Still muttering to himself, he rolled down the long sleeves of his shirt and buttoned the cuffs with indignance.

"Someone call the driver!" came Anna's active sharp voice. "I want this man taken to the station. I want to file a *denuncia*. This man is an animal. He's an animal and a liar. Someone please call quickly, before we reached the stop. I don't want this man to get away."

No one moved. All eyes were averted. The dark man's eyes flashed quickly over the crowd. It was passive. He was emboldened.

"Who do you think you are with your clothes and your sunglasses and your lies and *carabinieri*? You just wait till we get there and I tell them what fool stories you've been spreading. *They* all know," he declared, indicating the silent passive passengers. "And I know," he said, thumping his thumb on his chest. "And you know it too," he said, leaning forward, pointing his finger right into her sunglasses. He held this pose for a long moment, his finger lordly and masterful, till she shrank back a step. He moved forward a step, keeping the finger right there. Her trembling stopped. Something inside her died.

The dark man slowly drew his finger back to his side as if resheathing a weapon. A tear rolled out of the side of her sunglasses. A streak of mascara ran down to the corner of her mouth. Her lips were now quivering. The dark man watched intently. A smile played round his eyes now. He hoisted his pants up with both thumbs, and drew himself up taller.

"You're sick," she hissed to him alone, in dry ghastly tones. "You're... sick," she finished, her words tailing off to great sobs.

All posturing now drained out of him. No masks were now needed. No longer did his body act one way while his face acted another and his words tried to tell you what you were seeing. All was now integrated; just the animal now remained. Bringing his gargoyle-like face just an inch before hers, he put his forefinger at the pit of her throat, and spoke in low rotten tones:

"You talk real smart, lady." he said. "Real..." he jabbed the finger forward, "...smart." He jabbed again. "But there's no way I touched you and there's nobody ever want to touch you, and I'll tell you why that is." His voice dropped to a whisper. "You're a homely snaggle-tooth. You got that? Homely. Snaggle-tooth." He held his gargoyle head for one long moment before her, then leaned back his rail, jaunty and strong, hate pouring freely from both eyes.

Game, set, match for the dark man. The shell of a woman, dressed in smart clothes, stood like a ghost now, holding the rail. No more anger. No tears. No appeals. No *carabinieri*. The play was over.

Shame fell palpably upon the watching passengers. The bus rumbled on noisily. Inside it was silent.

Sensing this brooding, the dark man checked the buttons of both sleeve cuffs. He adjusted his collar and belt buckle. He touched his head here and there, with the nervous preening of a cat caught off-guard. He rang the bell for the next stop, then looked fixedly at the call-button.

One man looked at his watch quizzically then began winding it with great seriousness. Another peered at an ad for insurance, then set to pondering on the fine print. The other men dropped off, looked away, fell indifferent, or so pretended. Only the women kept watching Anna, like so many cats under duress, with ears flattened back but who still held their own, and kept seeing, through open eyes.

A woman with a shopping bag came forward. She paused before Anna. "*Mi scusi, cara...*" she began gently, as she put down her bag. She put one hand on Anna's forearm while the other went to encircle her waist. Anna shoved her away and kicked her bag over.

"Don't give me that *cara* don't touch me don't touch me *any of you!!!*" she shouted hoarsely, as her sunglasses swung round in a slow arc at these women.

Two women set to gathering the grapefruits and apples that had spilled out of the bag. They returned them to the bag with solemn grave movements. One grapefruit rolled near the stairwell, where it lay beside the shoe of the dark man. One woman stepped forward then stepped back. This grapefruit was left there.

Bus 64 came to its stop and its doors opened with a loud hiss. The dark man, until now so panther-like and controlled, sprang from the step and with shoves and flying elbows, barged through the crowd waiting to get on. Knocking several of them down, off he ran legs flying, back in the direction the bus had come from.

As she held onto her rail, Anna was an obstruction to the incoming tide. As new passengers pressed forward she was pried loose from her pole and was moved on down the aisle. There she stood among fresh passengers, all indifferent to the sun-glassed woman squeezed in among them.

Pretty as a Picture

Museo *Capitolina*. Nicoletta stepped down the museum stairs then crossed over to the bus-stop. And again, as always, that same deflated feeling came over her. How was it that just two hours in the gallery could make the world look so different? And why did it have to be that the world always come up lacking, the world second-best? The world in those paintings was so wonderfully ordered. Always the best was brought pleasingly to the fore. Flowers, bushes and trees, lakes and forests, clouds and mountains - all were selected then displayed with such sensitive intention, their colors combined in the most enchanting ways possible.

In the museum she had wandered happily from one room to another, met and cheered on all sides by harmonious scenes. Back here in the *piazza* though, not one thing was cheerful. How could she greet *this* world with the same open arms? In both worlds a tree was a tree, a cloud was a cloud and a building a building. But everything in this real world looked forlorn and haphazard, and sadly neglected. Here were the same Roman *palazzi* she'd just seen in the pictures, but they now had drain-pipes, antennae and electric wires, and storefronts with garish signs. The few trees she could even see were in scraggly half-health, disposed here and there looking lost, disarrayed. As for the sky - it was there - a flat blue - not much else could be said for it. Yes, this Rome was a poor double of the Rome in those pictures; it seemed everywhere random, diminished, banal.

Most dismaying of all were the people. In the paintings all were costumed and bejeweled, posed and composed, their every gesture calculated to its last expressive detail. And if the finery was wonderful, even better were the figures, so lavishly robed, or best of all, nude. What pleasure she took from the graceful posture of a woman's nakedness, or the sinewy muscle of the man's. Best of all was the body's summit, its crown: the human head. Heads with compelling physiognomies and spiritual faces, embedded eyes shining brightly with silent revelation.

What rude decline then, to these motley commuters, waiting beside her in ungainly repose. From the curbside she surveyed them as they stood against the grafffiti'd wall with its tattered posters. She found herself forcibly being reminded of something... what was it? Of a police line-up? No, that was not quite it. Yes, that's right! A psychiatric ward, where each was an unknowing caricature, a grotesque imitation - of himself. Here were no proud bodies expressive of noble interiors, but slouched ones, resigned and crooked ones, stuffed ones, compacted ones, abandoned ones - all fossils. Here were no searching eyes, no questing spark or nascent feeling. These eyes were heavy-lidded or vacant, or wistful or suspicious, or fearful or dead. Yes, she knew: waiting for a bus in the sun does not bring out one's best. But even making allowances, she knew she was seeing the foundation. And it was empty and ugly, and made her sober and sad.

What a hoax were all pictures and statues, with their shopworn Greek symmetries. They were fantasy, no more: teasing hints of ideals that existed nowhere save in gilded frames and museums. If art mirrored life, then that was not art in the museum. Surely *this* was art instead, looming above her this very moment: this big poster selling jeans. The figures were larger than any she had ever seen in a painting. And this poster was clearly valuable, housed in a steel frame that had night lights and protective glass. The reason for this considerable structure, was to present the Jeans Man and Jeans Woman, figures quite as iconic now as Christ and Madonna.

Wearing jeans but no shirt, the man's prize-fighter torso was flexed to maximum relief, captured in full chiaroscuro by some able photographer. His thug's face was brutish. His eyes stared out like a predator. His lips curled in a sneer. His jaws sprouted stubble. His hair was disordered. The Old Masters, she thought, would have known better where to put him. He was wasted in these jeans; he belonged in a painting. He should be Cain by the fire, devouring his slain brother's lamb. Or the soldier, plate in hand, with the Baptist's severed head. Or the son scornfully mocking wise old Noah's naked loins. Or just another face in the crowd that was hungry for a crucifixion.

His consort in the poster wore jeans just as he did. Her torso was unclothed also. But while his chest was bared fully, hers was half-hidden beneath artfully crossed arms, while her bold coy lidded eyes looked out teasingly, from above. She too would have her place in the paintings of the Masters. She'd be Salome. Or maybe Potiphar. Or a sybarite at Gomorrah. Or the woman at whom none were sufficiently pure to cast the first stone. What good was a museum, wondered Nicoletta, if it put her in dark moods like this one? What good was an ideal world, that was devoured so quickly by the real?

A tall Ethiopian woman walked up to the bus-stop and took her place at the graffiti'd wall. Nicoletta was drawn at once to her fine native garb. Folds of brightly colored fabric fell gracefully from her shoulders to her womanly broad hips, that were tilted in classic *contrapposto*, as she surely did not know. These folds were gathered at her waist by a bright scarlet sash, which then loosed them on downwards in cascades to her feet. This was the same toga Nicoletta had been looking at, just moments ago. Only now it was far better, incomparably better: it wasn't a white painted toga in some dreamed-up ancient scene. It was real, its bright hues keyed happily to the bright summer sky. She wore a turban that was happy also. And best of all, better than all of this - was her round mocha face and her plain open features, all patience and modesty, both calm and benign.

Nicoletta felt content now to linger at curbside - with this tall noble woman with the calm mocha face, so pleasing and bright against the fine summer sky. And such a fine sky it was, she now noticed, quite suddenly. So shimmery and sunny, so boundless and blue. The longer she gazed upon this dark toga'd woman, the brighter the sun blazed, the more boundless seemed the sky.

How lovely were the sun's rays, showering hot unseen light. Light that had showered down on everything, and everywhere, and always: before these cars, before these buildings, before this city, before herself. Words formed in her mind unbidden: Phaeton. Helios. Amen-Ra. Light's beauty showering down everywhere, profligate, indiscriminate. Light bathing smoggy streets filled with traffic. Bathing skewed bodies at a bus-stop. Washing buildings free of signs and wires. Washing everything now new and clean. Everything stripped naked. Everything now clothed in its true timeless raiment. She saw today's Rome as she knew it in her heart, but had briefly forgotten. Pretty as a picture.

Sacred Conversation

The crowd at the curbside pressed forward. Nicoletta moved peacefully among them as the bus doors hissed open. A wiry dark man sprang from the stairwell, shoving through them so violently that several people were knocked down. She was kneed hard in the leg, and saw his face as he crashed past her. Where could *this* fellow be placed? Judas rushing panicked to the tree for hanging? Or Cain once again, fleeing the scene of his crime? Her leg hurt as she boarded, but in moods such as this one, such things did not matter. She was scanning the passengers now, the best picture gallery of all.

Cow-eyed Corot women lounged in orange plastic seats, but with real life breeding in their fleshy limbs. A gnarled old man straight out of Rembrandt was stooped over, punching his ticket, his life etched on his furrowed face, miracles hovering all about him. Near the window stood a couple consulting their guidebook. The woman held it open and was reading to the man. The man's head was bent down, poised to listen. With the way they were standing, the angle of their heads, and their quiet shared focus, they looked straight out of one of those paintings, the kind called "*sacra conversazione.*"

Nicoletta stepped close up beside them, and turned her head and listened.

"It says those big buildings on both sides are done in the Venetian style," said the woman.

"That's Venice, right? I think I remember those skinny windows," the man replied.

"It's called *Piazza Venezia*. It says the little porch up on that building is where Mussolini gave his speeches."

"Some speeches. Rant and rave was more like it."

"The book says gave speeches."

"Mussolini. That ass."

"It says up that big staircase in the corner, there's a *piazza* by Michelangelo with an equestrian statue of Marcus Aurelius."

" A crustacean statue?"

"E-ques-trian. On a horse."

"And that huge white building with all the columns and statues is a monument to the unification of Italy…"

"Unification? I didn't know it was *un-unified* let alone unified. When does it say it was unified?"

"It doesn't say. It assumes you already know some European history."

"I don't care about unification anyway…"

"I knew you didn't."

"…as long as it has big sections on the moderate-priced restaurants in each city."

"Can you get a shot of the big white one when we go past it?"

"Since when did *you* care so much about unification?"

"I don't care either. It's the building I want a picture of. There's nothing like that back in Atlanta. As big: yes. But going upward instead of sideways."

"It's too wide to get in one shot. And I told you: I don't want to get fanatic about the camera on this trip."

"I'm not asking you to be a fanatic by taking one little picture. Anyway, behind that white building is the Roman Forum."

"Ok. And what else?"

"Uh... let's see... yes, the Colosseum too... wait, look! There it is, the Colosseum! Quick! Down that side street, see it there off in the distance?"

"It's black. Looks dirty."

"It's *old*. We'll be seeing it tomorrow. They've got it down here on Walking Tour #5."

"Number five? We've only been here for one day now."

"But we'll only be here for three. You've got to make choices."

"Choices? I don't mind choices but I'd like to be consulted once in a while. I don't want to get stranded at mid-day where there's only rip-off restaurants..."

"It looks small down that street but when you get there, I'll bet it's huge."

"...no rip-off restaurants and none of those skimpy bar sandwiches either. I didn't fly across the Atlantic Ocean to starve to death."

"You're not going to starve to death in Italy. It says that on one day as many as five hundred men and three thousand wild animals could be killed."

"Is this Venice *piazza* on a different walking tour than the Colosseum?"

"*Piazza Venezia.*"

"Ok. *Piazza Venezia.*"

"Yes. The Colosseum is on #5. This one's on #4."

"And the Forum is right behind the unification thing?"

"That's right."

"Is the Forum on #5 or #4?"

"Number four."

"So that means we're gonna miss the Roman Forum!?"

"If we do #5 as planned."

"As *you* planned."

"It's not carved in stone, dear. We can mix them up if we want to. Do half of a four and half of a five. It's not such a big problem."

"I can just imagine getting home and saying: 'Hey everybody, I just got back from Rome and I didn't see the Roman Forum.' You know: Friends, Romans, countrymen: lend me your ear!"

"Ears."

"How do you know?"

"I just remember, that's all."

"Ok. Ears."

"So: we'll do half of a four and then half of a five with the Forum - but I want you to read up on it tonight. Promise me. I don't want you walking around going: 'There's nothing to look at. It's all just ruins. It's just a bunch of rubble.' You do that all the time, you know."

"Don't exaggerate."

"You did it at Pompeii."

"You said it wasn't what you expected either. It wasn't big and it wasn't extensive. And apart from the guy frozen in his tracks by the lava it was dinky. Tell me it wasn't dinky. Tell me…"

"Well… it *was* pretty dinky."

"Dinky. Dinky and over-rated. The movie was much better. .."

"I know, you've told me the story five times: The volcano erupts. The lava's flowing between the man and his lover. He's reaching across the lava. It's burning away the little cliff she's standing on. He's urging her to jump. She can't decide whether to jump or not. The lava's getting higher. She jumps, but…"

"No need to get sarcastic. It was a good movie, that's all. You've never seen a movie you didn't get excited about?"

"But you did the same thing in Greece, and at those prehistoric Celtic homes we saw up near Innsbruck…"

"Homes? It was a bunch of holes in the ground with some boulders stuck in at the edges. I don't mind looking at old things but there's at least gotta be a *thing* there to be old!"

"At Stonehenge you said it was just a pile of rocks."

"Ok, so I'm not crazy about ruins. But that doesn't make me stupid."

"I didn't say you were stupid."

"If I were stupid we wouldn't even be here. We'd be at some Club Med at poolside with some darky pouring us gin and tonics."

"You know I don't like that word. It's 1994 now, you know."

"I know it's 1994 but I don't like being called stupid."

"I'm sorry dear..."

"So it's the Forum then, tomorrow. I'll keep my mouth shut. I promise. It'll be good a good place to limber up. These planes and buses are cramping my legs up and the Forum should get the kinks out. Friends, Romans, countrymen: give me liberty or give me death!"

"Patrick Henry."

"Show-off."

"You knew it too. Friends, Romans, countrymen, lend me your..."

"Ears."

"*Bravo.* You get a kiss for that."

"A kiss, and..."

"Ooh. Naughty boy."

"*Amore mia.*"

"*Mio.*"

"How do you know?"

"I just do."

"*Amore mio.*"

172

"No, *please*. Please don't do that here on the bus."

"What do you mean 'not on the bus'? This is Rome! This is where they invented it in the first place!"

"Invented what?"

"Take a guess."

"You *are* naughty."

"I may be stupid, but..."

"I didn't say you were stupid."

"I'll show you how stupid I am when we get back to the hotel room."

"You naughty boy."

"During *siesta*."

"That's Spain."

"During whatever-it's-called-here."

"It's called *intervallo*."

"Ok. *Intervallo*."

Mussolini's Balcony

Piazza Venezia. Rome's number one traffic hub. Cars, trucks, buses, taxis and motorcycles converge here, six abreast with no lanes, to fight their way round the rotary. For such fierce roaring vehicles in such anarchic masses, one man alone has been sent to keep order. On a little raised platform in this sea of machines, there he stands, beneath a tall white-domed helmet, waving two white-gloved hands giving shrill toots on a whistle. He makes quick pivots and palm thrusts, head snaps and arm jerks, looking less like a man than some smartly dressed insect. But such hordes are bearing down upon him - from the Parliament, from the Forum, and pressing out from the Tiber - that for all his exertion he's in large part decoration.

Unlike *Largo Argentina* whose ruins are not in plain view, *Piazza Venezia* offers ample diversion. On two of its sides rise broad-sided *palazzi*, with bright banners for art shows unfurled beneath Venetian-style windows. On a third side hulks the monument to a united Italy, with its endless columns and staircases and porticoes and statues and acres upon acres of bone white clean marble. Against today's bright blue sky, it looks like some factory-fresh Babylonia, or imperial Rome by Walt Disney. Straight across there's a bar festooned with the flags of many nations. And at the *piazza*'s hub is a green lawn flush with party-colored petunias. In this city of stone it's a festive effect, making the ride round the *piazza* like a circus carousel. It can take a good while to get around this jammed circle. But fortunately, our route takes us in near the policeman, then nips us quickly out the other side.

Bus 64 drifted into the *piazza*. Vinzo waited to be waved on. At the far side of the *piazza* he saw police cars and riot vans, and soldiers with shields leaning against striped saw-horses, smoking cigarettes. The traffic cop motioned Vinzo to pull up alongside him.

"All traffic's blocked off from the Parliament till two. We've got to reroute you down *Via del Corso*."

"What gives?"

"The usual manure. Some big shot is visiting; they don't want him bumped off. Everything's sealed off till he's off to the airport. Follow the 44 route to the station."

"*Stronzo* politicians," muttered Vinzo, giving a short wave-like salute.

"*Stronzo* politicians," muttered the policeman, returning the salute.

Vinzo merged into the six laneless lanes of the merry-go-round *piazza*, a clear deviation from the established route.

"What the..."

"What's he doing?"

"Is this driver retarded?"

"Look at this traffic!"

"This will take twenty minutes to get around."

"I haven't got time for this kind of *porceria*."

"He can't do this!"

Those near the front pressed forward to our driver.

"Where are you going?"

"This is the 64."

"I would have gotten off at the last stop."

"Let us out!"

Vinzo lifted one finger just the slightest bit off the steering wheel, and pointed at the police barricade in the distance. The passengers still pestered him of course, but to no effect. A more forceful temper, however, was brewing near the rear. Cesare Massimiliano, only blocks now from his important meeting, was in no mood for submission. Bulling his way forward, he stood on his tip-toes so his now-sweaty face loomed above the glass wall of the driver's cubicle. Though he resembled a dog on its hind legs begging, he spoke with menacing authority.

"Ho! You! What the hell is this? Pull over to one side there. Open those doors up. I've got to get out."

Vinzo hunkered down over his wheel.

"Don't play the deaf-mute with me, you barnacle. I'm not joking. WE want out!"

Well - mighty Cesare had uttered that most magic of words: WE. The crowd was emboldened, renewing its chorus of demands and abuse.

Vinzo swiveled around. His blank sullen eyes swept over them slowly. He looked up at the sign over the windshield: 'Do not speak to the driver.' His point made, he hunched back over, his beefy fore-arms crossed in an X over the steering wheel.

Agitated and impotent, the passengers shared their ire.

"My mother always told me I was born to do great things. But I spend half my life doing nothing, just standing here on buses."

"You weren't listening there, my friend. She didn't say 'great things'. She said you were born to grow old standing on buses in 'great places'."

"Hey – I've gone through this *piazza* every day now for ten years. I'd like someone to tell me one single thing great about it."

"I could care less about your great things or great places. I want my lunch. Lunch is great enough for me."

"You heard the man. We want out. That means all of us. That's the *vox popolo*. And when *vox popolo* speaks, a bus driver ought to listen."

"The hell with you and your schoolboy *vox popolo*. First things first: that means lunch!"

Sitting erect like a basalt pharoah, Ignazio Bruno watched this scene with disgust. His old still-strong body was trembling with anger. Why just imagine! A uniformed officer directs the traffic. An authorized bus driver obeys the officer. And now citizens were storming the driver, pelting him with insults, behaving like beasts, simply because his discharging of his duty did not favor their personal plans. Why, this was shameful. And revolting. He must be careful not to give way to anger though; it was bad for his heart. He switched off his hearing aid and looked away out the window.

Three floors above street level, projecting out from the *palazzo*, was a small narrow balcony, home to earth-shaking deeds. It was from this very porch that Mussolini addressed the thronged *piazza*, and Italians at their radios from Bolzano to Palermo. You could be sure that in *those* days there'd be no scene such as this one. Who would *dare* challenge a bus driver, let alone heckle and jeer him? Such disrespect was unthinkable. The world then had *order*.

Order was the basis, the bedrock, the foundation of true society. There were different ways it could be gotten, but what counts foremost is that you get it. When citizens are rightly educated, they understand rightly and obey rightly and will act for the common good. But when people are swine, jackals or vultures, each must be dealt with in his own language. For one it's the harness. For another the spur. To others one must speak with the whip, fist or bullet. What matters above all, is not to fear following through. If the line isn't drawn, things move quickly to chaos.

Looking up at the balcony, his mind drifted back in the ethers of time. It was '41, or maybe early '42, yes early '42, he was sure. They were garrisoned along with a German battalion just outside Addis Ababa. The British were advancing and were expected to attack within a fortnight. They were short on munitions. No reinforcements could be expected. They dug in for the siege. With hard fighting imminent, a terrible tension preyed upon the soldiers. The daytimes seemed endless but the night-times were worse. There were bugs. It was hot. There were even fist-fights over snoring three nights in a row.

Most intolerable of all was when the food went on rations. In the most heated times of combat, food had always been plentiful. You could well end up killed but you wouldn't go hungry. But now each man got one ration, early each morning. Some fell on their food like wolves, then grimly smoked and drank water till bedtime. Some nibbled like squirrels throughout the day. Others fasted till sundown, then sat down like pashas at banquets. But though each had his way, not one man was happy. Nothing makes a man nastier than not enough food.

On the fourth day of rationing, a German soldier's ration was stolen. The Germans were sure it was an Italian. The Italians, somewhat less sure, at least among themselves said it was a German. Another ration was stolen the next day. And the next day as well. Many soldiers now changed their habits. Some pashas now ate with the wolves. Some carried their rations with them on sentry duty, in vehicles, on patrol, or folded in their arms while they napped. When a ration was pinched a fourth and then a fifth time, it came to the attention of the two commanding officers.

Both battalions were called out side by side before their officers.

The German commandant stepped forward from two soldiers with carbines who flanked him on either side. In terse clipped tones he declared in German, that food theft would not be tolerated. It undermined morale. It weakened fighting cohesiveness. It was criminal. It would be punished. He demanded that the guilty man step forward, or that he be named by whoever knew him. A long silence followed, thick with undercurrents of feeling. No one came forward. He repeated his demand. Again no response. The Italian commander then briefly told his troops that the address was about food theft. He offered little translation, but little was needed. Everyone got the message.

The two officers returned to their quarters. After ten minutes they reappeared. The Italian commander now stepped forward. His message was the same, but with many more words. He rounded things off, cut off the sharp corners, and honeyed it here and there. Yes this theft was a bad thing, but no, it wasn't the end of the world, it was just a few meals. Yes the guilty man must come forward, but just to get this thing over with, to get on with the challenge before them. Besides, said the Italian commander, he now knew who the guilty man was. He had been seen and identified. So it would be better for him to come forward on his own, than to be forced to, by his officer. He made it sound like a schoolboy who needs to confess a prank for his own moral welfare. And implicit but unstated, was that the punishment would be light. He had no soldiers with carbines standing ready on each flank.

A long moment after this ruminating talk, an Italian soldier's hand went up. He looked just like the naughty schoolboy his commander had portrayed. He flashed a sheepish smile at his compatriots, as if expecting praise for some particularly bold kind of mischief.

His smile fast disappeared. Two Italians with carbines materialized at once. They shoved him straight over to a petrol tank, handcuffed him to its spigot, then left. The Italian commander walked over to the man, and with his booted right foot kicked the man with a strange ferocity, and apparent precision, for far longer than one could bear to watch. Ignazio could still see the man, who was named Carbone, or maybe Carboni, face-down in the dirt, his cuffed hands joined up over the spigot as if in prayer. Both battalions were dismissed. Ignazio was not sure if he ever saw Carboni again.

It was a clever ruse these commanders had hatched. But more impressive than their cunning was the result it produced. A wonderful calm descended over the soldiers. All the tension of the siege seemed dissolved. Men were soon back at their posts smiling again, joking freely. Cigarettes were smoked luxuriously. Rations were eaten at all hours and with keen satisfaction. Ignazio himself had several nights of deep sleep that seemed to release months of anxiety. The Italians and Germans both cursed the British now, not each other. And the attack, when it came, was decisively repulsed.

Drifting back from Ethiopia to *Piazza Venezia*, Ignazio gazed again at the scene before him. That businessman in the smart suit, the ringleader, opened his briefcase and took out one of those phones that still startled Ignazio each time he saw one. After punching the buttons angrily, he spoke vehemently, poking at the air. Squashed, helpless and angry, he was still giving commands. Ignazio switched his hearing aid back on. Someone was still arguing with the driver. Two women were still loudly indignant. A man beside them made extravagant gestures of disdain as he complained to his companion.

Ignazio Bruno watched and he listened. *O tempora! O mores!* Virgil's lamentation from his schooldays sprang to mind across a span of seven decades. He adjusted himself a shade more upright, and gripped his mahogany cane more tightly. He turned from the angry passengers and looked back out the window. The colossal monument to the fatherland loomed in white grandeur above him. On its distant steps burned the flame at the tomb of the unknown soldier. At each side of the flame stood a uniformed soldier, at attention. He felt a strong catch in his throat. He swallowed hard. Hot tears burned his eyes. He switched off his hearing aid. He was better off deaf.

The One Thing that Matters

A row of six seats across the back of the bus. With the engine right beneath them, it's hotter there. It's noisy. The seats rattle. You can smell oily fumes. Slouched in a seat in one corner, the lanky youth looked about sullenly - at the stupid old buildings moving too slowly past his window. At the stupid tourists with their stupid cameras. At the stupid people dressed up just to sit at their stupid desks in their stupid offices just to make stupid money. Yes how stupid it all was. Especially this waste-of-time ride on this hot stupid bus.

He'd had to stand for ages after that old coot had caned him way back at the hospital stop. And though this back seat was hot, at least he could relax some. He pushed his long plaits of hair back from his forehead and pinned them down with his headset, then switched on the tape player that was tucked in his breast pocket. Up the thin wire traveled the sound of wailing guitars, crashing cymbals, blaring horns and pounding drums. And a man's raspy voice that shrieked urgent words in his ears:

> Baby baby
>
> Do me baby
>
> Do me baby all night long.
>
> Gotta have it.
>
> Rock me baby.
>
> Rock me baby all night long.

The youth's torso began to rock slowly, first back and then forth, then from one side to the other. His two sneakers, big as clown shoes, began to tap up and down slowly. His fingertips played counterpoint on his kneecaps, which stuck out through the rips at each knee.

Gotta have it

Gotta have it

Gotta have that sweet thing

The lanky youth kept rocking and tapping with his feet and his fingers. But his movements soon took on an exasperated vehemence. The force coursing through his limbs was too great for such small movements. He looked trapped, morose, and pained. He twisted his head this way then that. He ran his fingers through his hair. He drummed his knees faster but still looked torn: bored and distracted on one hand, dumb to his own torment on the other. He leaned to one side and dug deep in his pocket. Out came a pen-knife that he opened gently, with care.

What a change now came over him with this knife now in hand. Just a moment ago he looked conflicted; he now looked composed. Looking purposeful and patient, he set to cutting at the wall right beside him. It was not easy to cut such tough plastic with a pen-knife. He brought his full weight to bear as he cut, scratched and gouged to form... who could say what?

How blithe and brazen, to carve the walls on a crowded bus! But he worked with too much dignity for a mere vandal. Indeed, the man sitting beside him looked over, to see what he was doing, then turned away, with seeming approval.

But what could inspire in him such keen focus? It must be some soccer team, or some rock group, or some girl he's become sweet on. Or maybe his own name. Or that back-in-vogue swastika.

The youth worked on with quiet intent. He paused to regard

his work, then went back to cutting. He paused again - then back to work. Then a few indifferent scratches — and a few more — was he done? He opened his pen-knife, then closed it, then pried it open and then closed it again - decisively. He was done. What he had carved was now revealed.

Why of course. How very obvious. It's a *cazzo* he's incised here — that most ubiquitous of *graffiti* in this still-pagan town. There's nowhere you can go without chancing upon his image, this upright young fellow who peeks out from all sides. *Cazzo* on the walls of the phone booth. *Cazzo* on the front of your apartment block. *Cazzo* on the subway cars and *cazzo* on their seats. *Cazzo* on stop signs, on sidewalks, on hydrants. *Cazzo* nuzzled up against the contours of women on billboards. *Cazzo* in bathrooms, on dumpsters, on lamp-posts and fountains and the shuttered doors of storefronts. And now *cazzo*, incised here on Bus 64.

The youth gazed at his handiwork. He didn't smile. Why he did it, he couldn't tell you, if you for some reason chanced to ask. He simply did it, as his friends simply *did it,* as did countless others he had never met. Like anonymous troops in a bannerless army, these youths pay allegiance to the one thing that matters. What has a young man, after all, that is really his own? He's a weed with no roots for a torturously long epoch. He owns nothing, he produces nothing, he earns nothing, he is nothing. While none need defer to him, he's subordinate to all. And so - he must assert what's his own and he does so with *cazzo*, which expresses a young man's many moods: angry, defiant, flippant and manic, riotous, irrepressible, incorrigible, destructive.

Last week he and his friend Mario spray-painted the grand-daddy of all *cazzi* on that big bearded statue by the duck-pond in the park. By moonlight they'd jumped the fence then climbed up on the pedestal. He had boosted up Mario then held his feet for two minutes in his cross-fingered hands. Mario did such a big *cazzo* that its balls filled the statue's whole hip area. Its tip reached to the solar plexus. Its jets radiated outwards like sun-rays, reaching the corners of both shoulders. He was amazed at the sureness of Mario's hand. Each ball was a perfect circle the same size as its brother. The shaft was perfectly vertical, its two side lines perfectly parallel. You would swear he'd used a ruler and compass.

The next day they'd gone back to watch the people strolling past it. They sat on a park bench acting casual and innocent, then cracking up while no one knew why. People had many different takes on this *cazzo*. Some stopped, cluck-clucked to themselves and looked mildly annoyed. Old folks could face it head on, yet walk by as if it wasn't there. Young couples sometimes smiled and pulled closer together. Or the one who saw it first would steer the other off in another direction. One girl held her hands like horse-blinders beside her grinning boyfriend's eyes. One youth began howling at it like a coyote. His girlfriend tugged him away growling on an imaginary leash, embarrassed but pleased. If just guys were together they would laugh and get loud, or trade punches and shoves. If it was just girls they would point, whisper, and giggle. One old man said that whoever did this should be fed to the sharks. No need to guard the borders, he added grimly. The barbarians arise now from our own soil.

The lanky youth wondered what he, Mario and the rest of the guys would do tonight. If Mario pinched that X-video they could start at his house and watch it. If his parents stayed home they could watch some action film instead. Then afterwards they'd hit the streets on their *motorini*. They'd zoom here then zoom there, and stop along the way for *gelato*. Then they could just hang for a while, and smoke some Marlboros. Then they could go out and do some more breezy zooming. You never knew what might happen these hot summer nights. They might set off fire-crackers. Or smoke dope-weed. Or try some pills. Or torch a dumpster. Or criss-cross sleek cars with long scratches from their keys.

The lanky youth looked about disgustedly as the bus poked on and on. He looked at the stupid tourists, the stupid workers, the stupid buildings that passed by too slowly. He ran his fingers through his hair and tossed his head to one side. But he no longer rocked and he no longer tapped. He just sat still and stewed in a thick sullen torpor, slumped in his corner full of hot oily fumes.

His tape player kept turning. It was still at full volume. Guitars, horns and drums were still traveling up the wire to his ears. The singer still shrieked urgently. But the youth wasn't listening. He knew this song only too well.

Gotta have it

I'm burning up

I'm burning up inside baby.

Can't live without it

Can't live without it.

Can't live without that sweet thing.

Name Day

Cesare Massimilliano fumed with frustration at this brute lummox driver. Taking his phone from his briefcase, he called his office and angrily directed Rita to call the Ministry to advise them of his delay. Jammed in this common crowd feeling impotent and explosive, his nose went up suddenly, like a hunting dog who has caught the scent. It was smoke. Definitely smoke. Which he ought not to be smelling. With a hundred-plus people trapped in this tin can by an obstinate ape, he had no wish to be stampeded.

Scusi, scusi, scusi... Cesare bulled his way back so he could chastise the offender. Probably some young punk he would straighten right out... *Scusi, scusi, scusi...* On the top step of the stairwell sat an old *barbona* swathed in layer upon layer of shawls, skirts and blankets. In her lap were cut roses with their stems wrapped in foil. She was drawing on a cigarette till the end glowed bright orange. She released the smoke in great volumes from her nose and mouth alternately; it hung round her head in a slow swirling cloud.

"*Senta,*" said Cesare brusquely, "No smoking here. You can't smoke here. You got that? Put it out."

The hag did not hear him, or acted as if she did not, anyway. Engrossed in her cigarette, she pulled on it repeatedly, making big smacking sounds with her lips. The cloud around her grew denser.

"You can't always be just *nice,*" Cesare said to the passengers nearby, both to remonstrate them for their passivity and to justify what he was about to do. The hag's forearm was held upwards, her wrist cocked to one side in a parody of sophistication. Cesare bent down behind her to take the cigarette from her hand, but she switched it deftly to her other hand without seeming to have even seen him.

"*Cazzo*," muttered Cesare, stepping quickly to her other side and then snatching away the cigarette.

The hag turned around and looked up at him squarely in the face. Her hooked nose almost met her pointed chin. On both sides of the nose shone two black pool-like eyes. They were not angry. They did not argue. They neither accused nor defended. She lay this open solemn gaze upon Cesare, in his white linen suit with the burning cigarette in his hand.

"No - smoking - on - buses," he stated, for himself and for those watching. He let the cigarette fall to the floor and ground it out with his tasseled loafer. The hag's eyes traveled up from his shoe till she was again looking at his face.

"What's your name?" she asked Cesare, in the kind patient tone one might use with a child.

Cesare emitted a little snort and flashed a smile at the passengers. 'What a jest!' said his smile. 'The wretch actually speaks, but what nonsense!'

"How strange," mused the *barbona* out loud, truly baffled. "Everybody has a name... everyone. But *here's* one who says he *has* none..."

Beside her was a little girl who stood flush against her mother, whose hands rested on her little shoulders. The old tramp turned to her. "Have you ever heard of such a thing, little dearie? Just imagine: a man with no name! You're quite right. It's incredible. But *you* have a name though. Little girls *always* have names."

The girl stiffened, threw a worried look at her mother, and said nothing.

"Won't you tell me what your name is?"

The little girl burrowed closer into her mother, who gripped her shoulders now more tightly.

"I won't bite you. I promise."

The little girl said nothing.

"Ok, then. How about this: I'll tell you *my* name, then you tell me *yours*. I'll go first - that's fair, isn't it? Ok, first my turn, here goes: my name is *Santa Caterina*, born the twentieth-fifth of November. Your name now please. Come on now. Please tell me. You promised."

The little girl had not promised anything but was now smiling shyly, at this strange woman who knew just the kind of games little girls like.

"*Santa Caterina, Santa Caterina*, you heard me. It's your turn. Your name is...?"

The little girl turned and buried her head bashfully against her mother's belly.

"*O dai, coraggio!*" chuckled the hag.

"Ok then - let's make a deal. For you, a very *good* deal. I'll give you this beautiful long-stemmed rose - and you tell me what your name is. How does *that* sound then?"

She took a rose from her pile and tickled the girl's bare calf with its bud. After more bashful squirming, the little girl looked up at her mother. 'Can I tell her?' her eyes asked. Her mother was suspicious. Her eyes said 'certainly not.' But something else in her must have felt differently, for her head nodded permission.

"Costanza," said the little girl.

"*Santa Costanza*! The twentieth-fifth of February!" the hag cried out. "Happy birthday *Santa Costanza*. Happy birthday you little dearie you." And she handed her her rose.

The girl looked up at her mother astonished. The mother's face softened some. For a wretched old *barbona* she certainly had quite a memory.

"And your mommy's name?" The girl looked up at her mother, once again for permission. The mother's face hardened. She smiled tightly and drew her girl closer.

"*Impossibile*," exclaimed the old woman. "Not another! After eighty-two long years, for the first time, in one day, I meet *two* people with no names!"

"Monica," came the clipped tone from the mother, wishing not to seem humorless.

"*Santa Monica*!" exclaimed the hag. "August twenty-seventh! Happy birthday to you also!"

And she extended a rose to the mother, who hesitated a good bit before taking it, but then shrugged and accepted it, with a smile, to prove she could humor this harmless mad hag.

It was Cesare's stop now. Careful not to let his white linen pant leg come in contact with the *barbona*, he stepped down past her with a huffiness that had no time to spare for demented old women. The new passengers getting on had to sidestep *Santa Caterina*. Some did so with smiles, some with frowns, others with fear or annoyance. All gave her wide berth on the stairwell. Once the bus doors were closed she at once lit a cigarette, and was soon inhaling deeply, exhaling slowly, smacking her lips and raising a dense smoke cloud around her.

"My, what *heat*!" she exclaimed, to nobody in particular. And as she smoked assiduously with one hand, she began to fan herself with the other. The smoke cloud around her flowed in gray fluid eddies.

She fanned herself more quickly but could not find relief. She reached down to the three hems of her various dresses and began flapping them for ventilation. This too proved insufficient. She pulled up the three dresses and gathered them high up near her lap. What a sight, now revealed, were this old street tramp's legs!

Like a terrain with many strong contrasts, these legs were dermatologically encyclopaedic. Well fatted and stark white, their blubberiness bespoke uselessness and age. The tissue was in some places bunched into waxy concavities and convexities, like small lunar landscapes. In others it was so smooth that one thought of babies, while in still others it was mottled and dried, forming fine sinuous fissures with a callous-like texture. This surface was well decorated: with fine-spun varicosities of black, ruby-red and blue; with moles, bumps, warts and nodules, and irritated follicles in a red rashy patchwork. From this varied topology sprouted long fine dark hairs matted tight to the skin, and long dried-out white ones in random directions, and coarse porcupine bristles that shone and looked healthy. Too strange to be repulsive, these legs were glorious in their factuality. The passengers all looked away, with contempt, shame or pity.

Santa Cristina did not notice. She was clearly more comfortable, from her woolen underwear to her laceless boots with the tongues sticking forward. She swung her two bared legs back and forth with a child's innocent pleasure. Relieved of discomfort, she returned to her theme.

"Don't think that a name, now, is just a word. No, no - it's the farthest thing from it. A name is *important*. And not just a little bit. We've got *saints'* names, you know, and that's not something to be taken lightly. *San-ta Ca-te-ri-na...*" She said her name slowly, enunciating each syllable distinctly. Then she lifted up her head, closed her eyes and smiled, as if communing with the good saint herself. She drew deeply on her cigarette and let the smoke trail out her nostrils. "*Santa*

Caterina", she said again. And then, "*Santa Costanza...* the daughter," she said in a slow rhythmic drone, like liturgy. "*Santa Monica...* the mother..." Her upturned old face now wore a beatific smile. She took another deep drag and exhaled the copious smoke slowly. "*Tutti santi*, all saints.., all in each other's good hands..." She moved her head slowly, as if dizzy with revelation.

The liturgy continued. "*Tutti santi, tutti santi. Santa Sofia*; September eighteenth; *auguri mama* - happy birthday. *San Giuseppe*; March fifteenth; *auguri papa* - happy birthday." Onward she went with the names of her family, rocking back and forth slowly: "*San Marcellino*; June second; *auguri fratellino. Santa Flavia*; May seventh. *Auguri mia Flavia; una brava sorella. San...*" At this name she stopped. And stopped rocking. She sucked powerfully at her cigarette till half its length blazed up fiercely. Her beatific face contracted to anguish. Her eyes squinched shut tightly. She held the smoke in her lungs for a frighteningly long time.

"*San...*" She tried again but could not finish. "*San... P-p-p... San p-p...*" she finally managed, with great difficulty, to get it out: "*San Placi-do*, October... fifth..." Then she stopped and chewed her upper lip, as her jaw began quivering. In a whisper she finally managed it: "*Caro Pla-ci-do. Povero... povero.* Such a wonderful... husband." She took to the cigarette quickly, puffing great clouds of smoke and smacking her lips. Then fell silent. The liturgy was over.

With grave delicacy she lowered her piled up dresses back down to her boot-tops. She looked up at *Santa Monica*, and with her head gestured toward the call button and mouthed a silent '*per favore*'. *Santa Monica* pushed at the call-button. The call-bell went 'ding'.

The hag reached up to clasp the rail, and with thrust and counterthrust, like a camel, rose up to her feet. As she bent back down to gather her roses, she winced suddenly as if from sharp pain. She clutched at the rail to stay upright. *Santa Monica* came forward quickly.

"Are you all right?"

"It's ok dearie," said the hag softly, superimposing, by force, a kind of smile upon her face. "It passes. It passes."

The bus stopped and the doors opened. The old woman went down sideways, taking each step with difficulty. When she was down on the sidewalk, the little girl called out: "*Ciao!*" she called out. "*Ciao ciao Santa Caterina!*"

The old tramp did not turn round. She was busy trying to light a cigarette with her roses still in her arms. Then she took a few steps away, and turned around with a grave expression. She blew some dense smoke with great intention into the still summer air, then shuffled on toward the church, where she would rest with her roses, till nightfall.

The Catacombs

Finalmente! Cesare Massimiliano finally set foot on the sidewalk. He pressed the creases of his pants, tugged the lapels of his white suit, preened at his hair, then looked at his watch. Twelve fifty-five. Not good at all, but not as bad as he'd thought. Caged in that bus time seemed scorchingly urgent. But here on the sidewalk, it slowed down and relaxed. Good *God* what a snit he had worked himself into! What a nightmare since he'd stepped out the door!

A brisk walk up the hill and he'd be fifty minutes late. Which was no sin. Within the bounds of forgiveness. Especially since he was a major player in this deal. He could already see himself flashing his winning smile as he walked into the meeting in his white linen suit. His finally arriving would create quite the stir!

Cesare set off up the main street, which wound a circuitous path up the hill to the Ministry at the top. Seeing a side-street that was much straighter, he took it at once. The noise of the traffic soon faded behind him. He began to feel that same flush of good feeling he'd felt back at his office. Ah, these wonderful Roman back streets! How long since he'd wandered them! *Che bella Roma! Che bel quartiere!* Crumbly old buildings on narrow cobbled streets, with bright garlands of laundry hanging by ropes from the windows. Little shops with interiors unimproved since the 60s. Old folks sitting in shaded doorways on rickety chairs with hemp bottoms. The sounds of clacking utensils and crockery before lunch-time. The laughter of children from the open windows. The butcher shop with the cat congregation, gathered faithful at the doorstep.

Upward climbed Cesare, his good spirits revived. When he got to the Ministry he'd first duck in the WC to spruce up and step free of a little something that was knocking. Probably *that's* what had so crazed him on that wretch of a bus! Whose guts wouldn't knot up in that tight nasty box?

Just ahead was a small bar. Better yet, he'd duck in, down a quick drink, hit the WC there, then push on. He'd need no detour, then, once inside the Ministry, and could march into his meeting at the top of his stride.

Beside the door on the sidewalk, a haggard old buzzard sat on a milk crate, his head in his hands. He didn't look up as Cesare strode past him inside. The bar was closet-sized and empty. So old grandad was the proprietor! That made perfect sense. The floor was warped linoleum. Six lonely liquor bottles stood on the dusty shelves behind the counter. The cash register was the kind with those press-down keys that go 'ka-chung!' Forget the drink. He'd just duck in the john. There was a door that said WC. He pulled it open. Good God - what a stair-well! It looked deep as a mineshaft. Each step was a foot high, and so narrow that he had to place his feet sideways. Thank God there was a rail, which he held onto tightly as he went down sideways, like a crab.

The door shut behind him, he was guided by a bare dim bulb at the base of the stairs. Down crab-walked Cesare till he got to the landing. There was a cardboard sign with a WC and an arrow drawn in crayon. He set off down the corridor.

What a junkyard was this dark wreck of a hallway! Doorless rust-ed freezer cases no longer filled with ice-cream, but with old dented cans of mayonnaise and ketchup. Piles of old phone-books on bro-ken-backed chairs. Display racks for hairspray showing women with bouffant hair-dos. An old-fashioned bicycle with no wheels. A broken meat slicer, a pile of milk crates. Tall plastic palms lying on their sides. Long cellophane packages filled with sliced bread turned to fur. The walls were old also. They were peeled, crumbly, and furred, with cob-webbed ceilings and countless pipes in a criss-cross thicket. Picking his way through the dirt and disorder, he half-expected rats to leap out at him.

At long last: a doorway. This must be bathroom. He opened the door - another stairway! Just as steep, just as dark, just as long as the first one! There was no turning back. He grabbed the rail and crab-stepped quickly. He was not surprised, at the next landing, to meet another crayoned arrow pointing down another long hallway. He set off, now intent.

This hallway too, was replete with old junk. He seemed to have stepped back even further in time. A graveyard of thick-walled selt-zer bottles with steel-levered spouts. Rusted cans without labels. A wood stove with the door open, overflowing with deflated inner tubes. Thick stained mattresses and rusted boxsprings. Boxes in crooked piles covered with sheets that formed high ghostly peaks. A pin-ball machine with wood flippers with yellowed newspapers stacked atop it. He bent over for a peek and saw Roosevelt and Churchill, and the fat pope before the skinny pope who was two popes before John.

How far had he gone from that first dim-lit landing! And far-ther still from the sleepy old bar with the sleepy old man sitting on the street's sunlit surface. He remembered the first time he had gone deep-sea diving. It was also his last time. As soon as the light from the surface seemed extinguished, he'd swum right to the top and crossed that sport off his list.

It certainly was eerie here. In some places the walls were those slim bricks you see in ruins. In others it was just crumbly earth that looked ready to collapse. This felt like the catacombs: creepy, disturb-ing. A place of sunless lives lived like moles passed in hiding and fear, threatened by torture, crucifixion. This long hallway now seemed ominous, the recesses in the walls filled with dark menacing depths. He hurried on anxiously, half-fearing to see a skull or some bones — or who knows, even worse. That Poe story came to mind - about the man sealed behind a wall and left to die in a wine cellar. What a sick fellow that Poe was... he sloughed the thought off uneasily.

At the end of the hallway a strong light was shining. A bright naked bulb flooded a white-tiled chamber. At long last: his destination! As he hurried along, a bad thought sprang to mind. It was a photo he had seen in the newspaper just last week. They had executed someone again in the States. The photo showed the electric chair - in a tiny bright-lit chamber at the end of a dark hall like this one. Skin diving and catacombs and electric chairs and Poe - a man could get nervous if he let his mind wander!

Cesare stepped into the room. A hole in the porcelain floor was flanked by two small raised islands. He hadn't seen one of these since he was in Istanbul, in the late 70s. Well - no point in fussing. He placed a foot on each island, lowered his pants to his ankles, peeled down his jockies and squatted for action. It struck him that he was framed perfectly in the wide open door. No one would come down here - but then, who could be sure? Swinging one foot off its island, he reached and with a hard push sent the slide bolt deep in the door jamb.

Cesare squatted back down, pleased with the intelligence of his bowels, now keen and willing, like a hunting dog who understood repose and then action. Action indeed! An avalanche of filth hurtled out like an express train. Peering down, he saw that the hole had gone hungry. He yanked the chain to clear the deck.

Good God, what strong plumbing! Who would believe such force possible? Powerful jets of water shot out from all sides, disintegrating the filth instantly, spraying his pants, shoes and bottom with dark streams of wet muck. But good God - they kept blasting! Kept spraying and spraying, undiminished, full blast! The hole filled up quickly. The water flooded his islands of safety. Pants still at his ankles, Cesare reached out for the slide-bolt.

What the hell... what was this? The slide bolt was stuck in the soft wood of the door jamb. His adrenalin surged. This was no time for jokes. He pressed his fingers and knuckles into the slide bolt. He clenched his eyes. He clamped his teeth. He gritted. He grunted - till his knuckles turned white and his finger skin burned and he didn't care if the bone broke.

The bolt would not to budge. A misty spray now came raining down from the ceiling water tank. There was no place to hide. It sprayed his head and his shoulders. His beige calf's leather briefcase turned an ugly dark brown. He pulled up his pants… both pant-legs were stained but the left one was slathered badly.

Cesare went at the slide bolt with fury. His skin tore away as the bolt gouged his knuckle. But the bolt still stayed stuck. And the mists kept on misting. And the jets sprayed on madly. Water coursed down his face. His white suit was sodden. Mucky water topped his shoetops. Could this really be happening, this absurd *porceria*? Should he cry out for help? Old grandad wouldn't hear him. He needed fresh clothes. He needed messages sent. He needed fast discrete action. Rita! Yes, Rita! Only dear faithful Rita could set things like this set straight!

Cesare turned his back to the tank from which mist was raining down. Hunching over his briefcase to protect the contracts inside, he took his phone out and punched the buttons. He crossed himself mentally, and gave a quick prayer of thanks.

"Hello," said Rita soothingly, in kind even tones. "You have reached the studio of Cesare Massimiliano. Signor Massimiliano isn't in. Your message is important to us. At the beep leave your name, number, and a brief…"

"*Porco*!!" cursed Cesare, sending his fist into the door-jamb.

"BEEE-P!" went the bright helpful tone in his ear.

WHOOOSH!!! went the jets, as they sprayed with full force.

G-LUURG!! went the muck, lapping up past his ankles, rising fast, *perilously* fast…

One Clean White Hand

Along *Via del Corso* the buildings come flush up to the sidewalk and these two lanes that bear slow constant traffic. Our bus is invaded by the foggy smell of diesel and acrid exhaust. Our noses wrinkle, our eyes scratch, our lungs breathe with caution. A bicyclist glides by wearing a white mask over his nose and mouth. A passenger up front sees him and slams shut his window. Those near him do nothing, preferring poisoned ventilation to none at all. But a woman further back thought this closed window was sensible. She stood up and closed hers, as did others further back and still others back from them. So on we go, inching down the *Corso*, with half the windows open, and half of them closed.

Philosophy can help here: take the good with the bad. After all: we like smoked peanuts, smoked ham, smoked salmon and smoked cheeses. So why not smoked oxygen? It's a taste you can acquire.

On the curb is a small metal trailer with some gadgets on its roof: a radar-like screen, a cupped weathervane that isn't turning, and three tall squiggly antennae. On the side of the trailer is stenciled 'Environmental Protection.' Some find it reassuring, to think that someone actually exists somewhere who is trying to do something to improve things. The more hard-boiled though, see through this stencil, screen and antennae - they're not taken in. They see money flowing in rivers into the pocket of some minister, who had this trailer set at curbside to look purposeful and impressive. But it's probably not plugged in, and if it were would be useless, like the pyrotechnics of the wizard of Oz.

Whether or not these gadgets work, though, no doubt there's a problem. Smog alerts go out regularly. Children and oldsters are advised to stay indoors, while the rest of us plod on and don't drop in too great numbers. Right behind this trailer is clear evidence of the problem – at least there was until yesterday. Flush up to the sidewalk stands a compact Baroque church. Dominating its square facade are two stone saints set in niches. One holds his hand to heaven. The other one offers alms. It was the second saint that absorbed the young priest as the bus rolled up nearer.

When he had first passed here five years ago, this church-front was black from exhaust fumes. From the crevices of each ornament to the folds of the saint's robes, lay such a dense black coat of grime that the church seemed cut from coal. Like many others who passed here, he felt ire at the public and church administrations that had allowed such a problem. But such was his priestly bent, that in this church he saw not malfeasance alone, but a much deeper manifestation of Evil. He felt sorrow for this world that knew nothing and made nothing that stayed whole, clean and fruitful, but sent each new creation to indecent corruption. This church was an emblem of this world's loveless ways. And such were his sensitivities, that it provoked in him much suffering. Why he alone seemed subject to such anguish, he had no idea. But each time he passed here and contemplated this forsaken black church, his throat caught, his heart ached, his eyes burned and teared. And as this pain would well up he'd feel kinship with Jesus, and feel blessed to be singled out for such suffering.

Passing by one Thursday this winter, he had been surprised to see that the hand of the saint offering alms had turned perfectly white. No, this was no miracle. Probably a chemical test as a prelude to cleaning the whole building. But Thursday after Thursday and month after month passed with no sign of labor. He concluded that the project had been called off, leaving behind the strange impression this one clean white hand.

So sensitive was this priest that this small change in the facade made a change in how he regarded it. Its utter blackness, before, had sparked pained sacred feelings. But this small splash of white now, that so significantly highlighted an alms-bearing hand, ignited more profound yearnings, causing his usual pained sensations to soar to new heights of wretchedness. So poignant seemed this church he had so heavily freighted with meaning, that he tried hard not to cry, grateful for being chosen to thus suffer.

Late winter he'd been surprised again. The restoration suggested by the white hand had actually begun! From one week to the next, intricate scaffolding had been erected, with a gauzy green material appended to it. The entire church now looked as if gift-wrapped, and was visible just in faint outlines. Each Thursday the priest passed now, the scene was quite different. Flat-bed trucks stood out front filled with all kinds of equipment, which jump-suited workers ferried back and forth as they steam-cleaned the building. Like most men, this priest was intrigued by this enterprise. Each time he passed now, his curiosity was so piqued by the practical marvels of this project, that he no longer had, and soon forgot, all his sacred bad feelings.

Work proceeded from the top down, and through the gauzy green wrap he could follow its progress. Winter passed to spring and spring then to summer. The clean stone shining through the green material moved down lower, ever lower. When he'd passed here last week, just cleaned white stone shone through. But even having seen this, he was quite unprepared for today's sight out his window. Gone were the trucks and workmen. On each side of the church lay neat stacks of dissembled scaffolding. Rising up from the sidewalk stood the facade of the church, fully exposed; all a stark pristine white. Each column and cornice, each relief and sculpture, all its many steps and ornaments, were now so uniformly white that all contrasts were bleached out. The church now looked washed-out and forceless, like an overexposed photo.

The two saints were white also. Deprived of all grime, their expressions were hard to make out, their beards looked like flat cut-outs, and their voluminous robes were inactive. He sought out the white hand - it was not to be seen, really. The hand was still white, but then so was the forearm and sleeve, and the whole saint and the niche he stood in. With the bus stopped in traffic, his eyes roved the facade over, scanning anxiously in search of… something. And though he could not say what he searched for, he searched earnestly, but found nothing. The thoughts, images and sensations that had always teemed inside him here, were now absent. As the bus pulled away he felt puzzled, lost and void.

The bus moved on slowly. Portly Giacomo dozed beside him. He looked about at his fellow passengers. No one moved. No one talked. No one seemed to be seeing. For a moment it seemed that everyone was dead, that this bus was a wax-work museum. A woman before him sat sideways. At the tip of her nose was a gum-drop-sized mole. All the lines of her face were drawn forward in a sneer that seemed to culminate in this mole, which because she so hated it, had revenged itself thus upon her. Beside her in the aisle stood a tall youth who looked romantic, like a renaissance troubadour. His left arm was palsied and tucked tight near his body. On the wrist of his right arm were bracelets of brass, of tooled leather, and cheap beads of many colors. He stood still as a portrait, exuding sad dreams and tragedy. Looking about in the bus further, he saw just one sign of life. An old woman's head shook with faint rapid tremors, as if her rivets were working loose and she'd soon fall to pieces.

Someone nearby had fresh-ground coffee. Its soothing smell stole into his nostrils. The image came to mind of himself at the kitchen table, eating breakfast before grade-school. His mother stood by his side, pouring her first cup of coffee. This image touched off something deep in his heart – too deep, too dear, and too painful, to reveal itself to him fully. It went off like a depth-charge. Tears sprang to his eyes. He clenched his eyes shut. The bleached awful church now filled up his whole skull. Like a plucked blood-drained chicken it now stood there, defiled, as cars streamed past with their uncaring drivers. He shut his eyes tighter, to exorcise that clean church. In his mind he cloaked it again in its dense coat of grime - except for the saint's hand, which stayed poignantly white. He held fast to this image as he forced back his tears. And sped quick thanks to God and felt sure God had heard him.

The Plan

Signor Fabrizio Sfortuno staggered up to the group gathered at the bus-stop. Soon one, then another, and finally all six moved away. He was left to one side, standing all by himself. *Signor* Sfortuno did not mind being isolated so rudely. He had not even noticed. He was too busy trying to remember his plan. It was hard to remember though, because his head pounded and his stomach hurt and the sun seemed to leech the strength right out of his bones. But these were just circumstances. He still had to try.

Bus 64 pulled up and the group all got on. *Signor* Sfortuno got on also. But he did so only because he saw everyone else getting on and because there was no sun blazing on the stairwell. He got on then, but not to go anywhere, for he was already where he needed to be, trying to remember his plan.

The passengers in the aisle drew back at the sight of him, putting what little distance was possible between him and themselves. This too he did not notice, but not because of his plan. He was absorbed now in the rail in his palm at the end of his upstretched arm. It felt cool, and it kept him from falling over. And then there it was again: that strange feeling came over him, as he stepped out of himself, drifted out beyond his body, into space. This happened to him often. It did not disturb him. Though just when he'd return was never quite clear.

He looked up and saw four raised forearms with four hands that were clutching the rail. He wondered whose they all were. And if one of them was his. One forearm was thin and tanned and had fine gold-spun hairs. Its wrist was encircled by two delicate gold chains. Beside it was a stout forearm thickly covered with rusty hairs. On its broad wrist was a watch full of buttons and dials. On the thick fingers of its strong hand were two massive rings with gems. The smooth hand beside it was hairless and unadorned, seeming boneless, amphibious. And next to that was a big gnarled hand with giant knuckles and swollen joints. Its skin was so caked with dirt that it shone, its filth crusted near to permanence.

The filth-caked hand moved. It touched the smooth hand beside it. The sensation of smoothness shot straight to the brain of *Signor* Sfortuno.

"*Squilibrato.*"

"Just keep your distance. He doesn't seem violent."

"It's ok. He's no addict."

"Probably just schizophrenic."

Only the dark crusted hand clutched the rail now. 'So…' thought *Signor* Sfortuno: this hand must be his.

The bus rumbled on. It did not matter where. The point was to keep trying to remember his plan. He'd been trying all morning and had remembered it briefly, but for one reason or another it just would not stay. There were spells when he thought he could remember, spells when he could not even remember to try to remember, and spells when he could try to remember, but found that he simply could not. It seemed always to elude him in one way or other, drowned out by the traffic, evaporated by the sun, sucked down into his aching stomach.

He had scant sense of the people around him, vague forms out there somewhere that were jostling all around him. Between two of these forms though, he saw something that made sense. On the floor down the aisle lay a plastic pen someone had dropped. And this pen seemed significant. The word 'plan' flashed through his mind. And he wanted this pen badly.

But how to get there, to get it? It looked tiny and distant, as if he were looking through the wrong end of binoculars. After some wondering, an answer arrived wordlessly. He dropped to his hands and knees and set out crawling, on all fours.

"*Cristo*, what's he up to now?"

"He might be sick."

"Probably doesn't belong to anybody."

"Damn shame; here it is 1994."

"Just keep clear and you'll be alright."

Signor Sfortuno heard none of this. He was lost in a dense forest filled with strange legs and shoes. Trousered legs with sandaled feet with toes topped with hairs. Bare smooth tan legs and tan feet with red painted nails. Skinny scaly legs on whose feet were shiny gold pumps with gold tassels. Squat fat legs, all hairy, with black blocky tied shoes. All these legs and these feet moved aside quickly as he groped forward.

And finally - he finally made it. He took the pen in his hand and sat down in the stairwell. A pleasant warmth flowed all over him, as the word "plan" rang like a bell in his foggy mind.

"*Porca madonna*! Now he's urinated."

"What a stink."

"Someone help him."

"Maybe he needs a doctor."

"Watch your shoes there. It's spreading."

"Call the driver."

Moments later, the doors opened. *Signor* Sfortuno felt a broad chest pressing tight against his back. Then those strong forearms with the rusty hairs reached around him, clasped at his chest, and lifted him up off the floor. He felt peaceful, warm and protected, and yielded with pleasure to this masterful guidance. The strong arms carried him down to the curbside, where it was again hot and sunny. There they lowered him down gently till he was balanced on his hands and knees. His left hand still clutched the pen. The word "plan" flashed again, although just for an instant.

He was suddenly choked by a cloud of acrid smoke. The bus moved off into the distance and was soon gone. Gone were the strong forearms with the thick rusty hairs. Gone was the strong chest that felt so good pressed against his back. The sun was again frying his skull. And again he was lost in a forest of legs and shoes. Only these legs moved by swiftly as he stood there on all fours, trying to decipher what these legs meant. A stray dog walked past him. It was on all fours just like him. This seemed some kind of indication. So he set off crawling, in the gutter, in the same direction as the dog. As good a place as any, to remember his plan.

After crawling a short way he came face to face with a car fender. He stopped following the dog then, which was actually alright, because it was shady there and his skull pounded less. He needed some rest anyway, so he fell fast asleep.

"How awful," said one.

"We'll tell a *vigile* if we see one," said another.

"They've got money for you–name-it but nothing for him."

"No place to put them all."

"We've got one in my neighborhood too. Always flat out on the sidewalk, right in front of the grocery."

On and on went the comments - all mouthings, all air.

Hours later, the street's cobbled stones pressed hard into his side, to remind him he was there. He was too tired though, to lift a limb. He opened his eyes just half-way. He found himself looking beneath the car at whose fender he had fallen asleep. Two feet from his face were two beautiful green eyes. They were outlined in mascara and were looking straight at him. It was an orange cat sitting in the top of a shoebox. Its pupils opened slowly to full circles then closed down to slits, opened to circles then closed down to slits. For a few moments he lay looking into these green mascara'd eyes. But he felt too weak to keep his eyes open. So he shut them and drifted off.

In the foggy darkness of his mind though, he still saw the orange cat as it sat in the top of a shoebox. And then it happened. Like a crack of lightning in a vast blackened sky, a spark was set off within him. Yes here was his answer. It had finally come clear. The word "plan" now proclaimed itself with decisive finality.

His weariness vanished. Rising to his knees he reached under the car and gave a swat at the cat, which scooted off in a flash. He took the top of the shoe-box in his big filth-caked hand, strode across the sidewalk to a doorstep, and sat down. Putting the box-top on his knees, he brought his head down beside its surface, and brought the pen-point beside his eyes. In laboriously scratched letters he wrote two crooked words: *PER VIVERE.* And after another long moment, he scratched one crooked word more: *GRAZIE.*

Buon Appetito!

I love to go a-wandering
Along the mountain track.
And as I go, I love to sing,
My knapsack on my back.
Val-de-ree! Val-de-raahh!!
Val-de-REEE!!!
Val-de-RAH HA HA HA HA HA
Val-de-Reee! Val-de-RAAH!!
My knapsack on my back.

Ah yes, to be young and footloose in the city of love! A teen-aged boy and girl squatting beside backpacks exchanged lively words in German. The strapping young fellow had blond hair, a straight nose, excellent teeth, ruddy tanned skin and a good-natured expression. He reached into his knapsack and took out two round rolls with slices of *mortadella* hanging out their sides. With a smile he handed one to his companion, who seemed cast from the same mold as him. Blond, suntanned, healthy and good-natured, with her hiking boots, muscular legs and khaki shorts, she looked ready for a long Alpine hike. As she reached for her sandwich, the gaping arm-holes of her sleeveless T-shirt showed the sides of her bosoms. They were evenly suntanned, besides being large.

Biting into their sandwiches with gusto, the two settled back against their knapsacks in relaxed contentedness. But theirs was no private meal. Millions of molecules of *mortadella* dispersed into the air, and within seconds were tickling the nostrils of the Romans around them. And the mere sight of visitors enjoying their food as were these two, prompted these Romans to their most charming of customs: each in his own way bid these guests *un buon appetito*.

A thin old woman in a housedress turned abruptly in the opposite direction – a gesture she hoped showed the exact degree of her displeasure. '*Bestia*, beasts', hissed the words across her old synapses. 'Vulgar beasts: that's what they are. They eat on our buses and sleep in our parks, wash their clothes in our fountains and dry them on bushes. They come here and act like *bestia*, then think I should curtsy while they chew *schwein* sitting on their haunches like baboons. *Che prepotenti!* What nerve! You'd think they owned the whole world! As if trying twice wasn't bad enough. The next time *they* march, I hope I'm long dead and gone.'

The thoughts of a young man nearby were a tad more magnanimous: 'Sure, go ahead: have a wonderful vacation bare-assed and fancy-free on the buses of *Bell'Italia*. But just wait till it's cold and they high-tail back home, where it's *zeig heil* and neckties and Audis in Dusseldorf.'

The gent beside him had economic concerns also, but was more puzzled than envious: 'What the heck…' he wondered as he watched them. 'If I had the power of the mark burning in my wallet, there's no way I'd be sitting on the floor of a bus eating a dry sandwich with nothing to drink. I'd be served at a table and eat *primo, secondo*… the works!, that I'd wash down with fine wine.'

Could it be that the young lady caught this last thought telepathically? For no sooner had he thought this, than she reached into her knapsack and took out a giant plastic bottle of Coke. She held it straight upside-down and took deep sucking glugs that sent big bubbles streaming upwards.

Her upraised arm caused her breasts to swell forward against her T-shirt, which did not escape the already rapt attention of a white-shirted man with a tattoo of a snake visible on one bicep, bushy out-of-date sideburns, and the cummerbund of a barman. 'Well would you just take a gander!' he said to himself with a snort. 'Only eleven-thirty in the morning and they're hungry as hogs. Probably been rutting like pigs all night long on the springy bed of some nice *pensione*. Then run off to see the sights while some *scemo* Italian washes their scummy sheets clean....'

Like thoughts were being entertained also, by others in the vicinity. But all these privately held observations, like the molecules of *mortadella*, were fortunately and harmlessly dispersed into the atmosphere. And if the backpackers sensed anything contrary around them, it did not curb their enjoyment.

"*Ees goot*," said the blonde fellow, nodding with satisfaction as he gnawed vigorously at his sandwich.

"*Ja, ees goot!*" she agreed, with a charming white smile, as she offered him the chalice filled with bubbly brown Coke.

Brief Delays

The box-like truck in front of us stopped suddenly. The driver's door opened, and down from the cab stepped a man in shorts and a T-shirt that was far too short to cover his far-distended gut. With the ponderous authority of a policeman and no expression, he held up one hand telling Vinzo to stop. On this two-laned street there was really no choice. From Vinzo's throat came a half-growl, half-curse.

As the pot-bellied man stood with his palm raised, the other cab door swung open. Out sprang a short wiry man, his spine so stooped that his arms hung down like an ape's. He loped to the rear of the truck, leapt up on the platform, opened a lock at his feet, stood on tiptoe to slide a bolt, then yanked a cable that raised the back of the truck like a curtain.

Inside the truck's shadowed interior hung the massive forms of carcasses. Along the side walls were sides of beef, the curved crescents of their rib cages glowing pale in the darkness. Along the rear wall were the silhouettes of hogs hung upside down by their trotters, their snouted heads all in profile, all equidistant from the floor.

The wiry man donned a plastic hooded coat and darted inside. Taking a gaffe, he lifted a side of beef off its hook and in one fluid movement draped it across his scrawny shoulders and back. Bent over at a right angle, he went back to the platform. The push of a button lowered him slowly to the ground. Before it touched down though, the skinny man clambered off. The side of beef moved quickly toward the butcher shop, two skinny legs running beneath it.

Two more carcasses scurried into the shop in the same way. The skinny legs then came running out, carrying their scrawny stooped owner in his blood-spattered coat. After the short ride up the lift, he hung his coat up, locked the door, swung down like a monkey, then scurried up front and jumped back in the cab.

Standing stock-still, still with his palm up and no expression, the driver gave a vague salute to thank Vinzo for his patience. Then he hauled his belly, with much effort, up the tall steps to his cab.

"Same to you *stronzo,*" muttered Vinzo, as his itchy foot set the bus back in motion.

Just half a block later, he heard a wild high-pitched siren. In his side mirror he saw a police car with flashing blue lights. It must one of those armed escorts that careen through Rome's streets ferrying big shots back and forth. Vinzo slowed down to hug the curb till the flashing light passed. But the police car swerved in front of him and braked with a screech. Three cops burst out quickly, their weapons drawn for action.

'*Porco Dio,*' thought Vinzo. There must be some fugitive on board who'd soon spray the bus with gunfire, with these trigger-happy cops shooting back.

Then a postal truck pulled alongside the police car. Vinzo sighed with relief. There'd be no crazy shoot-out after all. It was just the pension money being delivered to the post office.

"Had me worried there too, for a second," chuckled a passenger in the front stairwell.

But Vinzo said nothing. His alarm had diminished but by no means disappeared. Trapped in his cubicle, only the windshield separated him from these cops, who were not acting as if armed robbery were out of the question. Quite the contrary. One stood in the middle of the street. With one upraised hand he stopped all traffic, while with the other he held a machine-gun. The other two cops, in bullet-proof vests, quickly flanked the entrance to the post office. A fourth cop ran inside carrying a plump canvas sack.

The cop on the far side of the entrance was a thick-set, lantern-jawed brute perfectly cast for his role. Standing fixed as a fire hydrant, his eyes roved the sidewalk, the street, the stores opposite, nearby rooftops. He was the guard we see in the movies: the bank guard, or prison guard, the stock Nazi sentry, who at the first hint of danger springs at once to attack. And for his dumb courage he is rewarded: with a slit throat, a whack on the head, or a fusillade of bullets in the bulls-eye of his chest. The nearer policeman was not so well cast. With his skinny neck and skinny arms, he seemed lost in his peaked badged hat, holster, ammunition belt, and bullet-proof vest. Behind his round wire-rim glasses his eyes darted everywhere. But in him this was not vigilance, but fear. He could not stand still and he shifted his weapon side to side as he fingered it nervously.

The fourth cop soon emerged with a now-flaccid sack. Like puppets pulled by strings, the three cops were drawn back into the police car, their weapons still held ready on each step of their retreat. Once all four were inside, the siren was set back to shrieking. The postal truck and its escort sped off onwards on their rounds.

An old woman at the front fingered her pocketbook fretfully and was biting her lower lip.

"Our young boys, such young young boys," she said in a quavery voice, meaning the young skinny *carabiniere*. "Look what they have our boys doing. Such terrible things now they've got them doing!"

"Bet you're glad you drive a bus," quipped the fellow who had earlier tried to engage Vinzo in repartee. "Better tearing your hair out over traffic than worrying like those guys about getting a bullet through your gut." And he laughed heartily, inviting Vinzo to join in.

But Vinzo ignored this friendly overture just the same as the first one. He checked his mirror and flicked his turn signal, before easing the bus back out into traffic.

The Campari Girl

We're near *Piazza di Spagna* now. So she must be a model. Or maybe an actress. You don't see women like this on a city bus just like the rest of us. They must be shooting an ad or a film; you see that kind of thing here often: models posing in front of statues or fountains, movies being shot at sidewalk cafes. But where's the photographer? Where's the camera? They're nowhere to be seen...

She looks like the girl in the Campari ad, the planet-wide dream of the glamorous blonde. Very long smooth slim legs pumped high on red spike-heeled shoes. A very short, very clingy red dress with no straps that bares her very broad, very tanned shoulders, on which falls her very long, very silky, very very blonde hair. She's got arched penciled eyebrows, a pert upturned nose, and the obligatory high cheekbones. Nature is quite sparing with creatures like this one, and mints very few of them. In a fashion magazine you'd just turn the page, but in person, you just stare, for she really is... quite stunning! She must be famous, or at least rich. Haven't we seen her picture somewhere before?

This Campari Girl is quite tall. Her exceptional head stands alone above the heads all around her, up toward the ceiling. But her striking face, now so visible, is curiously impassive, oblivious to the stir she creates with her thoroughbred body and expanses of bared flesh.

Two women standing near her, themselves smartly dressed but quite ordinary, appraised the Campari Girl studiously. Was that dress real silk? How much did it cost? Was it tailored or off the rack? Were those her real lips or botox? Were those huge earrings costume jewelry? Could they possibly be real? Her hair was nice yes, but too much so, too perfectly flat, parted too simply up the middle. Yes her legs were exquisite, but those kneecaps were a touch knobby, the calves a bit too muscular. Those shoulders were quite broad, tending toward a man's more than a woman's. And those breasts were helped out lots by a quite clever brassiere. How many homes did she live in? How did she divide her time? Did she take many lovers? Was she married or kept, and to whom did she belong? Did she do it just for the money? Did she actually believe in love?

The men near the Campari Girl had no questions and were not picky, but were moved to diverse manly reflection. One had to forcibly drive out from his mind the image of his wife, which rose up before him in all her homeliness, and that of his daughter, tubby and bespectacled at five. A middle-aged married lawyer thought of the apartment he would rent her, the gifts he would buy, and the travels-on-the-side he could arrange surreptitiously. Three younger men found the Campari Girl a great inspiration. One, who was short, saw her lashed to him tightly by his octopus arms as he swam wriggling upstream between the rounded banks of her thighs. Another, who was tall, saw her as he liked to imagine all women: squirming like speared fish on his long pike-like member. The thoughts of the third man suggested no metaphor, nautical or otherwise. He was just sunk in hilt-deep and determinedly thrashed.

Everybody's thoughts though, were soon halted. After just one block, the Campari Girl got off. Off she went down a side street, her long flanks shifting side to side like the haunches of a racehorse. All she left behind was a few idle questions and some passing impressions. And three young men thrusting still, at the imagined summit of her long sun-tanned legs.

To See and Be Seen

Some people here seem to have stepped through a time-warp - old Romans being recycled with a mere change of costume. Take that bodyguard beside that car with those sinister dark windows, holster bulging beneath his silk suit-jacket. Such are his thick lips and strong nose and square build that you see a centurion with sword, standing guard by a chariot. Or that bent-over old man with a weathered face that's untroubled by thought. He's walking his dog on a leash, but you see him driving sheep on the *Via Appia*. Or that gentle woman with the brown eyes and the Dante nose. She would be washing clothes in the Tiber, or carrying fresh grapes in a basket.

We find one of these old types by his easel here, in *Piazza di Spagna*. His name is Pino. He'll draw your portrait in just twenty minutes. Rome, after all, was built not by churchmen and thinkers, but by craftsmen and artisans, laborers and masons - more by muscle and nerve than by brain or heart. No philosopher or priest made a thousand stone cherubs. They were chiseled by workmen who could swing a block-mallet the whole sweaty day through. Most sought not to express inner yearnings, but to make bodies whose limbs were correctly disposed and whose ears sat symmetrically on both sides of the head. There's no demand now for stone cherubs or marble popes or bronze wreathes, or wall-sized murals filled with figures. If there were, we'd find Pino on the scaffolds with a brush or a chisel.

As it is, he does portraits - quite the best in the *piazza*. They're technically sound but not much else. First he sketches in the forms till all is proportionate and in place. Then he methodically models these forms to their full three dimensions. In Pino's pictures the hair seems to grow from the skull - it's not just a blur or wild lines. He draws excellent eyes. Slightly over-sized, they are realized in detail, with whites, pupils and lashes, and a gleam of reflected light that he adds with white chalk. All eyes drawn by Pino are sweet or alluring, imposing or masterful. All his lips curve up subtly in confident smiles. The dull-witted become intelligent. The sourpuss becomes charming. The weak-chinned belong on Mt. Rushmore. All foible, all defect, all psychological underside have been banished.

Pino's the busiest artist in the *piazza*, but not on account of his portraits. You must see him to understand this. He has the arms of a blacksmith. He's got muscular legs and wears very short shorts. His torso is from Michelangelo, save the tank-top that clings to it. His face is fine-chiseled and classical, haughty and male, with wrap-around sunglasses that hide all expression. He's tanned a deep golden brown and has a wild mop of corkscrew curls. They're far too yellow to have been bleached that way by the sun - but with a face and body like Pino's, who dares snicker? Especially ladies who wish portraits; they most often choose Pino.

Beside Pino works Ettore. Ettore is his friend but has neither good looks nor talent. He's seedy and unshaven with long gawky limbs and a neck that sticks forward. His thinning hair goes uncombed and he's got two basic expressions: hunted, and sad. He has little knack for drawing, and tries to compensate for this with "atmosphere," using chalks of three colors he blends vigorously together. But his pictures on display look just smeared, blurred and dirty. People like being flattered and they don't like a mess. This is why Pino will soon head for lunch at a nearby *trattoria*, while Ettore will sit on the steps to eat pasta brought from home.

Up *Via Condotti* toward the Spanish Steps comes another figure through the time-warp: it's the conquerer, laden with booty. Only this was no brute bearing captured armor, or slave girls or gold. It was a female with shopping bags strapped in bunches on both arms, that bounce as if to drumbeat as she marches into the *piazza*. What a morning this had been for this aging *vincitrice*: she'd found a blouse and a necklace and two pairs of shoes, three scarves and two hats and some naughty lingerie. Well... perhaps 'warrior' is not quite right.

More like the wife of a senator who lived in a villa and was tended by slaves. But who now flew on jets and bought just what she wanted – a world of luxury at her command.

She paused at the fountain for her last look, on this visit to Italy, at her favorite *piazza*. The church's twin coral towers against the sky dark with clouds. Bright pink potted flowers in the fast changing light. The same vagabond youths were still strewn across the steps, with their hair, their guitars and their hang-dog expressions. At the bottom of the steps sat the artists at their easels... and her scanning eyes stopped the first moment she saw him: that tanned muscular artist with the blonde corkscrew curls. She leaned back against the fountain to regard him with more leisure. Her cumbersome shopping bags had turned suddenly light.

"Hey-O! Adonis. You've just become a blip on someone's radar screen," said Ettore.

"Where?"

"Nine o'clock. Left front fountain. Rich lizard. Fifty shopping bags."

"Oh *Jesu Cristo*."

"Definitely old enough to be your mother."

"I've got one already. It's getting near lunch."

"Complaints, such complaints. Forty thousand is good money."

"I'd still rather a good-looker."

"Send her to me then. I gotta eat too."

"My heart bleeds for you but I gotta protect the old broad. You can't draw worth a damn."

To this Ettore responded with an exceedingly vulgar gesture.

"You can't draw and you're an ugly toad."

"Anything else, *amico mio?*"

"Yeah. Beat it. She's coming over now. Vamoose."

"It must be love," said Ettore, making a vulgar gesture below the waist. "*Ciao bello.*"

"*Ciao* yourself you *bastardo*... see you later, okay?"

"Okay, *ciao.*"

"*Ciao ciao.*"

The woman strolled past the other displays and paused before Pino's. There were four samples of his work: two of women, one of a man, and one of a child. All four had the same strong contrasts of dark and light, the same smooth modeling, the same well-drawn eyes and smiling lips. They looked decisively like somebody, yet actually like nobody. She could not imagine anybody hanging one in their home.

"*Ti piace?*" asked Pino.

"Scoo—zee?"

"*Ho detto: 'ti piace?'*"

"Scoo-zee. *Sono francese.*"

"*Non parlo francese.* You speek english?"

"A leetle."

"I ask you like my peektures."

226

"Zay are... eenteresting," she said, striking a pose with one high-heeled shoe forward, as if appraising a masterwork.

"Why you say 'eenteresting' and not say 'pretty'? I make very pretty peektures. You sit down and we make you pretty peekture. Very special pretty peekture. Pretty peekture, pretty price. *Prego. Si accomodi.* We make *masterpiece* — okay yes? Please sit down *mon cheri.*"

She snorted inwardly at his shameless entreaties and craven '*mon cheri.*' But her snorts gave way to swoons as he came up alongside her and placed a magnificent strong hand, at the end of a magnificent bronze arm, oh so gently on her shoulder. He guided her toward the seat before his easel. She felt woozy - rather nice - like she'd just drunk champagne. The shopping bags were eased off her arms as one magnificent hand sat on her shoulder, while the other magnificent hand went round her hips and eased her down on the seat.

"Okay. *Madamoiselle* just relax now and Pino makes peekture. Look pass my shoulder; look at boat in the fountain. *Perfetto.* Hold your head... *bene, bene.*"

With four feet now between them, *mon cheri's* head cleared up slightly. Pino unrolled a fresh piece of paper which he tacked to his easel, his brown biceps bulging as his strong fingers worked. As he bent over and scrabbled about in his cigar box of charcoals, she looked down and marveled at the depth of his chest, the powerful column of his neck, and the wild untamedness of his corkscrew curls. The moment he sat up, she turned back to the fountain.

He began with many swift arcing gestures, one after another. He was at once absorbed in his task - as if she didn't even need to be there. She began to feel excluded, even testy. But then his hand stopped and his head lifted. He was looking straight at her. She took her eyes off his thighs, where they were drunkenly loitering, and looked again at the boat.

"Okay we all set now. We ready for you eyes. You take off sunglasses now, no? You no want pretty peekture just plastic. Pretty lady with sunglasses? Of course no hah hah, right?"

"What?.. these?.., n—no of course..." Poor *mon cheri*. She had forgotten she was even wearing them!

The moment they came off she felt everything change. There sat Pino the Magnificent, masterful and impassive behind wrap-around sunglasses. And there *she* sat, feeling naked, exposed – this was more than she had bargained for. His head stayed immobile, so she could not tell when he was looking at her or at the picture. When his drawing hand moved, he was probably looking down. It was then that she snatched looks at the whole length of his body. First his brown long-toed feet in their thonged leather sandals, then his tight muscled calves and his fine beveled knees, then his thighs, and those skimpy white shorts...

"The boat *per favore*. The boat *s'il vous plait*."

Her head snapped back toward the fountain. Her cheeks burned hotly. His tone had been neutral - neutral enough not to be mocking. But she knew what he was thinking, this tanned low-life Casanova: just another weak woman drooling before earth's handsomest creature. He probably thought she was here just to steal looks at his body. She laughed bitterly to herself and drew herself up straighter in her chair.

Go on, look all you want - thought a defiant *mon cheri*. I've got nothing to hide. This body was not young but it was all woman, still ripe. Male heads had turned her way at the beach this very summer. Go ahead, Casanova, she challenged him haughtily. She was very much a woman still, and one quite to be reckoned with. Her fine-featured face had great character. It had few wrinkles or sags and her forehead was lineless. Her neck was smooth also. She had no rooster's wobbly wags hanging slack from her chin. No jowls, no taut tendons, no dark pit of the throat. She had no dowager's hump and no old scarecrow arms, or those slack blimpy ones either, that hang loose off the bone. Her chest was still female - no cadaverous clavicle or bony sternum. Her breasts held their own and were shown to perfection, by her scalloped collar and her string of real pearls.

Let young girls fall in droves into his arms, interchangeable slim dolls from the same plastic mold. Under her dress was pure *woman*, save that scar where they took out what was nobody's business. She wasn't fooled by that statue-like face and those wrap-around glasses. She had felt it in his touch as he'd led her to her seat. She lowered her eyes to her tanned still-smooth legs. They were scaly, but what of it? They were trim as could be. Not a vein could be seen. She looked with pride at her brown feet with bright red nails in their gold high-heeled shoes, all so seamlessly pretty. Yes this swarthy low-lifer was no doubt rather enjoying himself. He had quite the deal to be gobbling her up so, from behind those big dark glasses. And getting paid in the bargain!

"Hokay we done now. I show *mon cheri* pretty peekture. You weel like it so much."

With a slow deliberate sashay, *mon cheri* walked up to his easel. Standing beside him, she let her leg press up negligently against his. The shared patch of heat traveled straight to her brain, another sip of champagne. He talked more nonsense about the peekture, more pretty thises and pretty thats. She could not follow his words since her head was half-reeling. With one long painted nail she pointed at the picture, mouthing long strings of words to which neither of them listened.

As these Romans walked by, seeing her casually at ease with this low virile type, her head felt like it was high in the clouds. How long did she stand there, her thigh against his, then her hand on his shoulder? An eternal fifteen seconds. When her allotted time was up, Pino stood up and began rolling up the picture.

"Extra very careful *please*," he said with great seriousness. "We put peekture in thees bag here, right on the top, like tomatoes in fruit shop. You peekture no crush, yes? It goes home real safe."

It all happened so fast… before she even knew it, she was marching away, shopping bags banging at her sides.

'Well *that* was a lark,' thought *mon cheri*, looking up at the sky. But what was this…? Big storm clouds had gathered quickly. It could pour any minute. Where were those taxis she had seen here this morning? There had been a mob of taxis and those festive horse-drawn carriages. Just one carriage was still here. She walked up to the driver, who was hard at work on a crossword puzzle.

"No taxis?" she asked.

"*Bo*," he replied, which expressed a combination of I–don't–know and I–can't–be–bothered–with–you.

She thought to ask him to drive her to the hotel in his carriage. But you don't make a taxi out of a carriage drawn by a horse with a red–tasseled mane.

"Bus? Grand Hotel?"

He pointed down a side street then went back to his puzzle.

Tak tak tak… off she went on high heels at a brisk determined pace. She never rode buses but you can't argue with storm-clouds. *Tak tak tak* went her heels, her bags bouncing at her sides. She marched quick to the bus–stop, pausing once, to jam her portrait in a trash can.

Pino meanwhile, was adding her bills to his thick wad of cash.

"A she–lizard in pearls," he said, shaking his head in dismay. "Probably sleeps in formaldehyde."

"No one ever told you don't bite the hand that feeds you?" asked Ettore, annoyed, looking sidelong at the cash."

"I don't bite at real hands. She had claws. You saw them."

"Claws you say *now*. I heard you back *then*. 'Oh pretty woman, I make you peekture. Very very pretty peekture. For very very pretty woman. Pretty lizard with pretty claws. I show you something very pretty." Ettore made as if to lower his zipper.

Pino laughed appreciatively. "You ugly toad you," he said, smiling warmly.

Ettore was just warming up. "Oh you sweet sweet fine lizard, you sweet sweet pickled lizard." He leered like a satyr. His mouth opened and his tongue flicked up and down.

"You're just jealous," said Pino. "You wish you could draw so you'd make good money like I do."

Ettore's gestures went below the waist again.

"But even if you could draw, you wouldn't have my money. You wanna know why?"

Ettore was too far gone licking and gesturing to come up with an answer.

Pino went on undeterred. "You wouldn't have my money 'cause you don't have my good looks. But don't let it bother you, my friend. Listen: It's gonna rain soon and I feel sorry for you, ugly toad that you are. So let me buy you a real lunch for a change: *primo, secondo, vino*, the whole works. It's my pleasure to take you, but on one condition..."

Ettore's active hands fell to his sides. His tongue disappeared. He put an imaginary key in his lips, turned it twice, then threw it away. He held up his hands as if facing a gun.

"*Bravo*. You got it," said Pino, as he folded his easel. "Let's get going. I'm starved. We gotta hustle. It's gonna rain."

Arm in arm climbed the two friends, up the steep Spanish Steps.

Tina and Gina

Tina was Gina's best friend. Gina was Tina's best friend. Tina wore jeans and sneakers. So did Gina. Gina wore a round-collared t-shirt. So did Tina. They both dressed like tomboys from their round collars down. All dolling up was lavished on their hair and their faces. Gina wore her yellow hair in a wild tousled mane that went half down her back. So did Tina. Tina was not blonde - but then neither was Gina. Tina's eye shadow and hoop earrings and hair-band were all green, like her sneakers. Gina wore the same, only hers were all turquoise. Gina wore lipstick with that dark line round the edges. So did Tina. Both Tina and Gina were lithe, tan and pretty. Both girls knew quite well they were pleasing young foxes.

Just four weeks ago they'd sat crammed in these same seats drawing line after line with a bright yellow marker in some dull heavy book. Thank God for vacations - what a pleasure, what reprieve, to sit back and watch the world from behind stylish new sunglasses. And why not, after all? When two girls are beach-bound it's a fine happy world.

"I can't believe it!" said Tina. "It was perfectly sunny when we left home."

"I can't believe it either," said Gina.

"It feels more like nightfall than daytime."

"Kind of spooky."

"I'll say spooky."

"It's going to pour any minute."

"I can't believe it".

"I can't believe it either".

"It might be different at the beach though."

"It could be."

"Maybe not."

"Shall we risk it?"

"Let's risk it."

"You think so?"

"I don't know; do you?"

To get to the beach took an hour by bus then an hour by train. But for Tina and Gina it most definitely was worth it. It was better than trying to listen to music while Tina's mama banged pots and chopped thousands of vegetables. Or trying to watch TV as Gina's mama lumbered about with her mop and bucket, washing the same floors she'd washed yesterday. Or trying to chat on the terrace while Tina's mama beat the rugs long after dust clouds stopped coming out of them. The beach was better, too, than walking around on frying-pan sidewalks and soft rubbery streets. This bus ride was worth it - if it just didn't rain.

What peace just to lie doing nothing and bake in the sun! It was just mid-July and they were nut-brown already. They weren't this dark last year till the first week in August. This year they'd already moved down faster with their sunscreen. They'd worked from factor twelve down to factor four. Today Tina planned to drop a double step down to factor two. Gina said she'd stop at four, thanks the same. She'd read something about a hole in the ozone layer. Tina said that was silly if you want the richest tan possible.

The girls rotated on their towels a quarter-turn every fifteen minutes. With each turn they would spray each other with cool water from a spritzer. They were careful to expose the tricky spots too: the insides of the arms and thighs, the palms and the webbing between the fingers. They kept the radio tuned to 103.4, Gina's favorite station. It was Tina's favorite also. As they lay on their backs they kept their eyes closed and smoked cigarettes, blowing hot smoke they could not see into the breeze passing by. Tina had started with Marlboros when she was twelve. So had Gina. Gina had just switched to some new ultra-thin menthol brand. So had Tina.

When they lay on their bellies they could read but they didn't. They would just look at pictures. Gina brought a huge fashion magazine with over three hundred pages. So did Tina. They both loved looking at tall slinky women wearing fabulous clothes and magnificent jewels, pampered queens of their beach, yacht or nightclub. They liked the fashion men also, standing off to one side - a suave man in a tux or some brute luscious savage.

"What would they do if they knew you went topless?" asked Tina.

"My mom would kill me. That's all," said Gina.

"What a dinosaur your mom is. Absolutely prehistoric. And your dad? What would he do?"

"He'd kill me too - but you know him. If he killed me, he'd *really* kill me. I'd be dead. Dead and buried."

"What a pig. You're probably right. And your *nonna*? What would she do?"

"*Nonna*? She wouldn't kill me."

"No she wouldn't. She's not the type."

"She'd just *die*, that's all."

"Probably right. Just keel over stone dead."

"Grammy's not pre-historic. She's *pre*-prehistoric."

"Maybe worse. Maybe pre-pre-pre-pre."

"And *your* mother?"

"She could care less. I could drop dead tomorrow for all she cared."

"And your father?"

"Same for him."

"You're real lucky."

"I suppose so."

"Elena says that last year, her and her mother *both* took off their tops."

"Fine for Elena. I wouldn't want to sit there all day looking at *my* mother with no top."

"Ditto here."

"She's not prehistoric but she looks like a dinosaur. Topless dinosaurs aren't pretty."

"I'll say dinosaurs! Pre-pre-pre-pre."

Their wearing no tops kept the beach nice and peaceful. If they kept their tops on they'd be pestered by boys who would hound them like dogs from the moment they arrived. Got a match? Got a cigarette? Got the time? What's your name? Where d'you live? Go to school? Come to this beach often? Then the frisbees would land on them and volleyballs bounce off them – along with shuttlecocks, soccer balls and sand. But like two eyes of warning, their bared breasts kept boys distant. It was funny how it worked that way. They were glad that it did.

Not that the boys would stop coming round. There was no cure for that. They were glad that there wasn't. They'd strut by all the same – with their smooth rooster chests and their wiry-haired legs and those sausages they're so proud of tucked in tight little trunks. And Tina and Gina could review this parade from behind big stylish sunglasses, immune from intrusion.

Bared breasts kept the boys away like some invisible shield. But the *voo-compra* just walked through it, undeterred, not unwelcome. The *voo-compra* were immigrants who hiked up and down the beaches selling goods piled on their shoulders: sarongs and sandals, towels and sunglasses, headbands and sunsuits, bracelets and beads. *Voo-compra:* you want to buy? *Voo-compra:* you want to buy? *Voo-compra, voo-compra:* the word itself sounded primitive, like some noise from the jungle. But a *voo-compra* is no boy. He doesn't joke. He doesn't smile. He doesn't do dumb juvenile things or stare rudely at your breasts.

Tina liked the Tunisians and Moroccans with their bandy iron legs and tightly muscled bodies, who looked like pirates with their piercing black eyes and their big mustaches and bandana-wrapped heads. How effortlessly they trekked down these beaches in the blazing hot sun with huge loads on their shoulders. She pictured herself riding behind one on a hazy white desert, swaying slowly back and forth to the camel's easy rhythms. Or herself in a great tent lit by torch-light on a sultry night. The tent flaps part. There he stands. His black eyes are flashing. He unchains his scimitar and comes panther-like toward her...

Gina too, liked these Arabs, but herself preferred the blacks. Lank-limbed and silent, patient and slow, they wore caps inset with mirrors and long embroidered caftans. Black as ink and mysterious, they seemed very romantic. She pictured sundown on a veranda looking out on the jungle. The pitch darkness filled up with the cries of wild animals. Inside, her man waited, long limbs black as night...

What a treat for the girls when the *voo-compra* would visit. Up he would come, so purposeful and strong beneath his ponderous load. He'd squat down beside them and get right down to business: 'Pretty sarong, real silk. Pretty hat, pretty price. Pretty suit, latest style. Pretty beads, make by hand.' How much better than the stores in the city, where bad-tempered clerks gave most young girls short shrift. But here it was different: an exciting dark man on his knees swathed in colorful fabrics, at your command! He'd take sheer sarongs and drape them over one arm, or wave them before them with a court-ier's flourish. And while he praised and presented, they could lie there and watch like two concubines in a harem, propped on one elbow wearing just their bottoms, as exotic and alluring as any model in a magazine.

They could lean back or sit up with their hands clasped behind their heads. And their breasts swayed and wobbled but a *voo-compra* shows nothing and goes on with his display. When they'd had their fill they'd say 'no not these colors', or 'I've got the same thing at home', or 'if only you had this in cotton'. Then they'd shake their heads sadly; it was time he moved on.

But for taking his time they would offer him a smoke - the best part of all. You held out the cigarette. He reached forward and took it. You held out your lighter – he would have to come nearer. He'd lean forward to come close, the white cigarette dangling from his thick dark pursed lips. He'd lean close as can be - but a *voo-compra* doesn't smile. As he took his first pull on the cigarette its end would glow orange and his eyes would glow also. But this glow in his eyes was not something you could see, for a *voo-compra* knows how to keep his fire all inside him. He'd lean back on his haunches, take few puffs and say *grazie*. Then off he would go on his bandy legs with his big pile of wares down the endless white beach.

"Do you think it's clearing up?"

"Try taking off your sunglasses."

"Not much of a difference."

"What do you think now?"

"Let's try not to think about it. It might be different when we get there... what do you think?"

"I don't know."

"Let's not think about it then."

"No turning back then. We decided."

"Absolutely."

"Say a prayer."

"Prayer said."

"Keep your fingers crossed."

"Fingers crossed."

Side by side with their sunglasses pushed back on their heads, Tina and Gina sat with their four hands with crossed fingers on their four blue-jeaned thighs. Their pretty faces clouded with worry as their mascara'd eyes searched the darkening sky. When they'd left home life was colorful and bright, like a wide-screen movie. It was a black-and-white photo now: small, static and dull. What good were radios or lip-gloss or sun glasses or bikinis? There's no justice at all when it rains on a beach day!

The Storm

Sorry Tina. Sorry Gina. Clouds that had been travelling inland all morning from Ostia arrived with great suddenness. The sun was blotted out by dark low-hanging clouds that were heavy with rain. Daylight vanished. It felt like sundown. Passengers peered out the windows. Some raised their eyes malevolently to the heavens. Some scanned the sidewalk, pedestrians' expressions, or the windshields of passing cars, to know when the drops fell in earnest. Some first drops had already fallen. Dark flecks kept increasing on an ochre wall nearby.

The general torpor on board the bus vanished with the storm's dramatic prelude. Restlessness swept through, as each anticipated his confrontation with the elements. Some wizened ones had heard the forecast, and known not to trust the smiling face of this morning's sun. With quiet triumph they fingered umbrellas extracted from briefcases and handbags. The unprepared peered out anxiously and worried - about dry clothes and expensive shoes, about make-up and delicate hairdos.

Krrr-AAKKK!!!! A great shaft of lightning split the sky, followed by an explosive clap of thunder. In seconds the storm went from imminent to full fury. Driving rain lashed the streets, sending pedestrians running for cover. Car headlights went on. Traffic slowed to a crawl. The streetlights came on. Car alarms wailed in unison, set off by the thunderclap. Bus 64 forged on into *Piazza Barberini*, looking less like a bus than a frigate plowing through stormy waters. Hunched over the wheel as he labored to navigate, our Vinzo was cast in a most flattering light. No longer an unshaven disagreeable bus driver, he was a sea captain at the helm, guiding the souls entrusted to him on a perilous journey.

In the center of the *piazza*, the Bernini faun held his conch shell heavenward, its tall stream of water jetting skywards, redundant, into the water-filled air. Our frigate forged on toward the bus-stop at the top of the *piazza*. At the stairwell, twelve passengers were tensed like paratroopers before a jump. Huddled up against a building near the bus-stop, twelve other citizens were waiting for the bus to draw near. What happened next should have been straightforward. Those waiting up against the building should wait for the passengers getting off to clear away. They could then cross the sidewalk quickly and mount the stairwell to dryness. But what was happening here instead?

The waiting citizens flocked to the bus doors the moment it arrived. Frenzied by the driving rain, they pressed, clamoring to get on. Hi-SSSS! The doors opened. The troopers inside, coiled like springs ready to sprint to dryness, found themselves face to face with the pressing throng. Goaded on by the rain pouring down the necks of their bowed heads, those outside pushed forward with self-justified zeal.

How ingenious is the umbrella. A portable roof; we can cheat the hostile elements. This homely device hooked over our arm speaks of comfort and convenience. Imagine the quiet joy with which the first umbrella was held aloft by its inventor. Could he ever have imagined how it would be used here today?

The battle lines were drawn. There was no turning back. Next came the scene when the charging armies meet and merge slowly into the mayhem of hand-to-hand combat. Gaetano Porzio, head up and chest out, held his umbrella point before him like the prow of an ice-cutter. His technique succeeded well; he cut right through toward the stairs. But he soon met his match in Dora Durone, disembarking. With such force did this fat-backed matron thrust her umbrella forward to open it, that Gaetano was jolted smack on the bridge of his nose, and staggered back three steps in pain. "Just be grateful," reasoned his wife later, as she rubbed salve into his wound. "One inch either way and you'd be out an eye!"

Franco Segurini too, was doing well, or so it seemed, disembarking. He stayed close behind a gorilla of a man, in whose wake he followed with ease. But once he stepped down, the gorilla swung his

242

umbrella open recklessly, flicking Franco's straw hat off his head and down into the gutter, where it was trampled to hay by the thundering hooves.

Camilla Cecina as well, had begun with sound tactics. Circling quickly round the line of scrimmage, she nimbly ducked two umbrellas and sprang forward to a free spot on the bottom step. But just as she caught the railing, her cheek was raked by an umbrella spoke-tip. It hooked off her new designer glasses and flung them rudely back into the storm.

Heads down like rams, bumping into and off to the side of one another, all soon were on board or had managed to fight free. The doors then hissed shut and the bus pulled away. Raindrops washed the curb clean of all signs of the clash.

The Horse with the Red-Tasseled Mane

Rivulets of rain now streamed off hats and umbrellas onto shoulders and calves down to ankles and feet. Wet bodies pressed against dry ones. The windows were all shut and quite quickly steamed over. The air was soon fetid, creating a subtle tense anxiety.

Bus 64 chugged slowly onward into the storm, up the hill of *Via Barberini*. Captain Vinzo was hunched forward struggling to see through the windshield, whose one lazy wiper swept side to side, insufficient. The rain-pounded street was now largely deserted. A lone Arab stood in a doorway, rolled-up carpets heaped on his shoulders, and a small one draped over his head. A *motorino* whizzed past up the hill, its two young riders shouting hilarities as they shook their drenched manes with glee. As the *motorino* disappeared up the hill into the storm, a strange sight loomed into view coming down in the opposite direction. A horse-drawn carriage for tourists came rolling swiftly down the hill. Up front sat its driver, hunched forward on his bench, urging his horse on with lashes from a riding crop. In the carriage's red-cushioned rear, three white-shirted Japanese sat huddled up against one another, trying to protect their video-cams from the downpour.

The horse was harnessed between two long rails that were attached to the carriage. Its fast-moving hooves kicked up continuous white splashes. Vinzo knew nothing about horses and had never driven a carriage, but he knew *this* horse was going too fast. It looked like the carriage was driving it into a momentum it was hard-pressed to keep up with. Its legs looked too skinny as they moved ever faster. Vinzo's left foot pressed the floor hard, as if vicarious bus brakes could slow down the carriage.

Then, just as he feared, the unthinkable happened. The horse's legs flew out from under it. It came skidding down the hill on its knees and folded haunches, still trapped between the rails with the carriage still in tow. Vinzo winced as the horse skidded a painfully long distance before finally coming to a stop. What a mess of a mess on this morning of messes!

The carriage driver was an old buzzard in a straw hat and a white shirt that his skinny arms stuck out of. He came down off his bench in the effortful way of the elderly, and walked with a limp to the front of the horse. Its forelegs were propped up in two angular peaks, its hooves on the asphalt. One knee was torn open. A patch of flesh had been gouged out neatly, like a divot by a golf club. The wound was filled with dark maroon blood and bits of gravel. A patch of bone gleamed out whitely.

"*Merde*," said the driver. Then he grimaced at the facades of the buildings around him, as if in each empty window someone had seen this injustice. He walked back to the horse's rear. One leg was folded beneath its body, which lay twisted to one side. He limped to where the reins and the harness had become tangled with its back legs. He grasped the rail alongside the horse and gave a weak tug of futility. The horse didn't move; he gave it a weak angry slap.

"*Merde*," he repeated.

Vinzo stopped and with two other men, got off the bus and ran over beside the horse. They yanked at the reins, twisting the horse's head side to side. They pulled at the rails, but the horse did not budge. The three Japanese got out of the carriage and stood in the downpour, looking unsure what to do.

"It's wound round back around the left leg," said Vinzo.

"I think he's just lying on it," said one man.

"If we could lift these side-runners out of the way or detach them from the harness, that might loosen things up," said the other.

"But they're attached to the reins so we gotta get the reins freed up first."

"But I told you - I think he's *sitting* on the reins. He's gotta stand up first, before anything else."

"Maybe the driver can release the whole harness so the tension wouldn't be so great."

"But you just said that you thought the reins had to be freed up first."

"I know, but now I'm saying something different."

"What's the driver say?"

"The hell with the driver. You saw him. He doesn't know shit about horses. This wouldn't have happened in the first place if he knew what the hell a horse was or what he was doing."

"The horse has gotta stand up first."

"But what if he can't, or if it hurts his leg?"

"If he can't stand he can't stand. If he hurts his leg he hurts his leg. The hell with the horse. It's not our horse anyway."

Having exhausted all words with no conclusion, they went back to wrestling with the harness, yanking the reins this way and that, and moving the side rails up, down, and sideways, and diagonally both ways. But the horse lay there still, bound-up and immobile. The three Japanese, who had gotten soaked as they dutifully watched, retreated to the shelter of a storefront.

A young woman with an umbrella came running from the bus. She went straight to the horse's blindered head. She wore a tortured look of concern that she hoped brought it comfort. The horse lifted its muzzle straight to the sky. Its eyes were wide open and doleful. They blinked from the rain. The woman held her umbrella up over its head. With her other hand she stroked its tousled bangs. The mane of the horse was braided, with a red tassel at the end of each braid. The braids were all tangled so she raked its mane with her fingertips.

"Good horsie, goo–od horsie," she said, in broad soothing tones. "You're a very good horsie, such a very good horsie." She glanced down and saw the wound with the white bone gleaming through. She winced and looked away, then raked its mane twice as fast. "Yes a very good horsie such a very good horsie you're a very good horsie" she said, speaking twice as fast also.

Two of the Japanese now came forward, leaving their companion at the store-front with their cameras. They watched the three men still struggling, and the woman cooing and stroking the horse's head. One of them, who was short, looked on with concern. The other, who was tall, wore a tight sardonic smile. The short one said something long and involved to the tall one. The tall one shot back a short question in a sharp voice. The short one shrugged. His concerned face went blank. The tall one said something curt and then dug out his wallet and took out a bill. He walked over behind the driver and tapped him on the shoulder. The driver looked at him with dull eyes. The tall man extended the bill with a short little bow. The driver's hand shot out like a frog's tongue and took it in.

"*Glazie*," said the tall one, with a short bow. The driver said nothing. He took a wad of bills held with a rubber band out of his pocket. He peeled off the rubber band, carefully wrapped the new bill around the wad, put the rubber band back on and put the wad in his pocket. Without a word he turned his back on the Japanese man and leaned back on the harness. The tall Japanese looked at the short one with a now-malicious smile. He gave a dry mean little laugh before striding to the sidewalk, the short one in tow.

Vinzo and the other man kept on struggling with the reins, harness and side-rails - to no avail. Then, running through the downpour from across the street, came the Arab who had taken shelter with his carpets. He was short, wiry and strong, with overlarge hands and a lined brown manly face. His eyes were black and flashing, his white smile showed a gold tooth. He wore a pencil-thin mustache and a maroon fez.

He went immediately to the wounded knee. Taking the foreleg in his hand, just above the hoof, he lifted it slowly and flexed it up and back twenty degrees. He repeated this movement, flexing it fifty degrees the second time. The third time he flexed it one hundred, then the full hundred and eighty degree extension. When the leg was fully extended, he flexed the foreleg joint twice, fully and smoothly, watching the horse's face intently the whole time. He then settled the hoof gently back onto the street.

He knelt in front of the horse and took its head between his two overlarge hands. He asked the horse a question loudly in Arabic. The horse made no reply. To this he laughed loudly, as if to say, 'What a devilish rogue you are!' Chuckling to himself, he walked back to where the other men were still struggling. When he squatted down beside them, they stood up and stepped back and crossed their arms tightly over their chests.

The Arab ignored them. He looked first at the harness, and its attachment to the rails and the carriage. He then put his hand on the side rail and slid his hand along it as he walked forward to the horse's head. Then he went back to the rear and looked at where the reins went under the horse, tracing their path attentively with his eyes, tugging them gently here and there. He finally stood up, with an air of satisfaction.

With a chuckle he called out something loud, again in Arabic, to the horse. And then sent a terrifically strong kick into the soft flesh of its haunches. The horse tossed its head, bared its teeth and gave a sharp high-pitched whinny. The Arab laughed, called out in Arabic, and then BANG BANG BANG BANG! gave four terrific kicks in succession. The horse whinnied with distress; it was alarmingly loud. But at the same time it made big clumsy movements with the whole of its body, pawed and scratched at the pavement, and clambered its way somehow onto all four skinny legs.

And there stood the good horsie, upright on all fours between two parallel rails. Its harness was in place. Its reins hung down neatly from both sides of its head. It snorted and shook its head. Its red tassels flicked side to side. It whinnied again loudly, as if eager to go home.

The Arab gave the horse a playful whack on the rump, then laughed loudly and called it a rogue again. With a flourish of an Arab hand salutation to all, he strode back to his carpets he had left in a doorway.

"Fuck of a horse," said our Vinzo, pushing his soaked hair back on his head as he headed back to the bus.

"I'll say," agreed one other man, as the third man nodded in agreement.

The girl with the umbrella stood beaming at the upright lively horsie, then went scampering off with a smile, after her driver.

With the effortful way of the elderly, the carriage driver climbed back in his carriage. He took his riding crop from its holder, and with a cry and a lashing snap beside the horse's red tasseled mane, set them both rolling downhill, trotting on through the storm.

Fleeced, Thank You

French!!! Someone here speaks French!? Does someone speak French here?" A woman pressed her way forcefully to the front of the bus. Her sun-tan and clothes, her jewelry and make-up all said 'big money', as did the designer shopping bags that hung in bunches on both arms.

"I do," said a young student-type, stepping forward.

"Good," said the woman, who seemed accustomed to taking charge.

"Please tell this driver someone has stolen my wallet. Gone right into my pocketbook and taken it right out."

The passengers were separated from the driver by a two-part glass partition. The student set his nose in the gap between the partitions and told Vinzo what had happened.

"What does he say?" said this aging *mon cheri*, standing behind him.

"He... well, he doesn't say anything."

"Tell him there's been a crime aboard his bus. It just happened. Just now. I got on just three stops back. Near *Piazza di Spagna*."

The student's nose went back to the partition.

"What does he say?"

"He says you have to go to the *Questura*."

"The *Questura?*"

"Police headquarters. When something happens here you have to… how do you say it? Go denounce it to the police. *Fare denuncia* we call it."

"'Later' is too late. This just happened. There'll be no point denouncing anything later. Tell him he should stop. Call a policeman. I seem to see one on every corner."

The nose returned to the partition.

"What does he say?"

"He doesn't say anything."

"Tell him I *want* him to do that. Tell him. Make it very clear."

The student, looking earnest, turned back to the partition.

"What did he say?"

"I think it's better I don't translate it," said the student, in neutral tones that sought to put the matter to rest. He was unsuccessful, however, at suppressing a wry smile.

"Then you tell him I want his name and I'll take his bus number and I'm going to report him just as soon as I get back to my hotel. That's a promise. You tell him that… What are you waiting for? Go on. Tell him."

Nose returned to partition. Vinzo's response was both lively and extensive.

"What is his name?"

"He didn't say."

252

"All that talk and he didn't say? What *did* he say then, with all those words?"

"I don't think I'd better translate that one for you either, *mademoiselle*," said the student.

"What. Did. He. Say," she commanded, in flat tones.

"Oh, nothing. Nothing really. Just a kind of... side comment of sorts. You know."

"But these people are all laughing now. They're laughing at me, I can tell, aren't they? That's plain enough to see. I'm not stupid you know."

"No really, it was... nothing about you. Romans just... like to... laugh a lot. Sometimes. You know what I mean?"

"I think I do — and now *you're* smiling too. You don't have to hide it. I can see. *You* think it's funny too then, my being robbed and getting no help from this oaf of a driver."

"No no - really! It's just that it's a... funny kind of... situation, that's all."

"Yes. I'm quite sure it is. Well whatever it is that oaf said to me, I want you to tell him that I say the same thing to him. You tell him that. Go on now. Tell him."

The student was reluctant to take part in this escalation.

"Well go on. What are you afraid of?"

The student turned resignedly to the partition. Perhaps he delivered her message, but definitely in too reasonable tones.

"Does he say anything to that?"

"No."

"Please tell him thank you. Tell him thank you very much. Thank you very much indeed."

The student's nose went to the partition. A terrible guttural outburst boomed forth from the driver's cubicle.

"And what did he say *that* time?"

"I think it's probably best you just get off at the next stop and try your luck at the *Questura*."

"He said that? Again?"

"Well...no. But I don't really want to say the words he said."

"Yes. I can well imagine. Okay then. Would you mind telling me what is *your* name?"

"Me? My name? It's Edoardo. Edoardo Carradorini."

"Well thank you anyway *Signor* Corradorini. You've been most helpful. I thank you all the same."

"Thank you. It was nothing. You're quite welcome yourself," said Edoardo.

The Last Judgment

*B*ravo! Serves her right!!' Arturo Velenato cheered inwardly at the driver's rude outburst. Why should he care she'd been so deaf, dumb and blind as to be fleeced by a pick-pocket? As if the whole world should stop just for her! Serves her right; why just look! Her one morning's shopping might pay his rent for a year - on her necklace alone he might live who-know-how-long? Yes that's how the rich are, though they're glutted with money: still righteous to hunt down the poor cur who's dared pinch some.

The rain had let up. She cut in front of the bus and walked past slowly, on purpose, making Vinzo stop short. Then she *tak-tak-takked* across the street on her gold high-heeled shoes making straight for the hotel with the five stars on its wall. As she entered the cavernous atrium whose statues stood in their niches, a bell-hop in tails appeared. He held the polished brass door open and gave a wind-up doll bow as she disappeared inside.

'That's right, rich-bitch rabbit. Just jump back in your hole. Back in the plush carefree world of the Grand Hotel with its bell-hops and drivers, its maids, cooks and waiters, where phone calls and signatures bring you all you desire as you float gently downstream on broad rivers of money.' His lips were drawn tight as his mouth hardened in a sneer. He suppressed a strong urge to spit but brought up phlegm just the same, which he enfolded with malice in a tissue from his pocket.

The bus rumbled on. Good-bye Grand Hotel. And good-bye to old buildings, to videocams and postcards, to caped soldiers on horseback bearing useless sabers, to bars with mirrors and marble, and sun-tanned high-flyers with cell phones - good-bye to the whole shining false stinking mess. From here on the bus slouched to the train station, and the Rome beyond it — to *his* Rome, the real Rome, where no tourist ever set foot.

For the money-bagged tourists, the station was a revolving door that led to better places. Going through *that* door they could pop up in Venice, where they strolled the canals feeling dreamy. Or on a terrace in Tuscany beneath a vine-shaded trellis, where the waiter pours *vernaccia* and awaits their approval. Or on a jet back to Zurich or Frankfort, L.A. or Paris, or wherever they amassed cash for their next trip abroad.

For Arturo this revolving door led to no sunshiney anywhere. It was a black hole that sucked him down to a sewerish subway that spat him out near the prison block he called home. Up the fifth of six staircases, on the sixteenth floor out of twenty, behind the ninth door on the right was his flat, #396. Behind the slide-bolted door were two small boxlike rooms with a sink, tub and toilet, a fridge, stove and TV and a few sticks of furniture. And no other living being. Where he'd be stuck the whole summer.

When he first got home he would feel almost grateful - just to sit in a soft chair with a cold beer and watch the bright changing pictures of TV. But after a while he'd have eaten and exhausted this small pleasure. His TV then said nothing. And the radio said nothing. And the magazines and newspapers said nothing also. He'd go out on his bird-perch-sized terrace with its cage-like steel fence. And look out at the apartment blocks that loomed around him, like monoliths in some moonscape.

Forks and knives clinked and clanked out from dozens of near-by windows. His neighbors' mouths loosed streams of nonsense, or boomed out laughs like hyenas. With the dead humid air he would feel he was on the wrong planet. He'd smoke cigarette after cigarette till they burnt at this tongue, then continue to smoke till his mouth tasted bad and his head throbbed with pain. After what seemed like forever, it would still just be ten. Families still would be animate, still clacking at their plates or shuffling about in their cells or crouched on chairs before TVs.

BLAM! BLAM! BLAM! came the gunshots from ten different windows, as ten TV blondes shrieked. From ten other windows came that lunatic canned laughter. From a dozen other windows came the anchor-man's stern voice, with the latest details of what you already knew: that the world was in chaos and that war, crime and money were the sun, moon and stars.

Alone on his terrace he would hope to tire early. But on summer nights with the windows open, he was kept awake by families who stayed up to all hours and seemed endlessly enthused by their TVs and fridges and inane talk and laughter. On and on they puttered aimlessly in their bright-lit small boxes in their lab-rat existence, punctuated often by the flushing of toilets. Men, women and children all jammed closely together: the incomparable bosom of the Great Italian Family.

Beside Arturo stood a couple with their guidebooks in hand, attentively tracing their fingers across a map. They were pale-skinned and fair-haired and no younger than forty, but with such naive faces and baby-fat that they looked prepubescent. What plump innocent swine, these two simpy nonentities, these two pale callow dumplings! What had *they* done to deserve globe-trotting vacations, save be born in the right place and time to make barrels of money? The fellow no doubt sat before a computer all day long on his womanish butt, punching buttons like a monkey just the way he'd been taught. His wife probably lounged sipping coffee with friends in the flower-filled garden of their beautiful home. She had a smile glazed on a face that cried out to be slapped, to jolt her from the cradle at least once before she died. And that dumb button on her blouse: the word 'I' and the word *Roma* with a red heart between them! Why who wouldn't love Rome, with such cash and stupidity, and this goose of a husband who could punch the right buttons?

Entering *Piazza della Repubblica*, the bus rumbled across the cobblestones around the famed fountain in its center. Many pointed and made remarks they imagined were thoughtful: yet another "wonderful" sight on a "wonderful" trip in this "wonderful" world that was flush with such pleasures. A nude faun in the middle held a big fish aloft. From the fish's mouth spouted water that spewed straight up in the air then fell back on the faun - whom it was slowly destroying. One leg was so corroded below the knee that just a steel bar remained, like the rusted bone of an amputee. Such a wonderful centerpiece, this dark rotted-legged leper!

On four sides of the faun there lounged four female nudes atop dumb grinning horses or absurd finny sea creatures. With passé fat-rumped bodies and coy vapid faces they seemed straight from sepia photos of old-fashioned pornography. They too looked diseased, like their consort the faun. Green algae grew like slime on their bodies, and from there spread to the fountain's rim. The whole thing belonged in some stagnant port on Lake Como: unwholesome, crepuscular, with the stink of low tide.

He looked back at the couple: still pointing at their map, still smiling their dumb smiles, still comfortable and complacent behind thickly-lensed glasses. The woman provoked in him particular contempt. He pictured her served like a suckling pig on a platter. Rudely slaughtered that morning, then flayed, baked and presented with her jaws pried wide open and an apple jammed inside - still smiling, as always, that insipid same smile.

He recalled now those films that all seemed alike on TV – the ones that end in mayhem and destruction as the Forces of Evil are vanquished. First, the villains being machine-gunned do macabre standing dances as the bullets rip through them. Bombs and grenades send their bodies hurtling high in the air off of bridges and rooftops and out windows and trucks that explode into flames. The Forces of Good, thank God, carry weapons that are always on target. Ruptured pipelines and gas tanks release deafening roars as whole buildings and districts are set raging with fire. As arsenals and munitions-dumps are kissed by the flames they shoot blistering fireballs blooming high in the sky. Set back from the scene stands the hero, untroubled. He knows all this violence is but righteous purification.

Yes this world merits such an end, thought Arturo Velenato. It deserves it for being the rotten mess it has become. But then what was this now?! The young plump suckling pig - she was turning his way, she was looking... at him! She stepped forward to speak - what could *she* want from *him*?

"Me skyoo-zee," she began, her vapid smile turned up two notches so her teeth gleamed white against her bubble-gum pink gums. She pointed on her map to *Piazza della Repubblica*, then pointed to the fountain passing by, then asked with the small trusting voice of a girl to her mother: "Pee-atz-uh de-la Ree-pub-lic?"

"*Si*," came the clipped word from Arturo's pinched lips as he inwardly seethed at these two helpless geese. Yes the only thing that would wipe the smiles off of faces like these, was the total destruction of this world that they slept in like some peaceful snug hammock. Now *that* was a film he'd be glad to direct, only his would be no movie, but reality, real life: Machine guns would strafe bars filled with smug sophisticates sipping *cappuccini*. Restaurants would be blasted and their contents spew forth in a hail of splintered tables, fractured crockery, broken bricks and shattered glass. Survivors would be cut down by a fusillade of forks and knives. Then raining down upon all would be smithereens of *antipasti* - to bespatter and make ludicrous their now lifeless corpses.

Then the earth would start trembling. Ten thousand old *palazzi* would crack open at their foundations, then collapse in slow motion till the last brick was leveled. Then the gas mains would blow and the streets gape wide open, as hellish flames flew out quickly to complete the great cleansing. With all human-kind now dead, the deep-scouring could proceed. All statues and fountains and arches and chapels and columns and relics would be crushed, torched and annihilated beyond all possible existence. No wonders to be gathered when the storm-clouds had passed. No fragments to be displayed in some sweet museum of the future. A dead phoenix, defeathered, broken-necked, putrefactive. A world met with justice. A world with no Rome.

Arturo's nostrils flared at the thought of his Armageddon. He looked about at the people standing peacefully all around him. How shocked they'd all be when they learned of their fate in those last frantic moments when they all got their due! The fair-haired man held a guidebook that said *Capella Sistina*. On its cover was a face from Michelangelo's Last Judgment. A stern prophet glared out from below two bushy bunched brows and a deep-furrowed forehead. His nostrils were flared and his lips were drawn back from his teeth bared with vengeance. The face was contorted with a terrible malevolence, which was all the more terrible since it was divinely inspired. Upon seeing this face, Arturo was struck suddenly and inordinately calm. It was like he had seen himself in a mirror.

For a moment he felt peace.

But his vile mood returned when the fair-haired man's free hand wandered to his wife's rounded rump, to which it gave calm caresses. She snuggled close up beside him. Her two smiling eyes in her child-like face peered up from beneath lowered lids. They beamed love at her husband, and spoke clearly of sex.

Arturo's head snapped away. He looked blindly out the window. Shock then wrath seized his bowels. To think that these two tepid mice, these two faceless jellyfish, could have *that*, could share *that!* This was more than he could bear, both to see or consider.

He saw his empty waiting flat. And the lone iron cot. He saw the broad bed that had been there till this Spring, with its oak head-board carved with small flowers. He saw the woman's body that had lain there. And the small boy's in the next room. Till she took the boy and left - with such excellent warning. You'd give more to a dog you pitched out for the night.

Arturo stole a glance - at the fair-haired man's hand on his fair-haired wife's flank. And his lip curled and his stomach burned as he cursed him and cursed her – but yes her, most of all. Her and her whole loathsome wicked cheating breed, he condemned yes condemned both to hell and oblivion with what strength he could muster in his black wounded heart.

Indoor Summer

The poor dear, thought Nicoletta with a wry smile, as the wealthy French woman who'd been robbed marched defiantly in front of the bus. She then chuckled out loud as the driver, forced to stop short, loosed a terrible guttural curse in dialect. Then she gazed out the window at the *piazza*, and its famed fountain. She knew this fountain already down to its smallest detail, but as with music one knows note for note, some nuance yet remained to be engraved in her heart. Today's nuance was comic: what a mismatch, she now realized, this *piazza* and its fountain! *Piazza della Repubblica* called for figures of soldiers and statesmen and guardian dieties, not this langorous ode to Eros from some romance-hazed past.

Atop a pedestal in the center of the wide circular basin, a nude faun hoisted onto his hip a fish large as himself, from whose lips water shot straight up, like a geyser. On the basin's circumference, nude women cavorted with merry-go-round horses and weird finny sea creatures. Jets that arced out from the fountain's center pummeled their breasts, backs and buttocks with a frothy white spray. These plump smiling women knew nothing of classical restraint. They arched, twisted and comported themselves like coquettes at pool-side. It's was all *fin di siecle* silliness and frivolous fun - till night-time fell black, banishing day's dry distractions. Some things can be seen only in starlight or moon-beams or full inky darkness, when the blood runs more turbid and one's yearnings more deep. Only then did this fountain revealed itself most truly, as a smoldering paean to sensuous love.

Smoldering. Sensuous. Love. Sensuous Love. How strange, thought Nicoletta, how this phrase came to mind. How her head thought it knew what her body did not. She'd been kissed by a boy, once. At this very same place. After a late film they had strolled round this fountain on whose railing, at intervals, couples sat and embraced. Was it by imitation alone she had found her way into his arms, her breasts spread on his chest as their hips and their thigh-fronts pressed up to each other? They had stood still for long moments – their bellows-like fronts speaking a slow silent language of expansion-contraction. She had listened to the splashing fountain as her eyes were closed tight. She felt magic. She felt mystery. She had not felt desire.

She had *seen* desire in the others. And it looked very different. They had dull lidded eyes and faces that swooned. Their limbs were entwined as if some drug now coursed thickly through their shared network of veins. Her embrace was not this. It was flameless. It led nowhere – but to that kiss she would always remember. He had stepped back from their embrace with the queerest of smiles – that showed kindness and affection mixed with what she had to admit was pity. He touched her lips with his fingers and kissed her once on the forehead, before walking her to the station where they'd parted as friends. That was rather some years past. There'd been no kisses since then. And none seemed forthcoming. Some girls, so it seemed, were not meant to have kisses. She had gradually become reconciled to herself being one of them.

What it would be like if she had a lover? Especially in hard times like these. Not the lover proposed by this fountain, whose geyser-like spray tickled undulant bodies. Rather – the lover-companion, the lover-friend, who could give her fresh strength in this summer of sorrows. Her image of her love was not two fires that burned higher, ever wilder. It was two candles side-by-side with two still quiet flames. But this too was just words. Nicoletta had no one. But at least in old Rome she'd found an unfailing kind of love.

You needed *some* kind of love in the neighborhood that she lived in. With its flat-faced block buildings, its streets lined with autos and dumpsters and no tree to be seen, it could as easily be Brussels or Hamburg or Belgrade or Detroit, or any of a thousand other grey urban warehouses. She could starve there with ease, though one didn't starve physically – that was well taken care of: only steps from her door there were shops choked with foods. There was furniture and televisions, clothes, banks and barbers, doctors and dentists, ice creams and bars. Your body lived well and could age fat and smiling – while your soul curled and withered in this most comfortable blight. This was why she'd gone downtown this morning – to be refreshed and revived by her wise ancient love.

Rome shamed and drove out from her all that was small: her mourned weaknesses and failings, her imprisonment in circumstance, the pinchedness and smallness that seemed to cling to her, and deprived her of her own good real stature. 'Look here,' said this city of ten thousand magnificences. 'I'm serene and indifferent, as greatness turns to dust in my entrails. Fling off all frets that would seem to consume you. Cast your small woes on my great common heap. I'm the mistress of cycles that move in great starry orbits. Step free of the small circles you have scratched all around you. All is well, and all passes. So come close and feast on my dead lovely remains.

She had once watched a gull perched on a buoy during a storm. Up and down the troughs of ever-steeper waves slid the buoy. It tipped far left then far right but the gull held its perch, merely shifting its weight so as to always stay upright. When the waves got so bad that the buoy was dunked under, the gull, with two wing-beats, was back home in the sky circling calmly aloft in the midst of the storm. It was this that Rome lent her – the heart to keep circling above her own small stormy seas.

She'd done well at the museum - now she headed back home. But before taking the subway she would stroll through the station, too. It was quite the low place and a bit frightening. Decent folks had to pass through but did not stop to linger. Yet this station too was a love of sorts, and it nourished her too, in its own peculiar way.

What people, what bodies, what faces she saw there! She was shocked every time by the rude human race. She saw white skins and black skins and yellow skins and brown, and a kaleidoscope of strange physiognomies. The Italians were here and the white Europeans and Americans, but they too looked strange in this strange mixed ensemble. Here were criminals and beggars and immigrants and peasants, from farms and the seaside and prairies and mountains, many torn from their element as they walked through the arcade. Here was a black woman on whose face was cut a design of blue welts. And a Berber strayed from his flocks, who looked awkward in trousers, his belongings in hand in a box tied with rope. Enveloped in the drone of the echoing loudspeakers, all these disparate people had nothing in common, save their tickets in hand and their eyes on the clock and a shocking self-absorption as they hurtled past one another to their separate destinies.

This was no place for a book or a picture, a song or prayer. Here was ignorance and motion and needful biology, lashed forward willy-nilly by invisible forces. Today all have tickets and passports and watches and shoes. But this is the same old Rome, old Cairo, same bazaar in Babylonia – the same ragged loose rabble at the edges of Empire. Sometimes as she stood there as the spectacle rushed by, she became so outwardly absorbed she forgot who she was. Among these thousands of people, who was *she*, Nicoletta? She had her small flat and her documents. She was a white educated Catholic. This was Italy, her home. But how real were these identities, and how much did they mean really? What if she were cast, with no credentials, into this rough human mob? This station seemed a jungle that was lawless and primitive and beyond all control, despite the so-highly-punctual movements of electrified trains.

Yet strangely and somehow, in this welter she found peace. In the mirror of the crowd she felt keenly who she was: as eccentric, as specific, as helpless as any Slav refugee or poor Eritrean. She was Nicoletta, with the pallid skin and thin frame and bespectacled pointed nose, with her deep introversion and aesthetic sensitivities. Delineated, here, in her true small dimensions, she could return to her nunnish life in her flat-faced box building on her outskirts of Brussels – heartened to pick up again with the life she'd been given. Classical

Rome first filled her and lifted her on high. The station then shrunk her, left her feeling just grateful.

Nicoletta opened her handbag. There was still time to jot a postcard she could mail from the station. She flipped quickly through the cards she had bought at the museum. She took out the card with her favorite of this morning. The dead Jesus was being carried by six disciples. Each looked strong enough to bear the litter, but not the anguish inside him. They were entering a cave that led deep into blackness, but the world outside, as well, was a world without sun. The disciples and Jesus were all pale and ghastly, as were the trees, rock and hills of the landscape they moved through. This ghastliness stood out strongly against heavy black shadows, which shot the scene through with a funereal air.

Nicoletta turned the card over and began to write quickly.

> *Dearest Veronica,*
> *Forgive the delay. I'm sorry to say I've got only bad news*
> *to report. Things are not expected to get better, and soon...*

She paused, turned the card over, and looked again at the picture. Then she looked back out the window, at the faun and the nymphs now receding in the distance. She put the card back and began flipping through the others.

Yes this one was better. A nymph with great flanks and full breasts stood waist-high in a lake. Bending over to one side, she was squeezing out water from her luxuriant black hair. Poorly concealed among the bushes beside the tree on whose branch hung her garments, a satyr peeked out. His face showed warm appreciation for her womanliness, which was echoed below by his upright red member. The nymph knew he was there but was not much concerned. She smiled sweetly to herself as she squeezed dry her tresses.

Yes this card was better.

She again set to writing.

Dearest Veronica,
Papa has come home now. The doctors say nothing more can be done. I do my best to keep him comfortable. Don't worry about me, please - I stay if not hopeful then cheerful. I sneak off to the museums - when I can - thus this post-card - do you like it? Enjoy the beaches. For me, I'm afraid, it's a long indoor summer. Till September.

Hugs and kisses,

Nicoletta

Old Porker and the *San Pietrini*

Rome's charm would be halved if its streets were not cobbled. We know this from other old towns that are smoothly paved over, whose slick streets just don't go with their old weathered buildings, just as sneakers look jarring on old ladies' feet. But we're usually too distracted to take pleasure in these streets' surface. When on foot, we must worry where we place our high heels, or beware that our shoe tips don't get chunks bitten out. We must steer clear of pit-holes and protuberances, wads of sputum and gnarled dog doos, all the while dodging traffic. Even when driving we're too busy wincing inwardly, as our tires and suspension are continually tormented.

Only in side moments does our attention slip free of the rigors of locomotion. Then these streets again glow with their cobbly old charm. They arouse in us nostalgia for horses and carriages, for gas-lights and torches - which we fondly remember though we never have seen them. The world then grows picturesque, as we rove these streets atop a life-sized mosaic.

Such art doesn't come easy. Water mains burst open and power lines oversizzle, phone wires go dead and all three need replacement. These streets must perpetually be hashed up and rehashed, and after each intervention its surface is not paved - it's recobbled. They're not cobblestones, really; they're stone cubes tapered at one end, like dark molars. They must be rapped into place by a man with a hammer. These tooth-like stones, long ago, earned an affectionate nickname. They are called *san pietrini*, the little rocks of the church.

Outside our bus window are three modern practitioners of this old workman's craft, on a patch of the street cordoned off by striped ribbons. One's a big muscular youth with the requisite brawn.

Another has a boy's skinny body but a man's craggy head. His bare torso is white as pizza dough, save his head, neck and forearms, which are deep leather brown.

"Rain's over, slugs. Back to work!" barked the voice of the third man.

"Damn Old Porker," muttered the brawny youth.

"Damn Porker," cursed the two-toned boy-man, as they reluctantly carried stones to their crew boss already kneeling in the dirt.

He was a huge sixtyish fellow in a sleeveless t-shirt and green work-pants. Atop his head was a kind of sailor's cap fashioned from the front page of today's paper. His right hand held a mallet with a clawed edge. As his left reached for a *san pietrino*, his right clawed the dirt to loosen it. As the left set the stone in place, his right rose up high, and at the top of its arc swiveled the mallet, then pounded down on the stone till it was driven in securely. This left hand and right hand were excellent partners. Stones went side by side neatly, with a swift even rhythm.

This efficient old workman, as we've just heard, goes by the name of Old Porker. He had first been dubbed Young Porker, when a schoolboy, on account of his flushed face and burly build - but most of all for his nose, whose extreme upward tilt let you look straight into his nostrils. The broken tooth of one boy, and the poisoned dog of another, attest to his displeasure with that name. But it stuck all the same. It was much too apt. At sixteen, Young Porker chanced to read that among mammals, the pig ruts most aggressively and indefatigably. From that moment on he wore his name like a crown. At the soccer game he would cry loudly, "...and Young Porker takes the field!" Or upon meeting new boys he would step forward, hand extended: "*Ciao*. Young Porker here," he would say, as he snorted and pawed the ground. His new pride in his namesake gave him confidence among females. By age thirty he was married and the father of four male piglets.

They were cute little boys, all with cute upturned snouts. Each Sunday, while three of them suffered sitting through Mass with their mother, one boy would be treated to a tour with his dad. Young Porker went on pilgrimage to the many sites he had worked on, since most people were at home and the streets were quite peaceful. "Just look at that!" Young Porker would say. "I laid these stones thirteen years ago and you still can't get a toothpick between them." Or "Look at this – still perfectly level!" And he would take a board from his car and lay it down length after length, and make proud boasts.

But Young Porker did not occupy himself entirely with self congratulation. He spent as much time critiquing the botched work of others. Where *san pietrini* had worked loose, drifted apart, or heaved up, he would discharge withering, heartfelt abuse. "Look at this," he would say, pointing to a concavity filled with water beside a sewer grating. "Would you just *look* at this!" he would cry out, with contempt and disbelief. He would then kick some of the standing water onto the grating, to demonstrate where it ought to be. Then he'd shake his head sadly. "*Idioti*," he would say, putting his head down before his son's face, and smacking the heel of his hand into his forehead. "A world filled with *idioti*!"

The more recent use of asphalt particularly disturbed him. Classic *san pietrini* are laid in small arcs that form a design of interlocking fans. The rhythmic design of these fans is a bit hypnotic and quite pleasing. To form fans though, takes effort. To make them interlock takes even more. Few work crews still bother. They lay the stones down helter-skelter. And rather than placing them so precisely that they stay in place by themselves, they drizzle asphalt loosely over them. It oozes down into the cracks but obscures many stone tops. "It's a *street* for Christ's sake, not a sundae," Young Porker would cry out to his son.

The crews sometimes lay rows at right angles that are orderly, but rather too much so. Laid in diagonals they look better, not so rigid at least, or boring. But even these effects lack the charm of these fine interlocking fans. Laying just such fans was the pride of Young Porker, who knew there was just *one* way to lay *san pietrini*. And so - on some desolate, dirty *vicolo* where the street heaved and the stones were all at random, there'd be eight perfect fans from when a new phone line was installed. Or on a broad stretch of *piazza* whose stones stood in straight military rows, there'd be a small patch of fans looking like butterflies poised for take-off.

Well into his late forties, Young Porker's body had still spoken of industry. His upturned nose, squared-off jaw, bandy legs and barrel chest made him look, even standing still, as if action was imminent. But some time after fifty, these taut lineaments gave way. A pouchy gullet loafed beneath his chin, mocking its last hint of determination. A blimpy paunch stood out further than his once forward-thrust chest. His bandy legs thickened to stumps. His strong arms became flabby thighs. It was as if his whole form had swollen up then been melted down into masses that sagged pendulously earthward. Only his nose still turned upwards, quite as porkishly as ever. It was time, though, for another name change. It took place gradually, over several years. No one could say just when, but Young Porker came to be Old Porker. He submitted to this change, for some reason, with nary a grunt.

But if his body looked less able, this appearance was misleading. On work crews several men often stand around watching as just one makes an effort. After all, there is so much else to do: one can lean against a pick or shovel, one can talk, scratch his head, ogle women, watch the cars driving by. One can tug at his balls, pick his nose or ears, or smoke a cigarette, or chew gum, or both. Old Porker, though, liked to work. And though age slowed him down - he didn't give off sparks as he had in his youth - he still worked and pushed others at a relentless, productive pace. And though copious sweat poured alarmingly off his flushed sagging flesh, his limbs stayed in motion, ever bent to some goal.

There's something poignant about aged men doing hard manual labor. This is not lost on tourists. At least once a week Old Porker is asked to pose before somebody's camera. He is not like a Vatican Swiss Guard, in bright elegance; no man sends his wife or daughter to pose smiling beside him. But all the same: in a leather-bound album in an elegant drawing room in London, you'll find a snapshot of Old Porker. Likewise in the album of a dentist in Dresden, in the slide collection of an architect in Rochester, an engineer in Oslo, a financier in Adelaide, and others as well - can be found the image of Old Porker, with his newspaper hat and his clawed mallet in hand, a sight well worth remembering from this city filled with treasures. No book or monograph celebrates him, no cultural fund supports him. On just a beer and salami sandwich he's a relentlessly vigilant guardian of a noble antique craft.

As he knelt in the dirt rapping stones into place, a coin struck his shoulder. He turned angrily to see where it came from. There, in the open front window of our Bus 64, was the shaggy baleful bison head of Vinzo, looking down at him.

"Vinzo you dog!" cried Old Porker, his cheeks rising to hard apples as his eyes squinched shut happily.

Vinzo's expression did not change. His buffalo head bobbed up and down slowly.

"What do you say there, Young Porker?"

Old Porker's cheeks grew redder and his squinched eyes twinkled brightly. He and Vinzo went back to grade school, before 'Young Porker' had even existed. Indeed, Vinzo was one of the few who knew Old Porker's real name - it was Lorenzo. And likewise Old Porker was among the few who had known Vinzo as Vicenzo — a clean skinny schoolboy, his hair combed neatly across his head. These old friends saw each other seldom: at church (perhaps) on Easter, at the horse races (by extreme coincidence), or at their parents' graves on All Soul's Day. But good will reigned between them. And it was with a pure brand of affection that they gazed at each other quietly, their faces and bodies weathered by these streets they had spent their lives on. It was hard to imagine Lorenzo and Vicenzo as squeaky-clean schoolboys or as pink smooth-bummed babies bringing joy to their families… and yet it was so, once, as it once was for us all.

"So how goes it?" asked Vinzo, in his guttural voice with no affect.

"Still humpin'," said Old Porker, nodding. "And you?"

"Same old shit. Can't complain," said our Vinzo.

The two men looked at each other and nodded. A long moment passed. Old Porker put his hands on his hips. Vinzo stole glances at the traffic light. Their conversation had reached its apex. Old Porker looked back at his workmen, who had at once both lit cigarettes. He suddenly brightened as he remembered something.

"Vinzo – I meant to tell you, I just read it...You know, the Japanese just invented a new bus. It drives by itself. You don't need a driver. It's gonna put you out of work, once they get the last kink worked out..."

Vinzo's chin jerked up defiantly. The pouch beneath it wobbled in alarm.

"What's that?" he asked, feeling threatened already.

"They can't figure out how to make a bus that's got hemor-rhoids!"

Old Porker abandoned himself to loud hearty chortling. His flesh folds all shook. His ruddy cheeks turned redder. He wiped a tear from the crinkly slit of one eye.

Vinzo made a quick vulgar gesture – a mere reflex; he was amused. And he also did something else that for us was quite shocking. For a full ten seconds, *minimum*, he relaxed and actually *smiled*.

But then cars started honking. Vinzo quickly recovered and looked annoyed, pissed and sullen.

"Till next time, Young Porker," he barked to Old Porker, giving a short rough salute.

"Yes SIR!" returned Old Porker, smacking his two heels together and lifting his massive form into a semblance of soldierly attention, an illusion greatly enhanced by his sailor's cap made from today's newspaper. He stood thus, at attention, till the bus was on its way. He then turned on his companions who were engrossed in their cigarettes.

"What are you standing there doing nothing? Let's get to it!" he barked, as he knelt in the dirt which he clawed with the mallet as he reached for a *san pietrino*.

"Damn Old Porker," muttered one, bending slowly to the task.

"Damn Porker," said the other, taking a last deep burning drag.

The End of the Line

Stazione Termini. So how shall we end, then - this book and this bus ride? Convention calls for climax, high drama, or violence, best of all. Some extraordinary event among the passengers. A murder, a break-down, or better yet, an accident. Or catastrophe on a larger scale: deadly lightning bolts that strike down; a terrorist bomb at the station.

But look: the rain-storm is over. The world's pacific, idyllic. The sun has come shining through and a gorgeous rainbow arcs over the station. A bus coming to a stop at a bus station beneath a rainbow? No drama, too saccharine, and contrived - albeit true. Even the station itself is anti-climax. No more stately columns or mighty statues. Nothing famous, old or beautiful. Just a modern box building with a big parking lot out front that would look just fine in Newark, or Dayton. On a building-top beyond the station we see a tall statue of Jesus, who blesses the waiting buses and the milling crowd. But we see him through the girders just erected on a nearby building-top, which will soon to sport a billboard that will blot him out from view.

The time of day conspires, as well, against a rousing finale. It's lunch-time. Relax-time. The mid-day nap, a tradition here for millennia, seems particularly sane on hot days like this one. Just look around at the animals; they're under no boss's lash, they're not asking anyone's permission to lie down. Cats curl up under cars, under dumpsters, in cool doorways. Dogs lie dead on their sides, tongues hanging out panting, or on their bellies with their haunches spread on a shaded sidewalk. Even the pigeons that strut and peck like wind-up dolls, tuck their beaks in and stand still, or strut slowly, as if their springs have run down.

Until not so very long ago, all partook in this ritual. At the end of the morning's toils one abandoned the stress of sustained verticality. One folded up one's limbs and sat down at the table. One sent ample foodstuffs down one's gullet. And as the blood rushed bellywards to meet the challenge, even being seated soon became onerous. One fled - slowly - to the ready bed, where one lay as still and thoughtless, for a few hours, as any pink-tongued panting hound. But encroaching modern rhythms have forced almost all of us from this timeless mold. We still tire and grow hot and hungry, but there's no armchair, no set table, and no couch or shuttered bedroom. Just the company of strangers as uncomfortable as we are, in crazed masses that must keep moving. So while the noon-day sun beats down nature into steamed helpless submission, we're still hell-bent to the forward drive of the mechanized stream.

It's not pleasant. We get cranky. Which is perhaps why Vinzo's so ill-humored as we near the end of the line. He's hot, hungry and constipated - and will soon be heading back again, to the Vatican. His bunched sweated brow overhangs tired eyes that yet seem menacing. There's more than discomfort here, or irritation. Something malevolent. An air of *vendetta*. But upon what can he revenge himself? On abstractions called 'fate', or 'modern times'? There's no dog here to kick at. Except for one, that is: it's the pedestrian.

As cities go, Rome is safe. Male or female, young or old, you can circulate most everywhere without fear. There is one place, however, where your life is imperiled - it's the zebra-crossing for pedestrians. It's the front line of a war that has raged here ever since the engine conquered the rhythms of nature. It's not just Vinzo who bullies frail humans with his big orange bus. It's a way of life now, a kind of free-for-all of blind vengeance for a paradise lost.

As in any war anywhere, both sides think they're right. After all, the pedestrian, at home, walks through his flat unimpeded. Chairs and shelves don't lunge out at him. Tables are stationary, deferential. With his eyes closed he can stumble to the bathroom. Chewing a sandwich he can walk from the kitchen. With the lights switched off he walks calmly bedward through dark halls. Once outside his chambers though, he's in a jungle and it's dangerous. He's checked and challenged at each step by resentful drivers in their steel machines.

The driver too, has his grievance. He didn't choose all this starting and stopping and cutting and honking, this prolonged nerve-wracking aggravation, in grim competition with creatures every bit as nasty as himself. He grows vengeful and malicious, feeling all the time righteous.

It's at the zebra-crossing that these two meet, where their grudges are most intensified. But with his frail human frame only, the pedestrian is no match for his foe. He can just weakly invoke civic respect as he sets out on his perilous journey across busy streets. But how dauntless is the human spirit! He becomes obstinate and contrary, insolent and willful - his unique brands of courage. He thrusts himself into moving traffic, even as drivers flash high beams and accelerate, beep horns and bear down upon him. It's Tienanmen Square writ large, on a thousand streets all day long, as driver and pedestrian challenge and torment one another in their shared realm of frustration.

Someone must be made to pay - as we see with Vinzo, as we enter now the home stretch. A mother crosses the street hand-in-hand with her small child, her head turning a continuous vigilant circuit. Her placid toddler moves beside her, all trust and obedience. Our bus bears down upon her, giving no sign of slowing down. She pulls her child forward hurriedly as the huge bus rushes past. An old woman sets out from the curb. One hand holds her pocketbook, the other waves a hanky over her head like a surrendering soldier who trusts he won't be shot. As Vinzo bears down upon her she keeps on with her walking slowly. But as his loud BEEEP! beats her eardrums, her old bow-legs get the message and run fast from the danger. Crossing the next block is a stiff-jointed man with a cane. He turns toward the bus with accusatory eyes bulging, sure that his piercing glare will stop this bus as surely as brakes. Vinzo missing him by mere whiskers, leaving him shaking his cane angrily in a cloud of exhaust.

Two teen-aged boys though, exult, skipping lightly out of the way at the very last second, like swallows sweeping before a car's grill. Vinzo's forced to swerve and touch his brakes, and mutters terrible oaths into the windshield. He's in a rush to the station for his short break for lunch. But it's not the sandwiches that call out to him, with their by-now wilted lettuce and waxy liquefied mayonnaise. He is in a rush because *it is time.* Three long days in the making. Two long hours ago, in a bar, he prayed for relief from his stagnant bowels. And *it is time* now. He's received a sign. He drives as fast as he's ever dared to.

He speeds into the parking lot and comes to a sudden stop behind two other Bus 64s that wait at curbside. As the pneumatic doors open with their loud hiss, our uniformed captain is the first to abandon ship. Among the crowds that mill around on the gummy asphalt beneath the blazing sun, an ungainly figure can be seen, trundling off into the distance, to the waiting porcelain mouth at the back of his favorite bar.

The rest of us disembark sluggishly and diffident, as we push on into the next phase of this much too hot day. The crowd waiting to get on board looks much keener than we do, fired up with hope they will get a seat. Students and workers, housewives and travelers, shoppers and idlers - all press close up near the doors as the last of us exit. They then dash headlong up the stairs toward the few empty seats. They scurry quickly, like rats. And pack the bus full in one minute.

Buona Notte!!

Roma - Caput Mundi - MCMXCII (1994 A.D.)
July 20th, 3:19 A.M.

Night has long fallen now, on this ancient city. Just hours ago manic, it now looks deserted. Only an occasional taxi rumbles up an empty avenue, while trash trucks with gargling maws circulate the labyrinth slowly, clearing the stage for the next day's pageant. Teeming no more with activity, Rome stands forth on its own now: seven hills crusted thickly with stone structures, beside a small river in a flat plain. The moon shines on these hills with no thought for these buildings, their histories, or their long-dead constructors.

All who dwell here lie in darkened chambers now, like the dead, until sunrise, when they will rise once again to animate these seven hills. Among the countless sleeping thousands are a few we've befriended, on that tedious bus-ride we took long ago, this morning:

Two priests lie in two small clean rooms. The young one lies awake wrestling with shameful thoughts. He does not seem to be winning. The older one lies on his back with his four limbs sprawled out, snoring loudly.

Maria Luigia sleeps with a second pillow on her head in her nicely furnished flat. The metal shutters have been drawn, the window gratings locked by key, the front door secured by two slide bolts that go deep into the walls and floor.

Bruno Ignazio rests well in his ironed pajamas that are buttoned to the neck. His mahogony cane rests against his night-table.

Cindy from the Feelings Group half-dozes as she lies uncomfortably on her side in the Hotel of the Emperors. Ted glumly watches John Wayne warn the bad guys in Italian. He's trying to get some fun out of it, but it's going to be a long night.

Guido Boccamoto lies temporarily silent. His false teeth sitting in a glass of water still vibrate from the day's action.

The young gypsy mother lies on a bare mattress in a trailer in the gypsy camp near the highway. Baby Lachlik sleeps in another trailer. He was just lent to her for the day, for her to suckle and beg money with.

Old Serena sleeps in her small room down the hall from her daughter and son-in-law. Their small baby sleeps in their room with them, but will soon have Serena's room all to itself.

The two healthy German teens are not asleep. They're clasped once again in the toils of Venus.

Six dark youths who wash windshields lie in sleeping bags on the hard floor of a *pensione* room with no curtains.

The patient in the stopped ambulance is asleep in the hospital. His vital signs are weak but he's been declared out of danger.

Ikabona lies in a church shelter among three long rows of immigrants on straw mats with clean sheets.

Ahmed rests in his *pensione*. By his night-table stands a framed photo of his wife and child back home.

Anna freshly henna'd her hair tonight, then put it in curlers. Though it took her a few months to get used to, she can now wear hair curlers to bed and sleep soundly.

Aldo rests well in his hotel room. He's all packed for an early take-off.

Emilio and his wife sleep up against one another like brown bears. The head of the swordfish stands upright in the cooler. Its eyes are wide open. Its beak seems to be smiling.

On a flattened carton beneath an arcade, Pantheon Rose lies covered, head included, with open newspapers. Only her feet in their laceless boots are sticking out.

Cesare Massimilliano's meeting had to be rescheduled. He flew straight to Brussels on important business. He's passed out in his five-star hotel room. The call-girl let herself out quietly without waking him.

The youth on the *motorino* lies in a chilled vault in the morgue. His girlfriend is home sleeping deeply, on heavy sedation.

Nicoletta rests lightly in a small room filled with pictures. She's moved the head of her bed beside the open door, to hear her father's call should he need her.

Pino sleeps in a single bed beside a blond Norwegian girl whose portrait he drew this afternoon.

Ettore sleeps in his childhood room; Mom and Dad sleep down the hall.

Mon Cheri rests between silk sheets in her suite in the Grand Hotel. The cosmetic mask she applied labors valiantly to rejuvenate her.

Tina rests in the top bunk of the room she shares with her younger sister. Gina rests in the bottom bunk of the room she shares with her older sister.

The horse with the red-tasseled mane stands on all fours in his stall on the outskirts of the city.

The lanky youth came in late with his head spinning from drugs and fell fast asleep fully clothed.

Arturo Velenato lays flat on his back on his cot. His eyes are closed but he's frowning, and does not look asleep.

Signor Fabrizio Sfortuno lies asleep against the travertine wall beneath a bridge.

The Man with the Port-Wine-Colored Scar rests in a small half-furnished flat, its closet filled with nice clothes.

The Man with the *Mano Morta* rests serene after an excellent late dinner. On his bare chest, on a chain, lie a red plastic pepper and a cross of pure gold.

The Campari Girl sleeps where? And with whom? In what stage of undress?

Old Porker lies snout up on his back with his wife snug against him.

Our Vinzo lies the same way, with his wife snug against him. He's happily married. Can you believe it?

And me? I'm awake still, gazing out the window at the sleeping city, chewing a pen top, writing stories. This last one's finally finished. I bid my reader, then, *buona notte*!!

www.ingramcontent.com/pod-product-compliance
Lightning Source LLC
Chambersburg PA
CBHW070321260626
47160CB00003B/910